HOKAS ON PATROL!

There were more than a hundred uniformed Hokas lined up at attention. But Alex's mind focussed on his spaceship. "My courier boat!" he wailed. "Jax, what have you done to her?" Her name had been painted out and replaced by *Fearless*, with the words *Space Patrol Ship Number One* below.

"Sorry, sir," the Hoka answered, "but you know that Space Patrolmen may requisition whatever is needed just by showing their badges."

"Who said so?" raged Alex.

"Tom Bracken of the Space Patrol, sir," said Jax. "He says it every day on the video."

"The danger is imminent, sir," added the second Hoka, who was dressed in an admiral's uniform. "The Malevonians are preparing their great push. We must stop the enemy." His voice barked out over the waiting ranks of teddy bears. "Ten-SHUN! Forward march!"

"But—but—but—" the human stammered.

The Hoka Admiral whispered to Jax. "Something wrong with the Coordinator, Captain? You suppose the Malevonians have gotten control of his mind?"

"Of course not," said Jax. "It's just his crusty way. He has a rough exterior but a heart of gold."

The Hokas tramped toward the ship's airlock. "Stop!" screamed Alex, racing after them.

"The Coordinator himself is coming with us!" yelled the Hoka Admiral in a burst of happiness.

Alex was caught up and carried into the ship. He heard the airlock clang shut behind him. Then the ship's drive went on, and Alex was thrown against a bulkhead and smashed into unconsciousness. . . .

POUL ANDERSON
Hoka! Hoka! HOKA!
GORDON R. DICKSON

HOKA! HOKA! HOKA!

This is a work of fiction. All the characters and events portrayed in this book are fictional, and any resemblance to real people or incidents is purely coincidental.

A Baen Book

Baen Publishing Enterprises
P.O. Box 1403
Riverdale, NY 10471

ISBN: 0-671-57774-3

Cover art by Stephen Hickman

First Baen printing, November 1998

Distributed by Simon & Schuster
1230 Avenue of the Americas
New York, NY 10020

Printed in the United States of America

Table of Contents

Table of Contents

PROLOGUE

From the *Encyclopaedia Galactica*, 11th edition:

TOKA: Brackney's Star III. The sun (NSC 7-190853426) is of type G2, located in Region Deneb, approximately 503 light-years from Sol. . . . The third planet appears Earthlike, to a sufficiently superficial observer. . . . There are three small moons, their League names being Uha, Buha, and Huha. As is customary in the case of inhabited planets, these derive from a major autochthonous language (see NOMENCLATURE: Astronomical). It was discovered too late that they mean, respectively, "Fat," "Drunk" and "Sluggish." . . .

At least "Toka" means "Earth." However, indigenous tongues have become little more than historical curiosities, displaced by whatever Terrestrial speech suits the role of the moment. . . .

Two intelligent species evolved, known today as the Hokas and the Slissii. The former are quasi-mammalian, the latter reptiloid. . . . Conflict was ineluctable. . . . It terminated after human explorers had come upon the system and the Interbeing League took charge. . . . In effect, the Slissii were bought out. Abandoning their home world *en masse*, they became free wanderers throughout civilization, to its detriment. (See SLISSII. See also COMPUTER CRIME; CONFIDENCE GAMES; EMBEZZLEMENT; GAMBLING: Crooked; MISREPRESENTATION; POLITICS.)

The ursinoid Hokas generally stayed in place. No nation of theirs refused to accept League tutelage, which of course has had the objective of raising their level of civilization to a point where autonomy and full membership can be granted. Rather, they all agreed with an eagerness which should have warned the Commissioners. . . .

The fact is that the Hokas are the most imaginative race of beings in known space, and doubtless in unknown space too. Any role that strikes their fancy they will play, individually or as a group, to the limits of the preposterous and beyond. This does not imply deficiency of intellect, for they are remarkably quick to learn. It does not even imply that they lose touch with reality; indeed, they have been heard to complain that reality often loses touch with them. It does demonstrate a completely protean personality. Added to that are a physical strength and energy astonishing in such comparatively small bodies. Thus, in the course of a few short years, the "demon teddy bears," to use a popular phrase for them, have covered their planet with an implausible kaleidoscope of harlequin societies describable only by some such metaphor as the foregoing. . . .

The Sheriff Of Canyon Gulch

It had been a very near thing. Alexander Jones spent several minutes enjoying the simple pleasure of still being alive.

Then he looked around.

It could almost have been Earth—almost, indeed, his own North America. He stood on a great prairie whose dun grasses rolled away beneath a high windy sky. A flock of birds, alarmed by his descent, clamored upward; they were not so very different from the birds he knew. A line of trees marked the river, a dying puff of steam the final berth of his scoutboat. In the hazy eastern distance he saw dim blue hills. Beyond those, he knew, were the mountains, and then the enormous dark forests, and finally the sea near which the *Draco* lay. A hell of a long ways to travel.

Nevertheless, he was uninjured, and on a planet almost the twin of his own. The air, gravity, bio-chemistry, the late-afternoon sun, could only be told from those of home with sensitive instruments. The rotational period was approximately 24 hours, the sidereal year nearly 12 months, the axial tilt a neat but not gaudy 11½ degrees. The fact that two small moons were in the sky and a third lurking somewhere else, that the continental outlines were an alien scrawl, that a snake coiled on a nearby rock had wings, that he was about 500 light-years from the Solar System—all this was mere detail. The veriest bagatelle. Alex laughed at it. The noise jarred so loud in this emptiness that he decided a decorous silence was more appropriate to his status as an officer and, by Act of Parliament as ratified locally by the United States Senate, a gentleman. Therefore he straightened his high-collared blue naval tunic, ran a nervous hand down the creases of his white naval trousers, buffed his shining naval boots on the spilled-out naval parachute, and reached for his emergency kit.

He neglected to comb his rumpled brown hair, and his lanky form did not exactly snap to attention. But he was, after all, quite alone. Not that he intended to remain in that possibly estimable condition. He shrugged the heavy packsack off his shoulders. It had been the only thing he grabbed besides the parachute when his boat failed, and the only thing he really needed. His hands fumbled it open and he reached in for the small but powerful radio which would bring help.

He drew out a book.

It looked unfamiliar, somehow . . . had they issued a new set of instructions since he was in boot camp? He opened it, looking for the section on Radios, Emergency, Use of. He read the first page he turned to:

"—apparently incredibly fortunate historical development was, of course, quite logical. The relative decline in politico-economic influence of the Northern Hemisphere during the later twentieth century, the shift of civilized dominance to a Southeast Asia-Indian Ocean region with more resources, did not, as alarmists at the time predicted, spell the end of Western civilization. Rather did it spell an upsurge of Anglo-Saxon democratic and libertarian influence, for the simple reason that this area, which now held the purse strings of Earth, was in turn primarily led by Australia and New Zealand, which nations retained their primordial loyalty to the British Crown. The consequent renascence and renewed growth of the British Commonwealth of Nations, the shaping of its councils into a truly world—even interplanetary—government, climaxed as it was by the American Accession, has naturally tended to fix Western culture, even in small details of everyday life, in the mold of that particular time, a tendency which was accentuated by the unexpectedly early invention of the faster-than-light secondary drive and repeated contact with truly different mentalities, and has produced in the Solar System a social stability which our forefathers would have considered positively Utopian and which the Service, working through the Interbeing League, has as its goal to bring to all sentient races—"

"*Guk!*" said Alex.

He snapped the book shut. Its title leered up at him:

EMPLOYEES' ORIENTATION
MANUAL
by Adalbert Parr,
Chief Cultural Commissioner
Cultural Development Service
Foreign Ministry
of the
United Commonwealths
League City, N.Z., Sol III

"Oh, no!" said Alex.

Frantically, he pawed through the pack. There must be a radio . . . a raythrower . . . a compass . . . one little can of beans?

He extracted some 5000 tightly bundled copies of CDS Form J-16-LKR, to be filled out in quadruplicate by applicant and submitted with attached Forms G776802 and W-2-ZGU.

Alex's snub-nosed face sagged open. His blue eyes revolved incredulously. There followed a long, dreadful moment in which he could only think how utterly useless the English language was when it came to describing issue-room clerks.

"Oh, hell," said Alexander Jones.

He got up and began to walk.

He woke slowly with the sunrise and lay there for a while wishing he hadn't. A long hike on an empty stomach followed by an uneasy attempt to sleep on the ground, plus the prospect of several thousand kilometers of the same, is not conducive to joy. And those animals, whatever they were, that had been yipping and howling all night sounded so damnably *hungry*.

"He looks human."

"Yeah. But he ain't dressed like no human."

Alex opened his eyes with a wild surmise. The drawling voices spoke . . . English!

He closed his eyes again, immediately. "No," he groaned.

"He's awake, Tex." The voices were high-pitched, slightly unreal. Alex curled up into the embryonic position and reflected on the peculiar horror of a squeaky drawl.

"Yeah. Git up, stranger. These hyar parts ain't healthy right now, nohow."

"No," gibbered Alex. "Tell me it isn't so. Tell me I've gone crazy, but deliver me from its being real!"

"I dunno." The voice was uncertain. "He don't talk like no human."

Alex decided there was no point in wishing them out of existence. They looked harmless, anyway—to everything except his sanity. He crawled to his feet, his bones seeming to grate against each other, and faced the natives.

The first expedition, he remembered, had reported two intelligent races, Hokas and Slissii, on this planet. And these must be Hokas. For small blessings, give praises! There were two of them, almost identical to the untrained Terrestrial eye: about a meter tall, tubby and golden-furred, with round blunt-muzzled heads and small black eyes. Except for the stubby-fingered hands, they resembled nothing so much as giant teddy bears.

The first expedition had, however, said nothing about their speaking English with a drawl. Or about their wearing the dress of Earth's 19th-century West.

All the American historical stereofilms he had ever seen gabbled in Alex's mind as he assessed their costumes. They wore—let's see, start at the top and work down and try to keep your reason in the process—ten-gallon hats with brims wider than their own shoulders, tremendous red bandannas, checked shirts of riotous hues, Levis, enormously flaring chaps, and high-heeled boots with outsize spurs. Two sagging cartridge belts on each plump waist supported heavy Colt six-shooters which almost dragged on the ground.

One of the natives was standing before the Earthman, the other was mounted nearby, holding the reins of the first one's—well—his animal. The beasts were about the size of a pony, and had four hoofed feet . . . also whiplike tails, long necks with beaked heads, and scaly green hides. But of course, thought Alex wildly, of course they bore Western saddles with lassos at the horns. Of course. Who ever heard of a cowboy without a lasso?

"Wa'l, I see yo're awake," said the standing Hoka. "Howdy, stranger, howdy." He extended his hand. "I'm Tex and my pardner here is Monty."

"Pleased to meet you," mumbled Alex, shaking hands in a dreamlike fashion. "I'm Alexander Jones."

"I dunno," said Monty dubiously. "He ain't named like no human."

"Are yo' human, Alexanderjones?" asked Tex.

The spaceman got a firm grip on himself and said, spacing his words with care: "I am Ensign Alexander Jones of the Terrestrial Interstellar Survey Service, attached to HMS *Draco*." Now it was the Hokas who looked lost. He added wearily: "In other words, I'm from Earth. I'm human. Satisfied?"

"I s'pose," said Monty, still doubtful. "But we'd better take yo' back to town with us an' let Slick talk to yo'. He'll know more about it. Cain't take no chances in these hyar times."

"Why not?" said Tex, with a surprising bitterness. "What we got to lose, anyhow? But come on, Alexanderjones, we'll go on to town. We shore don't want to be found by no Injun war parties."

"Injuns?" asked Alex.

"Shore. They're comin', you know. We'd better sashay along. My pony'll carry double."

Alex was not especially happy at riding a nervous reptile in a saddle built for a Hoka. Fortunately, the race was sufficiently broad in the beam for their seats to have spare room for a slim Earthman. The "pony" trotted ahead at a surprisingly fast and steady pace. Reptiles on Toka—so-called by the first expedition from the word for "earth" in the language of the most advanced Hoka society—seemed to be more highly evolved than in the Solar System. A fully developed four-chambered heart and a better nervous system made them almost equivalent to mammals.

Nevertheless, the creature stank.

Alex looked around. The prairie was just as big and, bare, his ship just as far away.

" 'Tain't none o' my business, I reckon," said Tex, "but how'd yo' happen to be hyar?"

"It's a long story," said Alex absent-mindedly. His thoughts at the moment were chiefly about food. "The *Draco* was out on Survey, mapping new planetary systems, and our course happened to take us close to this, star, your sun, which we knew had been visited once before. We thought we'd look in and check on conditions, as well as resting ourselves on an Earth-type world. I was one of the several who went out in scoutboats to skim over this continent. Something went wrong, my engines failed and I barely escaped

with my life. I parachuted out, and as bad luck would
have it, my boat crashed in a river. So—well—due
to various other circumstances, I just had to start
hiking back, toward my ship."

"Won't yore pardners come after yo'?"

"Sure, they'll search—but how likely are they to
find a shattered wreck on the bottom of a river, with
half a continent to investigate? I could, perhaps, have
grubbed a big SOS in the soil and hoped it would
be seen from the air, but what with the necessity of
hunting food and all . . . well, I figured my best chance
was to keep moving. But now I'm hungry enough to
eat a . . . a buffalo."

"Ain't likely to have buffalo meat in town," said the
Hoka imperturbably. "But we got good T-bone steaks."

"Oh," said Alex.

"Yo' wouldn't'a lasted long, hoofin' it," said Monty.
"Ain't got no gun."

"No, thanks to—Never mind!" said Alex. "I thought
I'd try to make a bow and some arrows."

"Bow an' arrers—Say!" Monty squinted suspiciously
at him. "What yo' been doin' around the Injuns?"

"I ain't—I haven't been near any Injuns, dammit!"

"Bows an' arrers in Injun weapons, stranger."

"I wish they was," mourned Tex. "We didn't have
no trouble back when only Hokas had six-guns. But
now the Injuns got 'em too, it's all up with us." A
tear trickled down his button nose.

If the cowboys are teddy bears, thought Alex, *then
who—or what—are the Indians?*

"It's lucky for yo' me an' Tex happened to pass by,"
said Monty. "We was out to see if we couldn't round
up a few more steers afore the Injuns get here. No
such luck, though. The greenskins done rustled 'em
all."

Greenskins! Alex remembered a detail in the report of the first expedition: two intelligent races, the mammalian Hokas and the reptilian Slissii. And the Slissii, being stronger and more warlike, preyed on the Hokas—

"Are the Injuns Slissii?" he asked.

"Wa'l, they're ornery, at least," said Monty.

"I mean . . . well . . . are they big tall beings, bigger than I am, but walking sort of stooped over . . . tails and fangs and green skins, and their talk is full of hissing noises?"

"Why, shore. What else?" Monty shook his head, puzzled. "If yo're a human, how come yo' don't even know what a Injun is?"

They had been plop-plopping toward a large and noisy dust cloud. As they neared, Alex saw the cause, a giant herd of—uh—

"Longhorn steers," explained Monty.

Well . . . yes . . . one long horn apiece, on the snout. But at least the red-haired, short-legged, barrel-bodied "cattle" were mammals. Alex made out brands on the flanks of some. The entire herd was being urged along by fast-riding Hoka cowboys.

"That's the X Bar X outfit," said Tex. "The Lone Rider decided to try an' drive 'em ahead o' the Injuns. But I'm afeered the greenskins'll catch up with him purty soon."

"He cain't do much else," answered Monty. "All the ranchers, just about, are drivin' their stock off the range. There just ain't any place short o' the Devil's Nose whar we can make a stand. I shore don't intend tryin' to stay in town an' hold off the Injuns, an' I don't think nobody else does either, in spite o' Slick an' the Lone Rider wantin' us to."

"Hey," objected Alex, "I thought you said the, er,

Lone Rider was fleeing. Now you say he wants to fight. Which is it?"

"Oh, the Lone Rider what owns the X Bar X is runnin', but the Lone Rider o' the Lazy T wants to stay. So do the Lone Rider o' Buffalo Stomp, the Really Lone Rider, an' the Loneliest Rider, but I'll bet they changes their minds when the Injuns gets as close to them as the varmints is to us right now."

Alex clutched his head to keep it from flying off his shoulders. "How many Lone Riders are there, anyway?" he shouted.

"How should I know?" shrugged Monty. "I knows at least ten myself. I gotta say," he added exasperatedly, "that English shore ain't got as many names as the old Hoka did. It gets gosh-awful tiresome to have a hundred other Montys around, or yell for Tex an' be asked which one."

They passed the bawling herd at a jog trot and topped a low rise. Beyond it lay a village, perhaps a dozen small frame houses and a single rutted street lined with square-built false-fronted structures. The place was jammed with Hokas—on foot, mounted, in covered wagons and buggies—refugees from the approaching Injuns, Alex decided. As he was carried down the hill, he saw a clumsily lettered sign:

WELCOME TO CANYON GULCH
Pop. Weekdays 212
Saturdays 1000

"We'll take yo' to Slick," said Monty above the hubbub. "He'll know what to do with yo'."

They forced their ponies slowly through the swirling, pressing, jabbering throng. The Hokas seemed to be a highly excitable race, given to arm-waving and shouting at the top of their lungs. There was no organization whatsoever to the evacuation, which proceeded slowly with its traffic tie-ups, arguments, gossip exchange, and exuberant pistol shooting into the air. Quite a few ponies and wagons stood deserted before the saloons, which formed an almost solid double row along the street.

Alex tried to remember what there had been in the report of the first expedition. It was a brief report, the ship had only been on Toka for a couple of months. But—yes—the Hokas were described as friendly, merry, amazingly quick to learn . . . and hopelessly inefficient. Only their walled sea-coast towns, in a state of bronze-age technology, had been able to stand off the Slissii; otherwise the reptiles were slowly but steadily conquering the scattered ursinoid tribes. A Hoka fought bravely when he was attacked, but shoved all thought of the enemy out of his cheerful mind whenever the danger was not immediately visible. It never occurred to the Hokas to band together in a massed offensive against the Slissii; such a race of individualists could never have formed an army anyway.

A nice, but rather ineffectual little people. Alex felt somewhat smug about his own height, his dashing spaceman's uniform, and the fighting, slugging, persevering human spirit which had carried man out to the stars. He felt like an elder brother.

He'd have to do something about this situation, give these comic-opera creatures a hand. Which might also involve a promotion for Alexander Braithwaite Jones, since Earth wanted a plentiful supply of planets with friendly dominant species, and the first report on the Injuns—Slissii, blast it!—made it unlikely that they could ever get along with mankind.

A. Jones, hero. Maybe then Tanni and I can—

He grew aware that a fat, elderly Hoka was gaping at him, together with the rest of Canyon Gulch. This particular one wore a large metal star pinned to his vest.

"Howdy, sheriff," said Tex, and snickered.

"Howdy, Tex, old pal," said the sheriff obsequiously. "An' my good old sidekick Monty too. Howdy, howdy, gents! Who's this hyar stranger—not a *human?*"

"Yep, that's what he says. Whar's Slick?"

"Which Slick?"

"*The* Slick, yo'—yo' sheriff!"

The fat Hoka winced. "I think he's in the back room o' the Paradise Saloon," he said. And humbly: "Uh, Tex . . . Monty . . . yo'll remember yore old pal come ee-lection day, won't yo'?"

"Reckon we might," said Tex genially. "Yo' been sheriff long enough."

"Oh, thank yo', boys, thank yo'! If only the others will have yore kind hearts—" The eddying crowd swept the sheriff away.

"What off Earth?" exclaimed Alex. "What the *hell* was he trying to get you to do?"

"Vote ag'in him come the next ee-lection, o' course," said Monty.

"Against him? But the sheriff . . . he runs the town . . . maybe?"

Tex and Monty looked bewildered. "Now I really wonder if yo're human after all," said Tex. "Why' the humans themselves taught us the sheriff is the dumbest man in town. Only we don't think it's fair a man should have to be called that all his life, so we chooses him once a y'ar."

"Buck there has been *ee*-lected sheriff three times runnin'," said Monty. "He's *really* dumb!"

"But who is this Slick?" cried Alex a trifle wildly.

"The town gambler, o' course."

"What have I got to do with a town gambler?"

Tex and Monty exchanged glances. "Look, now," said Monty with strained patience, "we done allowed for a lot with yo'. But when yo' don't even know what the officer is what runs a town, that's goin' just a little too far."

"Oh," said Alex. "A kind of city manager, then."

"Yo're plumb loco," said Monty firmly. "*Everbody* knows a town is run by a town gambler!"

Slick wore the uniform of his office: tight pants, a black coat, a checked vest, a white shirt with wing collar and string tie, a diamond stickpin, a derringer in one pocket and a pack of cards in the other. He looked tired and harried; he must have been under a tremendous strain in the last few days, but he welcomed Alex with eager volubility and led him into an office furnished in vaguely 19th-century style. Tex and Monty came along, barring the door against the trailing, chattering crowds.

"We'll rustle up some sandwiches for yo'," beamed Slick. He offered Alex a vile purple cigar of some local weed, lit one himself, and sat down behind the rolltop desk. "Now," he said, "when can we get help from yore human friends?"

"Not soon, I'm afraid," said Alex. "The *Draco* crew doesn't know about this. They'll be spending all their time flying around in search of me. Unless they chance to find me here, which isn't likely, they won't even learn about the Injun war."

"How long they figger to be here?"

"Oh, they'll wait at least a month before giving me up for dead and leaving the planet."

"We can get yo' to the seacoast in that time, by hard ridin', but it'd mean takin' a short cut through some territory which the Injuns is between us and it." Slick paused courteously while Alex untangled that one. "Yo'd hardly have a chance to sneak through. So, it looks like the only way we can get yo' to yore friends is to beat the Injuns. Only we can't beat the Injuns without help from yore friends."

Gloom.

To change the subject, Alex tried to learn some Hoka history. He succeeded beyond expectations, Slick proving surprisingly intelligent and well-informed.

The first expedition had landed thirty-odd years ago. At the time, its report had drawn little Earthly interest; there were so many new planets in the vastness of the galaxy. Only now, with the *Draco* as a forerunner, was the League making any attempt to organize this frontier section of space.

The first Earthmen had been met with eager admiration by the Hoka tribe near whose village they landed. The autochthones were linguistic adepts, and between their natural abilities and modern psychography had learned English in a matter of days. To them, the humans were almost gods, though like most primitives they were willing to frolic with their deities.

Came the fatal evening. The expedition had set up an outdoor stereoscreen to entertain itself with films. Hitherto the Hokas had been interested but rather puzzled spectators. Now, tonight, at Wesley's insistence, an old film was reshown. It was a Western.

Most spacemen develop hobbies on their long voyages. Wesley's was the old American West. But he looked at it through romantic lenses; he had a huge stack of novels and magazines but very little factual material.

The Hokas saw the film and went wild.

The captain finally decided that their delirious, ecstatic reaction was due to this being something they could understand. Drawing-room comedies and interplanetary adventures meant little to them in terms of their own experience, but here was a country like their own, heroes who fought savage enemies, great herds of animals, gaudy costumes—

And it occurred to the captain and to Wesley that this race could find very practical use for certain elements of the old Western culture. The Hokas had been farmers, scratching a meager living out of prairie soil never meant to be plowed; they went about on foot, their tools were bronze and stone—they could do much better for themselves, given some help.

The ship's metallurgists had had no trouble reconstructing the old guns, Colt and derringer and carbine. The Hokas had to be taught how to smelt iron, make steel and gunpowder, handle lathes and mills; but here again, native quickness and psychographic instruction combined to make them learn easily. Likewise they leaped at the concept of domesticating the wild beasts they had hitherto herded.

Before the ship left, Hokas were breaking "ponies" to the saddle and rounding up "longhorns." They were making treaties with the more civilized agricultural and maritime cities of the coast, arranging to ship meat in exchange for wood, grain, and manufactured goods. And they were gleefully slaughtering every Slissii warband that came against them.

As a final step, just before he left, Wesley gave his collection of books and magazines to the Hokas.

None of this had been in the ponderous official

report Alex read: only the notation that the ursinoids had been shown steel metallurgy, the use of chemical weapons, and the benefits of certain economic forms. It had been hoped that with this aid they could subdue the dangerous Slissii, so that if man finally started coming here regularly, he wouldn't have a war on his hands.

Alex could fill in the rest. Hoka enthusiasm had run wild. The new way of life was, after all, very practical and well adapted to the plains—so why not go all the way, be just like the human godlings in every respect? Talk English with the stereofilm accent, adopt human names, human dress, human mannerisms, dissolve the old tribal organizations and replace them with ranches and towns—it followed very naturally. And it was so much more fun.

The books and magazines couldn't circulate far; most of the new gospel went by word of mouth. Thus certain oversimplifications crept in.

Three decades passed. The Hokas matured rapidly, a second generation which had been born to Western ways was already prominent in the population. The past was all but forgotten. The Hokas spread westward across the plains, driving the Slissii before them.

Until, of course, the Slissii learned how to make firearms too. Then, with their greater military talent, they raised an army of confederated tribes and proceeded to shove the Hokas back. This time they would probably continue till they had sacked the very cities of the coast. The bravery of individual Hokas was no match for superior numbers better organized.

And one of the Injun armies was now roaring down on Canyon Gulch. It could not be many kilometers away, and there was nothing to stop it. The Hokas gathered their families and belongings from the isolated ranch houses and fled. But with typical inefficiency, most of the refugees fled no further than this town; then they stopped and discussed whether to make a stand or hurry onward, and meanwhile they had just one more little drink. . . .

"You mean you haven't even *tried* to fight?" asked Alex.

"What could we do?" answered Slick. "Half the folks 'ud be ag'in the idea an' wouldn't have nothin' to do with it. Half o' those what did come would each have their own little scheme, an' when we didn't follow it they'd get mad an' walk off. That don't leave none too many."

"Couldn't you, as the leader, think of some compromise—some plan which would satisfy everybody?"

"O' course not," said Slick stiffly. "My own plan is the only right one."

"Oh, Lord!" Alex bit savagely at the sandwich in his hand. The food had restored his strength and the fluid fire the Hokas called whiskey had given him a warm, courageous glow.

"The basic trouble is, your people just don't know how to arrange a battle," he said. "Humans do."

"Yo're a powerful fightin' outfit," agreed Slick. There was an adoration in his beady eyes which Alex had complacently noticed on most of the faces in town. He decided he rather liked it. But a demi-god has his obligations.

"What you need is a leader whom everyone will follow without question," he went on. "Namely me."

"Yo' mean—" Slick drew a sharp breath. *"Yo'?"*

Alex nodded briskly. "Am I right, that the Injuns

are all on foot? Yes? Good. Then I know, from Earth history, what to do, There must be several thousand Hoka males around, and they all have some kind of firearms. The Injuns won't be prepared for a fast, tight cavalry charge. It'll split their army wide open."

"Wa'l, I'll be hornswoggled," murmured Slick. Even Tex and Monty looked properly awed.

Suddenly Slick began turning handsprings about the office. "Yahoo!" he cried. "I'm a rootin', tootin' son of a gun, I was born with a pistol in each hand an' I teethed on rattlesnakes!" He did a series of cartwheels. "My daddy was a catamount and my mother was a alligator. I can ran faster backward than anybody else can run forrad, I can jump over the outermost moon with one hand tied behind me, I can fill an inside straight every time I draw, an' if any sidewinder here says it ain't so I'll fill him so full o' lead they'll mine him!"

"What the hell?" gasped Alex, dodging.

"The old human war-cry," explained Tex, who had apparently resigned himself to his hero's peculiar ignorances.

"Let's go!" whooped Slick, and threw open the office door. A tumultuous crowd surged outside. The gambler filled his lungs and roared squeakily:

"Saddle yore hosses, gents, an' load yore six-guns! We got us a human, an' he's gonna lead us all out to wipe the Injuns off the range!"

The Hokas cheered till the false fronts quivered around them, danced, somersaulted, and fired their guns into the air. Alex shook Slick and wailed: "— no, no, you bloody fool, not now! We have to study the situation, send out scouts, make a plan—"

Too late. His impetuous admirers swept him out into the street. He couldn't be heard above the falsetto din. He tried to keep his footing and was only vaguely aware of anything else. Someone gave him a six-shooter, and he strapped it on as if in a dream. Someone else gave him a lasso, and he made out the voice: "Rope yoreself a bronc, Earthman, an' let's go!"

"Rope—" Alex grew groggily aware that there was a corral just behind the saloon. The half-wild reptile ponies galloped about inside it, excited by the noise. Hokas were deftly whirling their lariats forth to catch their personal mounts.

"Go ahead!" urged the voice. "Ain't got no time to lose."

Alex studied the cowboy nearest him. Lassoing didn't look so hard. You held the rope here and here, then you swung the noose around your head like *this*—

He pulled and came crashing to the ground. Through whirling dust, he saw that he had lassoed himself.

Tex pulled him to his feet and dusted him off. "I . . . I don't ride herd at home," he mumbled. Tex made no reply.

"I got a bronc for yo'," cried another Hoka, reeling in his lariat. "A real spirited mustang!"

Alex looked at the pony. It looked back. It had an evilly glittering little eye. At the risk of making a snap judgment, he decided he didn't like it very much. There might be personality conflicts between him and it.

"Come on, let's git goin'!" cried Slick impatiently. He was astraddle a beast which still bucked and reared, but he hardly seemed to notice.

Alex shuddered, closed his eyes, wondered what he had done to deserve this, and wobbled over to the pony. Several Hokas had joined to saddle it for him. He climbed aboard. The Hokas released the animal. There was a personality conflict.

Alex had a sudden feeling of rising and spinning on a meteor that twisted beneath him. He grabbed for the saddle horn. The front feet came down with a ten-gee thump and he lost his stirrups. Something on the order of a nuclear shell seemed to explode in his vicinity.

Though it came up and hit him with unnecessary hardness, he had never known anything so friendly as the ground just then.

"Oof!" said Alex and lay still.

A shocked, unbelieving silence fell on the Hokas. The human hadn't been able to use a rope—now he had set a new record for the shortest time in a saddle—*what sort of human was this, anyway?*

Alex sat up and looked into a ring of shocked fuzzy faces. He gave them a weak smile. "I'm not a horseman either," he said.

"What the hell are yo', then?" stormed Monty. "Yo' cain't rope, yo' cain't ride, yo' cain't talk right, yo' cain't shoot—"

"Now hold on!" Alex climbed to somewhat unsteady feet. "I admit I'm not used to a lot of things here, because we do it differently on Earth. But I can outshoot any man . . . er, any Hoka of you any day in the week and twice on Sundays!"

Some of the natives looked happy again, but Monty only sneered. "Yeah?"

"Yeah. I'll prove it." Alex looked about for a suitable target. For a change, he had no worries. He was one of the best raythrower marksmen in the Fleet. "Throw up a coin. I'll plug it through the middle."

The Hokas began looking awed. Alex gathered that

they weren't very good shots by any standards but their own. Slick beamed, took a silver dollar from his pocket, and spun it into the air. Alex drew and fired.

Unfortunately, raythrowers don't have recoil. Revolvers do.

Alex went over on his back. The bullet broke a window in the Last Chance Bar & Grill.

The Hokas began to laugh. It was a bitter kind of merriment.

"Buck!" cried Slick. "Buck . . . yo' thar, sheriff . . . c'mere!"

"Yes, sir, Mister Slick, sir?"

"I don't think we need yo' for sheriff no longer, Buck. I think we just found ourselves another one. Gimme yore badge!"

When Alex regained his feet, the star gleamed on his tunic. And, of course, his proposed counter-attack had been forgotten.

He mooched glumly into Pizen's Saloon. During the past few hours, the town had slowly drained itself of refugees as the Injuns came horribly closer; but there were still a few delaying for one more drink. Alex was looking for such company.

Being official buffoon wasn't too bad in itself. The Hokas weren't cruel to those whom the gods had afflicted. But—well—he had just ruined human prestige on this continent. The Service wouldn't appreciate that.

Not that he would be seeing much of the Service in the near future. He couldn't possibly reach the *Draco* now before she left—without passing through territory held by the same Injuns whose army was advancing on Canyon Gulch. It might be years till another expedition landed. He might even be marooned here for life. Though come to think of it, that wouldn't be a lot worse than the disgrace which would attend his return.

Gloom.

"Here, sheriff, let me buy yo' a drink," said a voice at his elbow.

"Thanks," said Alex. The Hokas did have the pleasant rule that the sheriff was always treated when he entered a saloon. He had been taking heavy advantage of the custom, though it didn't seem to lighten his depression much.

The Hoka beside him was a very aged specimen, toothless and creaky. "I'm from Childish way," he introduced himself. "They call me the Childish Kid. Howdy, sheriff."

Alex shook hands, dully.

They elbowed their way to the bar. Alex had to stoop under Hoka ceilings, but otherwise the rococo fittings were earnestly faithful to their fictional prototypes—including a small stage where three scantily clad Hoka females were going through a song-and-dance number while a bespectacled male pounded a rickety piano.

The Childish Kid leered. "I know those gals," he sighed. "Some fillies, hey? Stacked, don't yo' think?"

"Uh . . . yes," agreed Alex. Hoka females had four mammaries apiece. "Quite."

"Zunami an' Goda an' Torigi, that's their names. If I warn't so danged old—"

"How come they have, er, non-English names?" inquired Alex.

"We had to keep the old Hoka names for our wimmin," said the Childish Kid. He scratched his balding head. "It's bad enough with the men, havin' a hundred Hopalongs in the same county . . . but how the hell can yo' tell yore wimmin apart when they're all named Jane?"

"We have some named 'Hey, you' as well," said Alex grimly. "And a lot more called 'Yes, dear.'"

His head was beginning to spin. This Hoka brew was potent stuff.

Nearby stood two cowboys, arguing with alcoholic loudness. They were typical Hokas, which meant that to Alex their tubby forms were scarcely to be distinguished from each other. "I know them two, they're from my old outfit," said the Childish Kid. "That one's Slim, an' t'other's Shorty."

"Oh," said Alex.

Brooding over his glass, he listened to the quarrel for lack of anything better to do. It had degenerated to the name-calling stage. "Careful what yo' say, Slim," said Shorty, trying to narrow his round little eyes. "I'm a powerful dangerous hombre."

"You ain't no powerful dangerous hombre," sneered Slim.

"I am so too a powerful dangerous hombre!" squeaked Shorty.

"Yo're a fathead what ought to be kicked by a jackass," said Slim, "an' I'm just the one what can do it."

"When yo' call me that," said Shorty, "smile!"

"I said yo're a fathead what ought to be kicked by a jackass," repeated Slim, and smiled.

Suddenly the saloon was full of the roar of pistols. Sheer reflex threw Alex to the floor. A ricocheting slug whanged nastily by his ear. The thunder barked again and again. He hugged the floor and prayed.

Silence came. Reeking smoke swirled through the air. Hokas crept from behind tables and the bar and resumed drinking, casually. Alex looked for the corpses. He saw only Slim and Shorty, putting away their emptied guns.

"Wa'l, that's that," said Shorty. "I'll buy this round."

"Thanks, pardner," said Slim. "I'll get the next one."

Alex bugged his eyes at the Childish, Kid. "Nobody was hurt!" he chattered hysterically.

"O' course not," said the ancient Hoka. "Slim an' Shorty is old pals." He spread his hands. "Kind o' a funny human custom, that. It don't make much sense that every man should sling lead at every other man once a month. But I reckon maybe it makes 'em braver, huh?"

"Uh-huh," said Alex.

Others drifted over to talk with him. Opinion seemed about equally divided over whether he wasn't a human at all or whether humankind simply wasn't what the legends had cracked it up to be. But in spite of their disappointment, they bore him no ill will and stood him drinks. Alex accepted thirstily. He couldn't think of anything else to do.

It might have been an hour later, or two hours or ten, that Slick came into the saloon. His voice rose over the hubbub: "A scout just brung me the latest word, gents. The Injuns ain't no more'n five miles away an comin' fast. We'll all have to git a move on."

The cowboys swallowed their drinks, smashed their glasses, and boiled from the building in a wave of excitement. "Gotta calm the boys down," muttered the Childish Kid, "or we could git a riot." With great presence of mind, he shot out the lights.

"Yo' fool!" bellowed Slick. "It's broad daylight outside!"

Alex lingered aimlessly by the saloon, until the gambler tugged at his sleeve. "We're short o' cowhands an' we got a big herd to move," ordered Slick. "Get yoreself a *gentle pony* an' see if yo' can help."

"Okay," hiccoughed Alex. It would be good to know he was doing something useful, however little. Maybe he would be defeated at the next election.

He traced a wavering course to the corral. Someone led forth a shambling wreck of a mount, too old to be anything but docile. Alex groped after the stirrup. It evaded him. "C'mere," he said sharply. "C'mere, shtirrip. Ten-*shun!* For'ard marsh!"

"Here yo' are." A Hoka who flickered around the edges . . . ghost Hoka? Hoka Superior? the Hoka after Hoka? . . . assisted him into the saddle. "By Pecos Bill, yo're drunk as a skunk!"

"No," said Alex. "I am shober. It's all Toka whish ish drunk So only drunks on Toka ish shober. Tha's right. Yunnershtan'? Only shober men on Toka ish uh drunks—"

His pony floated through a pink mist in some or other direction. "I'm a lo-o-o-one cowboy!" sang Alex. "I'm thuh loneliesh lone cowboy in these here parts."

He grew amorphously aware of the herd. The cattle were nervous, they rolled their eyes and lowed and pawed the ground. A small band of Hokas galloped around them, swearing, waving their hats, trying to get the animals going in the right path.

"I'm an ol' cowhand, from thuh Rio Grande!" bawled Alex.

"Not so loud!" snapped a Tex-Hoka. "These critters are spooky enough as it is."

"You wanna get 'em goin', don'cha?" answered Alex. "We gotta get going. The greenskins are coming. Simple to get going. Like this. See?"

He drew his six-shooter, fired into the air, and let out the loudest screech he had in him. "Yahoo!"

"Yo' crazy fool!"

"Yahoo!" Alex plunged toward the herd, shooting little and shouting. "Ride 'em, cowboy! Get along, dogies! Yippee!"

The herd, of course, stampeded.

Like a red tide, it suddenly broke past the thin Hoka line. The riders scattered, there was death in those thousands of hoofs, their universe was filled with roaring and rushing and thunder. The earth shook!

"Yahoo!" caroled Alexander Jones. He rode behind the longhorns, still shooting. "Git along, git along! Hiyo, Silver!"

"Oh, my God," groaned Slick. "Oh, my God! The tumbleweed-headed idiot's got 'em stampeded *straight toward the Injuns*—"

"After 'em!" shouted a Hopalong-Hoka. "Mebbe we can still turn the herd! We cain't let the Injuns git all that beef!"

"An' we'll have a little necktie party too," said a Lone Rider-Hoka. "I'll bet that thar Alexanderjones is a Injun spy planted to do this very job."

The cowboys spurred their mounts. A Hoka brain had no room for two thoughts at once. If they were trying to head off a stampede, the fact that they were riding full tilt toward an overwhelming enemy simply did not occur to them.

"Whoopee-ti-yi-yo-o-o-o!" warbled Alex, somewhere in the storm of dust.

Caught by the peculiar time-sense of intoxication, he seemed almost at once to burst over a long low hill. And beyond were the Slissii.

The reptile warriors went afoot, not being built for riding—but they could outrun a Hoka pony. The tyrannosaurian forms were naked, save for war paint and feathers such as primitives throughout the galaxy wear, but they were armed with guns as well as lances, bows, and axes. Their host formed a great compact mass, tightly disciplined to the rhythm of the thudding signal drums. There were thousands of them . . . and a hundred cowboys, at most, galloped blindly toward their ranks.

Alex saw none of this. Being behind the stampede, he didn't see it hit the Injun army.

Nobody really did. The catastrophe was just too big.

When the Hokas arrived on the scene, the Injuns—such of them as had not simply been mashed flat—were scattered over the entire visible prairie. Slick wondered if they would ever stop running.

"At 'em, boys!" he yelled. "Go mop 'em up!"

The Hoka band sped forward. A few small Injun groups sounded their war-hisses and tried to rally for a stand, but it was too late, they were too demoralized, the Hokas cut them down. Others were chased as they fled, lassoed and hog-tied by wildly cheering teddy bears.

Presently Tex rode up to Slick. Dragging behind his pony at a lariat's end was a huge Injun, still struggling and cursing. "I think I got their chief," he reported.

The town gambler nodded happily. "Yep, you have. He's wearin' a high chief's paint. Swell! With him for a hostage, we can make t'other Injuns talk turkey—not that they're gonna bother this hyar country for a long time to come."

As a matter of fact, Canyon Gulch has entered the military textbooks with Cannae, Waterloo, and Xfisthgung as an example of total and crushing victory.

Slowly, the Hokas began to gather about Alex. The utter awe shone in their eyes.

"*He* done it," whispered Monty. "All the time he was playin' dumb, he knew a way to stop the Injuns—"

"Yo' mean, make 'em bite the dust," corrected Slick solemnly.

"Bite the dust," agreed Monty. "He done it single-handed! Gents, I reckon we should'a knowed better'n to go mistrustin' o' a . . . *human!*"

Alex swayed in the saddle. A violent sickness gathered itself within him. And he reflected that he had caused a stampede, lost an entire herd of cattle, sacrificed all Hoka faith in the Terrestrial race for all time to come. If the natives hanged him, he thought grayly, it was no more than he deserved.

He opened his eyes and looked into Slick's adoring face.

"Yo' saved us," said the little Hoka. He reached out and took the sheriff's badge off Alex's tunic. Then, gravely, he handed over his derringer and playing cards. "Yo' saved us all, human. So, as long as yo're, here, yo're the town gambler o' Canyon Gulch."

Alex blinked. He looked around. He saw the assembled Hokas, and the captive Slissii, and the trampled field of ruin . . . why, why—they had won!

Now he could get to the *Draco*. With human assistance, the Hoka race could soon force a permanent peace settlement on their ancient foes. And Ensign Alexander Braithwaite Jones was a hero.

"Saved you?" he muttered. His tongue still wasn't under very close control. "Oh. Saved you. Yes, I did, didn't I? Saved you. Nice of me." He waved a hand. "No, no. Don't mention it. *Noblesse oblige,* and all that sort of thing."

An acute pain in his unaccustomed gluteal muscles

spoiled the effect. He groaned. "I'm walking back to town. I won't be able to sit down for a week as it is!"

And the rescuer of Canyon Gulch dismounted, missed the stirrup, and fell flat on his face.

"Yo' know," murmured someone thoughtfully. "maybe that's the way humans get off their hosses. Maybe we should all—"

Interlude I

Foreign Ministry
of the
United Commonwealths

Cultural Development Service
Earth Headquarters
Interdepartmental No. 19847364
2/3/75

FROM: Adalbert Parr, Chief Cultural Commissioner

TO: Hardman Terwilliger, Head Administrator, Personnel Office, New Cultures Section, Extraterrestrial Adjustment and Assignment Branch

SUBJECT: Tokan Autochthones, Development of, Cultural

REFERENCES: (a) TISS Report 17281, (b) TISS Report 28485, (c) Prelim. Psych. Rep. 12971-B, (d) CDS

Regs. (rev.), Vol. XVIII, Sec. 49, Par. 2-c

1. You are hereby advised that the Tokan ursinoids, as originally reported in Ref. (a) and subsequently in Ref. (b), have agreed to send a delegation to EHQ to consider guidance. Details in Ref. (b), especially as regards mineral deposits on planet and strategic location of star in area where civilization is rapidly expanding, indicate that acceptance of such status by the aforementioned is highly desirable from the standpoint of achieving the objectives of the League and this Service.

2. Of course, the party of six whom HMS *Draco* of Ref. (b) have brought to Sol can legally speak only for their own small city-states, but empirical evidence given in Ref. (c) suggests that no great difficulty will be experienced in co-ordinating the rest of the planet once such a foothold has been gained.

3. The Tokan delegation is now in quarantine Callisto Reception Center, but is expected to reach Earthport Prime on 5th inst. at 0947 hours GMT.

4. You are therefore directed to prepare suitable quarters and entertainment for the aforementioned with a view to inducing them to accept ward status for their people, stressing the preferability of our protection and guidance to whatever precarious and backward autonomy their nations may possess at the moment.

5. In accordance with Ref. (d), you are further directed to nominate a suitable plenipotentiary in event of affirmative decision by Tokans.

6. However, Refs. (a), (b), and (c) do show this to be quite an unusual case. It is by no means certain

that any of our own career personnel would be an ideal choice for the position, but rather someone already possessing a degree of familiarity with the Tokan situation is to be recommended for at least temporary appointment.

AP/grd

Foreign Ministry
of the
United Commonwealths

Cultural Development Service
Earth Headquarters
Interdepartmental No. 19847372
2/3/75

FROM: Hardman Terwilliger, P.O., N.C.S., E.T.A.A.B.

TO: Adalbert Parr, C.C.C.

SUBJECT: Tokan Autochthones, Entertainment of and
Plenipotentiary for, Arrangement of

REFERENCES: (a) Interd. No. 19847364, (b) TISS
Personnel File J-965731-s3

1. Note is hereby taken of Ref. (a).
2. In compliance therewith, have arranged suitable
   quarters for Tokan delegation in the Official
   Hostel, and appointed Miss Doralene Rawlings
   of my personal staff Official Hostess to the
   aforementioned.
3. In view of allegedly unusual Tokan character and
   recommendation that experienced persons be
   found to deal with them, have also arranged with
   TISS HQ to borrow Ensign Alexander Braithwaite
   Jones to serve as Official Host. As shown in Ref.
   (b), Ensign Jones has probably had more experience
   with Tokans than any other available human.
   Indeed, he is doubtless an expert on their
   psychology, though showed commendable modesty
   in disclaiming any such abilities whatsoever when

his furlough was cancelled with orders to report to undersigned.

4. Your recommendation noted re appointment of plenipotentiary; but must remind your office that, while it possesses powers of review, all actual appointments fall under jurisdiction of this office, which must follow its own judgment exclusively.

HT/pa

Don Jones

"Don't go—" said Tanni Hostrup, kissing Alexander Jones frantically.

"I've got to—" said Alex, kissing Tanni frantically.

"You mustn't—"

"I must—"

"I love you so much—"

"I love you too—"

We will spare you the rest of this dialogue. One reconciliation between lovers is very much like another.

The trouble was that while Tanni was a highly desirable specimen, both physically—being the possessor of long sunlight-colored hair, eyes like North Martian summer skies, a pertly beautiful face and a figure describable objectively by a complex assemblage of high-order curves and subjectively by an explosion in a fireworks factory—and mentally, being spirited, intelligent, cultured, and good-humored . . . she suffered from one minor vice which recent circumstances had blown into a major one. (If this sentence is complicated, it is because a girl like Tanni touches off extremely complicated reactions in a healthy man like Alex.)

She was unreasonably jealous.

Though stunning, she had only emerged of late from a gawky and lonesome adolescence. The scars of insecurity were not quite healed over. They showed as a too-quick readiness to assume that her fiancé lived up to the roving reputation of all spacemen.

Now actually, in spite of writing poems now and then, Alex was a rather steadfast young chap. But his record, as far as Tanni was concerned, was against him.

On a sunny afternoon two years before, he had been spending furlough time in Krog's Fish Restaurant in Copenhagen. Tanni walked by just as a capitalized Meal was commencing. Alex abandoned a cold glass of Hof and a plate of Limfjord oysters to take off after her—an infallible sign of true love. The same love lent his tongue an unaccustomed glibness. Though the immediate result, a whispered "Ja, *min elskede*" while the Tivoli roller-coaster poised for an especially fell swoop, was excellent: its long-range effects were troublesome. If this American spaceman could win her so swiftly, brooded Tanni, why would not the same techniques work elsewhere? The laws of nature are constant, even on the remotest planets.

She did him an injustice. He had, in fact, been looking for a job which would pay enough for him to get married and also permit him to live with his wife, instead of merely visiting her on meager Earthside leaves. So far he had not succeeded.

We have now given Alex and Tanni enough time

to say their good-byes. After all, they expected to meet again the next day.

He kissed her a last lingering once and stepped through the door, over the flange, onto the elevated walkway. It soared in one magnificent arch from this apartment building to the League hostel where Alex was quartered; the view of towers, traffic, sky, and New Zealand's distant mountains was famous throughout the civilized galaxy; but Alex turned to wave at the blonde girl in the door.

"Who's the blossom?" inquired a familiar husky voice at his shoulder.

He glanced around. A foreboding chill twined about his vertebrae. This was an unusual phenomenon, for the Canadian lass, Doralene Rawlings, was generally believed to raise the temperature three degrees C. in any room where men were present. She was tall, strong, supple, red-haired, green-eyed, unmistakably mammalian, and addicted to skin-tight tunics and half-kneelength skirts. Alex, however, had had his troubles on her account.

"My fiancée," he said coldly. "We're engaged."

"It figures," said Doralene. She took his arm in her normal companionable manner. "Well, let's get back and make ready for the occasion, eh?"

"Please!" Alex pulled away from her. "You don't understand," he added when she gave him a hurt look. "That party the other night . . . you remember, we got to talking on the terrace, and then you wanted me to learn that new dance—"

"Which one?" she asked. "I was showing you several. You've been away from Earth a long time, spaceman, and you had a lot to catch up on."

Alex blushed. "I mean the . . . the one you said was derived from the Pilsudski's Star III fertility rite."

"Oh, yes." Doralene sighed reminiscently. "That one."

"That one," said Alex, "happened to be what you were teaching me when Tanni found us. She'd just gotten back to Earth herself after a good many months—vacationing on New Podunk—and, well—" He shuffled his feet. "I only got matters straightened out today."

"Oh, I see." Doralene smiled compassionately. "I'm sorry." She cocked her head at him. "You know, Alex, you're cute."

And, with that impulsiveness which so many men found so delightful, she kissed him.

"Yipe!" said Alex.

"Oh, dear," said Doralene. "I forgot."

"Well, please see to it that you remember." Alex began walking very fast toward the hostel. Her long smooth legs matched his strides easily.

"After all," he fumbled, "I thought you and, er, Hardman Terwilliger were, uh—"

"Him?" Doralene laughed. "Hardman better go up five grades in the Service before he starts talking to *me* about love." She stretched herself voluptuously. "I don't understand why you're in such a rush to get married, Alex. Play the field a while longer— like me. Hardman's only useful for wangling me soft assignments like this one." Then, for just a moment, quite a different light flickered in her eyes, and she added with unnecessary quickness: "Oh, don't think I'm mercenary about it. I do like him. He's kind of cute in a stuffed-shirt way. Almost like your Hokas."

"They're not *my* Hokas," clipped Alex. "And as for their being cute, I could tell you a thing or two!"

"Nonsense," said Doralene, shaking back her mane of ruddy hair. "They're just pure cuteness, with their adorable button noses and little round tummies, sitting there all in a row and simply eating up that opera. I'm quite unprofessional about them."

Alex jumped.

"Opera?" he demanded sharply. "You don't mean . . . horse opera?"

"Why, no. The San Francisco Opera was in town, and I took them down to see it a couple of nights ago. *Don Giovanni.*" She stared at him. "What's the matter with horse operas?"

Alex gulped. "They react to stories about cowboys and Indians," he said.

So far things had gone smoothly enough. The delegation was not from the Wild West but from the more prosperous and socially advanced confederation of maritime city-states. Apart from a tendency to wear striped pants, top hats, and morning coats everywhere—even to bed—the Hokas had been very well-behaved.

Alex realized, however, that he had been quite derelict in his duty. The assignment was to keep the delegates happy . . . but calm. Introduce them in the most favorable way to the amenities of civilization. Persuade them to accept low status and the long upward grind toward full acceptance, autonomy, and League membership.

But when she heard he was on Earth, Tanni had taken an apartment right in the city to be near him. And, well, Doralene had been very kind about squiring his charges around for him. But of course, if trouble came up while he was neglecting his task, it could mean court-martial, dishonorable discharge, and even an ensign's lousy pay was better than no pay at all—

He entered the enormous hostel building with Doralene and took the gravshaft up to the floor where he, she, and the Hokas had their adjoining suites.

As he stepped into the ornate corridor, a light flashed and a robotic voice said: "Ensign Jones, sir, there is an urgent call for you." With the remorseless literal-mindedness of all machinery, a portable visio unit had already rolled up to save the few seconds it would take him to get inside his own quarters.

"Oh?" Wondering, Alex stepped forward.

"I better go on ahead," said Doralene. "Have to get our Hokas all tidied up for this dinner tonight."

"Right." Alex nodded and bent over the visio. Tanni's face sprang onto the screen. There were big pathetic tears in her eyes. There was also a cannibalistic screech in her voice.

"Alex!"

"Eep!" said Alex.

"I saw you with that woman!"

"Yipe! But . . . but darling—" stammered Alex. "It was only Doralene . . . you never let me explain before, but she works with me—lives right here—"

"WHAT?"

"Oh, Lord! Look, she's assigned to, this job with me—"

"Why?"

"Why . . . why . . . well, I need an assistant . . . well, actually, just between the two of us, she has pull with Hardman Terwilliger and—"

"And she used it to get assigned to a job with you. I know!" Tanni's charming Danish accent became less suggestive of dances on the greensward than of a Viking chief telling his men to break out the battle axes. "Well, she's not going to get away with it. I'm coming right over there and—"

"You can't!" yelped Alex. "It's against regulations! I'll be court-martialled if they find a woman in my rooms—"

"Except that Doralene woman, of course," snarled Tanni.

"But she *works* here!"

"What does she work at, besides you?"

"Look here," gabbled Alex, "there are these Victorian-type regulations on the books. Left over from the Puritan Party administration fifty years ago. Ordinarily they're just ignored . . . so much ignored that no one's ever bothered to change them. But Terwilliger—my supervisor while I'm on this blasted assignment—well, he heard about that episode at the party too. The one with, well, us, you know. He won't admit it, but he's obviously in love with Doralene . . . wildly jealous. He told me if I ever broke the morality regulations he'd report me to my CO for dereliction of duty and—and—oh, gosh, he's coming over here now! Tonight! Dinner party for the Hokas—supposed to be small, intimate thing between alien delegates and CDS official—can you see how you'd foul the whole thing up by making a scene and—"

"I don't care!"

"No! Wait! Wait, Tanni, honey, please!" wailed Alex. "Listen, you've got it all wrong. Doralene told me herself she isn't interested in getting married. She's just playing the field—"

"*Oh!*" shrieked Tanni.

And cut the connection.

After a frantic attempt to call back, Alex turned and sprinted for the door of the Tokan suite.

"Doralene!" he howled, bursting in. "You've got to help me—you—us . . . huh?"

The place seemed to be deserted by all except one small Hoka.

Somehow, this pudgy being had gotten dressed

in crimson trunk hose, black velvet doublet, puff-sleeved shirt, cloak, and boots, not to forget the tall plumed hat which he now removed from his panda-like head in order to sweep the carpet with a low bow.

"Ah, Illustrissimo!" he squeaked. The English which he had learned so recently and so well had suddenly become thickly accented, with a tendency to wander off into bars of melody. "You are returned."

"Of course I are returned . . . am returned . . . I'm back!" puffed Alex. "Where's Miss Rawlings? What's happened to the others? Why are you all costumed up like that, Ardu?"

"Ah, 'Lustrissimo!" warbled the Hoka reproachfully. "Do you not recognize your faithful Leporello?"

"Lepo—huh?"

"Your servant, Don Giovanni. Your assistant in the unnumbered amorous escapades which have made you the terror of husbands and fathers from Lisbon to Athens." The Hoka struck a pose with one hand extended and the other on his pot belly, and burst into song:

> *"Gaily he within is sporting.*
> *I must keep off all intrusion,*
> *For his lordship needs seclusion—"*

"Stop!" yelled Alex. And as the Hoka obediently quit singing, he rattled: "You mean me? Don Giovanni? I'm Don Giovanni?"

"In the Spanish sometimes referred to as Don Juan," amplified the self-appointed Leporello.

Alex clutched after reality, which seemed to be eluding him. "But that's just an opera!"

"*Cospetto!* Has your lordship been so trounced by

an indignant husband that your lordship's memory has failed him?"

"No such thing!" screamed Alex. "Where's Miss Rawlings?"

"Hist!" said Leporello slyly, laying a stubby finger to his black nose. "Ah, the beautiful Zerlina."

"All right," gritted Alex. "The beautiful Zerlina. Where is she?"

Leporello stood on tiptoe and whispered hoarsely: "She is within."

"Within? Within what, for Betelgeuse's sake?"

"Within your chambers, of course, Illustrissimo."

"My chambers?" Alex charged off, skidded to a halt, decided that her chambers—oops, rooms!—were meant, and turned left in the hallway instead of right.

Mozartian tweedlings came through the door as he leaned on the chime button. "Doralene!" he cried "Open up! What's happening here?"

The door was flung wide. Five Hokas stood there in Renaissance costume, violins tucked under their chins or flutes to their lips or— "Seducer! Ravisher! Cuckolder!" they squeaked.

One of them put down his oboe, drew a wicked-looking rapier, and lunged. "Help!" yelled Alex, giving ground.

Leporello came trotting forth, slammed the door in the faces of his fellow delegates, and called soothingly: "Excellencies, Excellencies! It is no use. My master, that rascal, has just made his escape."

They seemed willing enough to accept this. The music resumed and one of them broke into an aria swearing vengeance upon a certain unknown assailant and murderer.

"Whew!" shuddered Alex. "What's got into them?"

"The Signor means Don Ottavio and the other

husbands, fathers, brothers, and lovers of the women he has ruined?" asked Leporello.

"Yes . . . I mean no! Now, look here! What's become of Doralene?"

"Did I not inform your lordship, the beautiful damsel was in his chambers?" replied Leporello. He dug his elbow familiarly into Alex's ribs, and winked. "Surely your lordship would not wish her to be any place else, would your lordship?"

"Oh, NO!" Alex smote his brow.

"That's what I thought," beamed Leporello.

Alex spun about, reached the door of his own rooms, jerked it open, and charged through. "Doralene!" he yelled from the entry. "Where are you?"

"Alex?" trilled a voice from further in. "I'm here."

He dashed ahead, braked, and yipped. Her voice had come from his bathroom.

"What are you doing in there?" he shouted. "What's going on here? Have those Hokas gone crazy?"

A happy feminine laugh bubbled through the panels. "Aren't they cute?" purred Doralene. "They were just wild about that opera. Of course, I'd already told them they were Earth's guests and could send out for anything they wanted, so they must have called the library and a costumer and a music shop and—"

"But . . . you mean they *believe* all this?"

"Well, more or less, Alex. Haven't you read the preliminary psychological reports? It seems that Hokas have a hitherto unknown type of mind—given to accepting any colorful fantasy as if it were real . . . nobody knows, yet, whether they actually and literally believe it at the time, or just play a role to the hilt, but it comes to the same thing. They're also very quick to learn anything at all, so—"

Alex held tight to his whirling head.

"Oh, by the way," went on Doralene carelessly. "Hardman just called. He's got an emergency session later tonight, so we're going to have dinner early. He ought to be here any minute now."

"Now?" squeaked Alex. He got a fresh grip on himself. "But what are you doing in my bathroom?"

"Taking a shower, of course," replied Doralene's voice. "I couldn't dress in my own suite with the Hokas falling all over me. They were waiting for Don Giovanni . . . isn't it just darling? . . . they're convinced he'll show up sooner or later in any young woman's chambers. I'll be out in a minute—that is," her voice finished cheerfully, "unless you want to come in and scrub my back."

"Yipe!" said Alex.

"Do you mean yipe—yes, or yipe—no?" inquired Doralene's voice.

"I mean yipe n—"

Bong, bing, bong went the doorchimes.

"Wait!" cried Alex in agony. "Don't move— I mean, don't come out!"

"Why not?"

"Never mind why not!" Alex dashed off.

As he re-entered his living room, he heard Tanni's wrathful tones from the entry. "Where is he?"

"Mean you my master?" wavered Leporello's high-pitched recitative.

"I mean him, that deceitful . . . that deserter—" She choked.

"Ah!" said Leporello wisely. "You must be Donna Elvira."

"What?"

"Come, come, Zelenza, I am privy to all my master's secrets. "

"You're what?" said Tanni. Her English was fluent, but had its limitations as yet.

"My master," said Leporello, misunderstanding. "Don Giovanni. Sometimes in the Spanish referred to as Don Juan."

"Don Juan!" "claimed Tanni in a fire-breathing manner. "Yes, that's just what he is! A miserable, deceitful Don Juan."

"Are you Spanish, too?" asked Leporello, interested.

Tanni burst into tears.

"Ah!" said Leporello. "Time for me to sing the comforting aria." His voice soared:

> *"Gentle lady, this list I would show you*
> *Of the fair ones my master has courted:*
> *Here you'll find them all duly assorted*
> *In my writing, will't please you to look.*
> *In fair Italy, six hundred and forty,*
> *Germany, two hundred and thirty-one,*
> *A hundred in France—"*

Shaken, Alex tiptoed backward. If he could only find a way out—

With a sudden feeling of shock, he checked himself and shook his head to clear it. What was this fantastic spell the Hokas seemed to cast? It must be their own hypnotic solemnity. For a minute he had actually been thinking of himself as Don Giovanni.

This was intolerable! Was he a man or a figment of some Hoka's inflamed imagination? Wheeling about, he marched back into the living room. Tanni had just entered, brushing Leporello aside.

"Alex!" She hesitated, with fire in her eyes.

Bong, bing, bong went the door again, followed a second later by the booming voice of Hardman

Terwilliger, unseen in the entry. "Well, well, well! And where is everybody?"

"Yipe!" gasped Alex. "Tanni, hide! It's him!"

"Never mind him," she said, grimly. "This Hoka has been telling me some things about you and what I want to know is—"

With visions of court-martial dancing through his head to the sound of muffled drums, Alex pushed her into Leporello's arms. "Hide her!" he whispered. "Get rid of her . . . lock her in the study at the rear. . . . I'll explain later, darling—"

"I—" Tanni got no further. Leporello's hand closed about her mouth and Leporello's astonishing Hoka strength lifted her off her feet. He whisked her away barely in time.

Terwilliger entered the living room, carrying a package. He was a heavy-set ginger-haired man in his late thirties, who had never quite decided whether a bluff comradely heartiness or a stiff official dignity was more suitable. The former would in fact have been the most natural to him, but some fifteen years of climbing the bureaucratic stairway had left their mark.

His red face split in a hail-fellow let's-let-bygones-be-bygones smile. "Hello, there, Jones!" he trumpeted. "Got a cooler for this? Magnum of champagne I brought along, for you and Doralene and myself. Understand the, ah, Tokans prefer their native beverage, but no reason for us to stint ourselves, eh? Daresay the catering machines will fix a decent enough dinner, but, the appropriation doesn't allow for champagne, so, tum-te-tum . . . take care of your stomach, I always say, and your stomach will take care of you."

Alex bolted an artificial grin to his own face. "Thank

you, sir," he wheezed. "Ah (pant, pant) . . . excuse my not being in uniform . . . you did come unexpectedly early."

"Quite all right, quite all right." Terwilliger rubbed his hands and looked about him. "Pleasant digs here, eh? Cut above spaceship on Survey, what? Is Dory ready yet?"

"Dory? Er . . . Miss Rawlings? She's getting dressed, I, I believe—" said Alex, casting a worried glance down the hall toward his bathroom door.

"Ah? Dressing? Ho, ho!" said Terwilliger, turning, if possible, a shade redder in the face than usual. "Perhaps I ought to take her a glass of the gloom-chaser, eh? Haw!" He dug Alex in the ribs, sending the younger man tottering off balance. "I say, what a woman, eh? What a shape! What—"

"I'd better put this bottle in the cooler," said Alex, and dashed for the kitchen.

He swerved just in time to avoid colliding with Doralene, as she stepped out of his bedroom clad in a shimmering dinner gown which hugged her form like a mountain climber not quite able to reach the ultimate peaks.

"Oops! Watch it, boy," she said. "Where's the fire— oh, hullo, Hardy."

Alex looked around, swallowing. Terwilliger's rubicund features appeared to have lost some of their good humor. His eyes swiveled from Alex to Doralene to the bedroom door and back.

"How do you do," he said frozenly.

"Ha, ha!" said Alex. "Guess what happened! The Hokas took over Dor— Miss Rawlings' rooms, so she had to dress in mine. Isn't that funny?"

"Ha-ha!" laughed Doralene.

"Ha!" said Terwilliger.

"What did you say, Hardy?" cooed Doralene.

"Just 'ha,' " snapped Terwilliger. "Man has a right to say 'ha' if he wants to, eh?"

"What's wrong with you, anyway?" asked the girl.

"Nothing wrong with me!"

"Oh yes, there's something wrong with you—"

"Will the gentlefolk have a small drink before dinner?" fluted Leporello, emerging from the kitchen. The savory odors which followed him showed that the catering service robots were hard at work on the meal. Leporello carried a tray bearing three tall glasses and a bottle of extraterrestrial manufacture.

As he passed Alex, he said in a *sotto voce* audible for several meters: "I have locked the importunate damsel away to await your pleasure, Illustrissimo."

"What's this?" Terwilliger started.

"Oh, that!" floundered Alex. "*The Importunate Damsel.* Novel by, uh, Wolfgang Amadeus. Very interesting. Lend it to you when I'm through with it— Have a drink!"

He took one off the tray himself. Automatically, the other two humans followed suit. Terwilliger raised his stonily, took a sip, choked, and lowered it with tears in his prominent pale eyes.

"A native Tokan beverage?" he asked in a strangled voice.

"Uh . . . yes," said Alex wretchedly, after tasting and wincing. "It's pretty strong—not quite to Terrestrial taste. . . . I'll get some Dubonnet or—"

"No, no," said Terwilliger. In a rough aside: "Don't you know, you bloody fool, you never refuse a non-League alien's gift? No telling how some of 'em will react. We'll drink this if it burns our guts out."

"It could be worse, really," murmured Doralene

around a thoughtful sip. But then, she was a very husky young woman.

"Ah, Ser Masetto," burbled the Hoka servant to Terwilliger, "take courage. You may only be a peasant, but what is rank compared to honest worth? What, even, is the disgrace in losing your beloved to my master? There is no woman living who could resist him."

"*Eh?*" exploded Terwilliger.

"Er . . . excuse me . . . put the champagne in the cooler," mumbled Alex. "Ardu—Leporello, I mean— a word with you."

When they were in the kitchen, he demanded the key to the study. Leporello broke out another bottle and followed him down the short passageway, remarking that Donna Elvira would need consolation.

Alex unlocked the door. Tanni stood there with sparks in her lovely eyes and small jets of steam appearing to come from her chiseled nostrils. "Well!" she began.

"Now, wait—" croaked Alex. "Here; honey, take this—" Blindly, he snatched the bottle from Leporello and thrust it into her hands. "I'm sorry," he gibbered, "but you shouldn't have come in the first place . . . could ruin me . . . you've got to keep quiet, lie doggo in here till Terwilliger goes home. Then we can straighten out this mess."

"But—" protested Tanni.

"Do you want to get me court-martialled?" groaned Alex.

He closed the door in her face and sped back to the living room.

The conversation between Terwilliger and Doralene had grown somewhat acrimonious in his brief absence. As he entered, a shrill "Now you look here, Hardman

Terwilliger—" broke off, and the two stared glumly at their glasses. The boss raised his with a defiant air and tossed the contents off at a gulp. The effect was spoiled by his choking as said contents sank its claws into his gullet. Doralene sneered, swallowed her own drink likewise, and didn't turn a single red hair.

"Uh . . . is dinner ready yet, Leporello?" groped Alex.

"At once, Signor," bowed the Hoka. "And their other Excellencies?"

"What other Excellencies?"

"The husbands, brothers, fathers, and lovers of the women you have seduced, ravished, and—"

"Yes, yes, of course," interrupted Alex as Terwilliger turned his head to stare at him.

"Then best that your Excellency wear this mask." Leporello whipped a black domino from his doublet and extended it. Alex put it on in a numbed, unthinking fashion. Leporello trotted out the main door to give the word.

A swelling chorus of *Finch'han dal vino* rose and five Hokas poured in, engulfed the humans for a moment, and washed on into the dining room, still singing.

"What's been going on here, anyway?" demanded Terwilliger. "What's all this with costumery and . . . and opera, and masks, and—"

"Oh, don't be such a bore, Hardy," said Doralene. She giggled. "I think it's fun."

Terwilliger bristled. "Oh, so I'm a bore now, am I?"

"No . . . yes . . . don't *be* like this!"

"I'll be any way I jolly well please," said Terwilliger sullenly. He poured himself another glassful, grabbed the bottle by the neck, and marched on into the dining room. Alex escorted Doralene, as if through a lobster-and-ice-cream dream.

It would have seemed a pleasing sight under happier circumstances: the snowy tablecloth, the glittering silver, the candles, the bottles, the gaily clad Hokas seated there waving their instruments, swilling merrily, and extemporizing a drinking song full of grace notes. The RoboServs rolled about offering appetizers, not too badly handicapped by Leporello's assistance, and sunset light streamed through the tall plastic windows. It ought to have been a picture of gracious living.

Terwilliger sat down at the head of the table and took a moody gulp of liquor. Doralene sat at his right and took a moody gulp for herself. Alex, at his left, sweating under the mask, realized that the Hoka hell-brew was taking effect on them. Already it had numbed taste buds and judgment enough so that they didn't understand what they were drinking and what a wallop was being prepared.

"Wouldn't you like to switch to this vermouth?" he suggested.

"No," said Terwilliger.

"Well, the clear soup looks good—"

"Don't want any clear soup."

"*Perbacco!*" squeaked the sword-bearing Hoka who had apparently assumed the part of Don Ottavio. "This Masetto is a man of parts. He would rather drink than eat. Drink to Ser Masetto!"

"Ah," said another Hoka pityingly, "who would not seek to drown his sorrows, whose intended bride is soon to be seduced by the unspeakable villain Don Giovanni . . . if, indeed, she has not already succumbed to his lure?"

"What?" barked Terwilliger, jerking in his chair. "What's going on here?"

"I don't know," said Doralene, perhaps a bit to quickly.

Terwilliger's eyes narrowed as he stared at her. "Who is this Giovanni chap, anyhow?" he demanded.

"Ah," said Don Ottavio, "who, indeed?" He looked straight at Alex's dominoed face. "Perhaps you, anonymous sir, know where we may find the villain to punish him for his crimes?"

"No," said Alex weakly. "He went that-a-way . . . I mean, no, I don't."

"It's no use, anyway," said the mournful Hoka. "There is no mortal man who can overcome Don Giovanni. You are but inviting your own death, Don Ottavio."

"Nevertheless," said Don Ottavio firmly, "I have sworn vengeance." He hopped up on his chair, put one foot on the table, spread his arms dramatically, and burst into song:

> *Che giuramento, oh Dei!*
> *Che giuramento, oh Dei!*
> *Che barbarao momento!*
> *Tra cento affetti e cento—*

"Uh . . . er . . . see here," shouted Alex above the racket. "Terwilliger . . . ah . . . this is supposed to be an official dinner, and I haven't yet presented the delegates—"

"Yes," said Terwilliger darkly, tossing off another draught. "It was *supposed* to be an official dinner."

"Have some salad?" pleaded Alex as a tray rolled by with the next course.

"What use is salad?" mumbled Doralene, draining

her glass and singing to Leporello to refill it. "I should sit here and listen to a certain gazabo crunching salad in his big fat mouth?"

"May I ask to what gazabo you refer, Miss Rawlings?" said Terwilliger with elaborate overtones.

"Never mind," said Doralene. "It might not be polite to say."

Terwilliger quivered. His eyes swung to Alex and grew smoky.

"You!" he rasped.

"Me?" said Alex.

"You!" repeated Terwilliger, breathing heavily.

"Leave him alone!" said Doralene.

Terwilliger returned his bleared gaze to her. "Ah so!" he said. "Now it comes out! Dressing in here— ha!"

"Oh!" cried Doralene. "Are you insin— are you insin-shin—" She drew herself up in her seat. Her décolletage, already strained, threatened to burst its moorings altogether. "How dare you!"

"Why, Miss Rawlings, what *are* you thinking of?" leered Terwilliger unpleasantly.

"Now, now, wait—" sputtered Alex. "I don't undersand—I didn't have anything to do with—"

"My master speaks truth, Ser Masetto," murmured Leporello, leaning over Terwilliger's shoulder to pour him another glassful. "He was out seducing another wench at the time."

"*What?*" roared Terwilliger.

"Excuse us, Masetto," piped a couple of Hokas. They got up and brushed past him and toddled out of the room.

"WHAT'S GOING ON HERE?" bellowed Terwilliger. "What you been doing behind my back, Jones? Are you an incompetent, a lecher, a lechment incompeter . . . an incompeter lech . . . or . . . or both? What is all this?"

"I'd better check on them," stammered Alex. He scrambled to his feet and dove after the two Hokas who had left.

Shuddering, he inspected the inner doors. Noises came from his bedroom. He entered.

A large statue in green marble loomed by the dresser. He recognized it as belonging to the Progress of Man series which lined the tenth-floor main corridor. This one represented John W. Campbell. Somehow . . . oh God . . . *when* had the Hokas stolen it?

The two whom he sought stood with brushes and a bucket of whitewash, happily splashing it on the statue.

"What are you doing?" choked Alex.

"Ah, Signor," beamed one. "Obviously matters are approaching a climax. It seems only proper that we prepare the statue of the Commandant for an appropriately ghastly entrance."

"No!" Alex snatched the bucket away from them. "Absolutely not. We don't do that."

"Why not, Signor?" asked a small wide-eyed being.

"Because . . . because . . . it's not the first of the month," said Alex desperately. "Statues of Commandants only get whitewashed on the first of the month, not like statues of Admirals, who get whitewashed on the fifteenth or the twentieth. That's because Admirals have more salt on them—" He realized suddenly that he was babbling, and with a strong effort pulled himself together. "Now do go back to the dinner party," he begged.

Somewhat disappointed, but willing as always to oblige, the painters obeyed. Alex stood for a moment wondering where he could put the bucket—no use leaving temptation around—ah, yes. He took it into the bathroom and balanced it precariously on the medicine chest, out of the short Hoka reach.

Loud, disputatious human voices came from the dining room. Alex was in no hurry to intervene. He slipped down the little hallway and stuck his head in the study door. It would not have surprised him much to have gotten it bitten off.

A warm and wobbly shape collapsed softly on his neck. "Oh, Alesh," breathed Tanni. "Sh' been sho long—"

Alex stared at her. She stared back, through tangled golden locks. She giggled. "Oh, Alesh," she said. "Alesh, dear, tha' li'l bottle shtuff . . . so *strong* . . . hol' onna me, honey—"

His eyes lit on the half-emptied bottle. He saw it had not, as he had assumed, been blown on Earth. The label said:

OLD PANTHER SWEAT
Made in Montana by Panthers

"Oh, no!" he moaned.

"Oh, yes," said Tanni. "Kiss me."

"JONES!" thundered Terwilliger. "Where are YOU? C'mere!"

"*Sig du elsker mig,*" pleaded Tanni.

"JONES!"

"Now . . . now just sit here . . . I'll be right back— just take it easy—" Somehow, Alex untangled himself from his suddenly octopus-like beloved and stumbled back to the living room.

Terwilliger, his face hardly distinguishable from the boiled lobster which Leporello was urging on him, sat weaving in his chair. He fixed a swollen and bloodshot eye on Alex. "Jones!" he woofed. "Where you been?"

"Oh . . . the Commandant . . . whitewash, you know," stuttered Alex with a feeble smile, sliding back into his seat.

"Whash— whish— Be. That. As. It. May. Jones," said Terwilliger, "I hold you responsible. High times I looked— I mean, *high time* I looked inna conditions here. Noss gregligence! Underculture aliens . . . prospec'ive wards o' League, d'you hear, allowed t' run riot an' . . . run riot. Mos' reprehensible." He sat for a moment repeating "reprehensible," obviously to be sure he had it right. The Hokas joined in with voice and instruments, and an impromptu cantata was getting under way when Terwilliger shifted gears and went on:

"Al'ays had . . . sof' spot f' you, Jones. But now . . . neglec' o' duty . . . slip me this rotgut, hope make me drunk so I wouldn' notice . . . highly immoral, lecher an' so forth—Nothin' personal, un'erstan'!" he added quickly. "Nothin' personal. If you've ruined woman I love—nothin' personal . . . feel sorry f' you, Doralene, him an' his hundreds of, uh, uh—"

"Paramours, Signor," supplied Leporello.

"Thank you. Paramours. You'll be outvoted, I'm afraid, Doralene. But i'sh your business." Terwilliger climbed slowly to his feet. "If I report you f' dereliction o' duty, Jones . . . recommen' court-martial—nothin' personal. Don' misun'erstan'. 'S jus' f' good o' the Service." He turned majestically on his heel. It was a well-chosen exit line, marred only by the fact that he kept on turning and asked plaintively: "Which way's uh bathroom?"

"Not love," snuffled Doralene into her glass. "Go

up five grades 'fore talk to me o' love. Suffed shtirt . . . stuffed shirt! Cute, though. Could'a loved him—" She began to cry. Terwilliger gyrated slowly out.

"Doralene!" howled Alex, oblivious to the interested gaze of the surrounding Hokas. "Doralene, what happened?"

He stood up as she came tearfully around the table. "Quarrel," she said. "Shirred stuff! *Believed* wha' those Hokas was sayin'— Oh, Alex!" And throwing her arms about his neck and her face against his tunic, she broke into noisy sobs.

"Doralene . . . now, Doralene, please—" he begged.

A Valkyrie shriek interrupted him. He yanked his eyes around and saw Tanni advancing on them.

"Bravo!" cheered the Hokas.

"That woman!" bawled Tanni. "All uh time I was waitin' and waitin' for you, all alone, you an!— Oh!"

"Whozis?" queried Doralene, fuzzy-voiced.

"My dear Ottavio," murmured one of the Hokas, "considering how the ladies cluster about him could it be that our mysterious masked friend is none other than . . . him?"

"Cospetto!" A furry hand dropped to a sword. "Think you so?"

"Ye-e-e-e-es," said another Hoka in A flat.

"I happen t' be Ens'n Jones' fian-she," said Tanni to Doralene.

"Oh, izzat so?" said Doralene, still holding on to Alex.

"It is past time we had our revenge, Signores," said a Hoka, "I, for one, don't like being cuckolded."

"But you're not married, Don Vittorio," pointed out another one reasonably. "How do you know if you haven't tried—"

"Yes," said Tanni. "That izzo."

"Now, girls," chattered Alex. "Girls, girls—"

"Wanna make somethin' of it, beanpole?" growled Doralene.

"*Beanpole!*" screamed Tanni. "Why, you fat frump—"

"After all," said a Hoka, "it's my honor that's at stake."

"How did it get there?" asked Don Vittorio.

"I have my suspicions," said the first one, darkly.

A crash from the inner suite was followed by a weird, strangled, gargling cry. The humans half turned to see what it was. But they had too much else to think about.

"What did you call me?" spat Doralene.

"The thing is," said Don Ottavio, "how can I discover his true identity as long as he has that mask on?"

"I call' you uh frat fump," said Tanni, returning to the pressing business at hand.

"You could ask him to take it off," suggested Don Vittorio.

"Why, you li'l squirt—" snarled Doralene.

"Girls, girls, girls!" Alex wrung his hands.

"Pardon me." Someone tugged at his sleeve. He looked down into Don Ottavio's round golden-furred face.

"Yes?" he asked.

"Would you do me the favor of removing your mask, sir?" requested the Hoka.

"How 'ud you enjoy uh poke inna nose?" said Tanni.

"Girls, girls—" Absently, Alex removed the domino "Tanni, Dory, now wait, wait just a—"

"*Perbacco! 'Tis* he! At the villain! Hew him down!'

With a roar of epithets, the Hokas came swarming around the table at Alex. Don Ottavio's rapier whizzed in front of his nose. He yelped and jumped back. The other Hokas formed a line, cleared their throats, and broke into the Soldiers' Chorus from *Faust.*

Don Ottavio halted his ominous advance. "That doesn't sound right, Signores," he complained.

"I know," said Don Vittorio. "But we haven't really had time to prepare—"

"Ho-yo-to-ho?" suggested the smallest Hoka.

Don Ottavio turned and bowed at Alex. "Perhaps your Excellency knows a suitably bloodthirsty chorus to which to meet your doom?" he inquired politely.

Frantic, Alex looked about for a weapon. He didn't know if the Hokas would really kill him or not—they were the kindliest race he had ever met, ordinarily, but they were so hopped up on this grand opera jag right now that— He backed into a corner.

"No!" cried Tanni, running toward him. "Stop that, you little monster! Don't you dare!"

Leporello caught her by the arms. "Don't worry, Zelenza," he said. "Your honor is about to be avenged. He never paid me enough anyway."

Tanni kicked and writhed to no avail. "But I don't want my honor avenged!" she sobbed.

"Dammit," shouted Alex, "her honor doesn't *need* avenging! I'm not— I didn't—"

He broke off. So did the Hokas. One and all stood frozen at the noises coming toward the room . . . the sound of slow, heavy footfalls.

Through the door, arms extended, grisly white, tottered a Shape.

It was Hardman Terwilliger, liberally coated with whitewash.

"Blop-blup-bluh!" he said, waving his dripping hands at them.

The Hokas' eyes lit up.

"The Man in Stone!" squeaked Don Ottavio. "The Commandant!"

Happily shrilling dismay, he and his friends fell back from the apparition. Leporello dived conscientiously under the table. "Help!" cried Don Vittorio.

"I'm palsied with fright," said another. "See how I tremble."

"I'm shuddering, myself," said the one beside him in a confidential tone. "It's more gruesome."

The smallest Hoka went rigid as a board and, holding his stance, toppled over backward to land with a thud. Stiff on the carpet, he opened one beady black eye.

"I fainted," he explained, and closed it again.

Alex's lurching brain made a final convulsive leap. One way to straighten out this mess—at least to save a few fragments—

He sprang past the petrified girls, to the table. One hand seized a bottle of the murderous Hoka liquor and emptied it on the floor. Another threw a candle on top of it. A cool but satisfactorily hellish blue alcohol flame jumped up.

He reeled back to the gaping Terwilliger. "Quick!" he whispered. "When I fall, drag me out of here."

"Eh? What?" sputtered the bureaucrat. "Wha's uh meanin' o' this, Jones? What—" His eyes fell on Tanni, standing beside Doralene. "My God," he whispered in awe. "The man's insatiable."

"Drag me off to eternal damnation, you idiot!" hissed Alex.

Terwilliger remained dazed. Alex swore under his breath. Then he emitted one last, anguished scream and fell against the whitewashed man, throwing the shoulder block he had learned on the football fields of the Academy. Don Giovanni and the Statue went crashing out the dining room door.

All kindly gods be praised! As he got an arm around Terwilliger's throat to keep him quiet, Alex heard Tanni—his own dear sweet intelligent wonderful Tanni, sobered by his need of her—pick up the cue. She stepped to the door, closed it, and cried in an awful voice:

"Such is the end of those who do evil! To such an end, the wicked have ever come and ever will!"

The Hokas must have retrieved their instruments, for as Alex struggled with Terwilliger, he heard the operatic finale rise to a doomful burst and die away again.

It was followed by thunderous clapping and squeaky cries of: *"Da capo!"*

"No, dear friends," said Tanni. "It is all over now. Don Giovanni has perished as he so richly deserved. Now hadn't you better go to your rooms and get a good night's sleep?"

"Sì, Zelenza," agreed Leporello.

"After all, tomorrow you will be having all kinds of important conferences with high interplanetary officials."

"Mysterious conferences?"

"Very mysterious."

"Then goodnight, Miss Hostrup," said Ardu gallantly.

Small feet pattered out through the main door.

Alex released Terwilliger. "Shall we join the ladies?" he panted.

"You'll pay for this, Jones!" stormed Terwilliger as they went back into the living room. "Discredit whole mission . . . make a farce . . . slip me this rotgut—" His wandering eye came to light on a disheveled Tanni and Doralene, who were wearily accepting coffee from a RoboServ. "Yes, an' lechery . . . drag in blondes soon's m' back's turned—"

"Shut up!" roared Alex.

The whitewash rose on Terwilliger's neck. "What?"

"I said shut up." Alex strode over to Tanni and put an arm about her waist. She sighed and snuggled up to him. "Miss Hostrup happens to be my fiancée. I haven't done a damned thing I shouldn't have, and you'd have known it if you weren't so filthy-minded suspicious, and I can prove it. If you'd known what you were supposed to know about Hoka psychology, you'd never have believed those yarns. And I didn't ask for this job in the first place. It was your big bright idea to yank me in off my furlough and hand it to me."

"But—"

"Shut up, I said! I'm not through with you yet, Terwilliger. You never gave me any restrictions to observe in entertaining the Hokas, so this mess tonight is your fault, and it was Miss Hostrup and I who pulled your isotopes out of the pile. I didn't try to get you drunk, either, you melodramatic excuse-monger. Did I hold you by the nose and pour that wet lightning down your throat? I did not. I even asked you to drink something else. I didn't upset a pail of whitewash on my own clumsy head and track up this suite, either!"

Alex stepped forward, fists doubled. "Terwilliger," he finished, "if you want to try and make trouble for me, go ahead. Just go ahead! I've got the real story of what happened here tonight, with witnesses, and I can spread it from here to the Lesser Magellanic Cloud!"

"That's telling him, sweetheart," said Tanni.

"Uh," said Doralene with rather less enthusiasm.

Terwilliger turned pale beneath his whitewash. "So!" he said. "It's blackmail!"

As a matter of fact, it was, and Alex felt ashamed of himself. But he couldn't see any alternative. He had, after all, been neglecting this assignment in order to be with Tanni—that much could be proven, if Terwilliger did press charges—so the only thing to do was silence the man with the threat of making him a galactic laughing-stock.

"Shall we say . . . a bargain?" puffed Alex in what he hoped was a suitably villainous manner.

Terwilliger began to swell alarmingly. "No," he said thickly, "we shall not."

His voice rose to a quarterdeck bellow. *"Publish and be damned! The Service is muh career, but if y' think I got so li'l honor that I'd give in t' blackmail—"*

"Sweetheart!" trilled Doralene, hurling herself into his arms.

"Huh?" said Terwilliger after he had picked himself up.

Doralene wiped whitewash off her face. "Oh, darling," she said, "here I always thought you were jus' a shuffed stirt—"

"Perhaps I am a snuffed skirt," said Terwilliger doggedly, "but thuh fack remains—"

"Oh, but you aren't! I see it now. You're a *man!* Oh, darlin', you don' wanna make a big mess o' things an' get y'self in trouble an' poor Alex an' Tanni . . . they're in love, darling, jus' like us!"

"Like us?" whispered Terwilliger, not daring to believe.

Doralene squelched into his arms. Silently, Alex and Tanni left the room.

They were in the study, half an hour or so later, when Terwilliger knocked on the door and entered.

"Ah," he beamed, scattering good humor and flakes of dried whitewash. "Ah, there, Jones. No hard feelings, I trust? There's something that just occurred to me. How would you like to be a plenipotentiary—?"

And he stood, watching good humor and
rubicund cheeks. "Ah, Miss Jones, we
had for long . . . much . . . since the time, and
occurred to me, how would you like to be a
plainsman—"

Interlude II

**Foreign Ministry
of the
United Commonwealths**

Cultural Development Service
Earth Headquarters
5/5/75

Ens. Alexander B. Jones (TISS, ret.) New Cultures
Section, E.A.A.B. CDS Building Prime, Annex 18
League City, N.Z.

My dear Mr. Jones:

Enclosed is your official appointment as Plenipotentiary of the Interbeing League to Culture
X-73-Z-218-r, otherwise known (in English translation of the indigenous name) as the Five and a

Half Cities, said culture being located on the planet officially designated Toka or Brackney's Star III. You will note that your jurisdiction will automatically be expanded to include any other societies on this world which may apply for ward status; and the preliminary studies and propaganda results indicate that all autochthonous nations will be eager to do so as soon as exposed to League civilization. Thus your territory should, within a few years at most, include the entire planet. My heartiest congratulations and best wishes for a long and successful career in the Service.

As an "old hand" "who knows the ropes," and by way of duty from seniors such as myself to "new chums" such as yourself, perhaps I may be permitted to extend a *verbum sapienti,* as it were. A great tradition binds us of the CDS together—not only here at Earth Headquarters, but wherever the flag of civilization waves, and even on airless worlds where the flag of civilization does not wave at all. Little honored and unsung (except, of course, on Thrrrwhilia, whose inhabitants have somewhat of a mania for musical limericks), we carry on our daily rounds, long-suffering but unrelenting in our efforts to raise the primitive. And of all fully civilized races, it is humankind, the predominant species whose culture sets the tone of the entire League, that most feels the impact of *noblesse oblige.*

You have now joined us in assuming the Earthman's Burden.

We must remind ourselves, always and forever, to be patient with the innocent sub-civilized being. We shall often find his attitude uncosmic, his mind naively fumbling in its attempt to grasp the nuances of that which we teach him. He gazes at us with clear unknowing eyes that plead with us to show him the right way, the civilized way—the way, in short, of the Interbeing League. We must not fail that trust.

Perhaps he will seem slow to adopt our ways. Especially at first, he will tend to be shy, retiring, afraid to push himself forward, to suggest things to us. And when this happens, we must draw him out of himself. (N.B.: The use of this metaphor is not recommended in the presence of shelled or carapaced beings.) We must take him by the hand (or paw, or tentacle, as the case may be); we must put his small, hesitating shoulder or equivalent thereof to the wheel of progress, encouraging him in his faltering attempts to adopt our most basic ways while simultaneously guarding him against those aspects of civilization which are beyond his present ability to understand and/or cope with.

It is a hard task. We who labor in this vineyard will not gather the fruits of those same trees we plant; it takes more than one lifetime to elevate a whole world to readiness for full status, autonomy, and representation in the League. Our chief reward is the rich sense of personal achievement; the knowledge that ultimately, however much some of them at present may resent certain necessary restrictions, we shall each have the undying gratitude of an entire intelligent species; and, in the words of that great poet whose prescient spirit animates our entire endeavor, "the judgment of your peers!"—i.e., your fellows in the Service.

For the present, then, I leave you with the motto

of the Service, which is now yours: *Whatsoever a man soweth, that shall he also reap.* (Gal., vi, 7)

Very truly yours,
Adalbert Parr
Chief Cultural Commissioner

N.B.:   Immediately upon arrival at your post of duty, you will complete Forms W-43921-j, G-64390, and X-89-A-7645, and return them to this office.

AP/grd

In Hoka Signo Vinces

"Snort!" snorted Alexander Jones.

"What, dear?" inquired Tanni.

"It's those Pornians," he grumbled from behind the newsfax sheet he was holding, still damp off the subspace receiver. "They've finished building that battleship, and now they're putting her into space."

"How awful!" said Tanni musically.

Alex lowered the newssheet and gazed fondly at her blonde beauty. He could never quite get over the exaltation of being married to her. And when in addition, he—still a very young man, only a few months ago mere ensign in Survey—was made plenipotentiary, with the rank and pay of an ambassador, it was not even a very believable situation.

So far his duties had been light: to reside here in the coastal city-state Mixumaxu, introducing the natives gradually to modern technology, leading them toward the eventual formation of their own world government, and so on. Of course, as the Terrestrial cultural mission expanded their activities and brought more of the planet under his supervision, the work would increase; already there were a fiendish lot of reports to file. And even ambassadorial quarters on a new planet were not quite the ideal home for a recent bride, and the Hokas were—well—a little odd, to say the least. But it could have been a lot worse, too. Mixumaxu was fairly civilized, and had a delightful climate. The Hokas, far from chafing at their subordinate status, were falling all over themselves to be friendly and helpful and . . . yes, their only fault was that excessive enthusiasm, too much imagination, too much tendency to go hog-wild over any new concept, too little ability to distinguish fiction from fact—

"I think that's terrible," said Tanni indignantly. "You'd think the other planetary governments would get together and stop them."

"What?" asked Alex, jerked back from his musings.

"Those Pornians and their space dreadnaught."

"Oh, that!" said Alex. "Well, you see, the trouble is, after the last war all the civilized races agreed to complete disarmament except for small interplanetary police forces. There's no military to speak of anywhere in the known parts of the galaxy, and the taxpayers wouldn't stand for any. Damn fool thing, too—" Alex started to fume again. "We need some kind of *interstellar* police to stop fanatic racialists like those Pornians from building weapons. Why, something like this ship could spoil a hundred years of peace and goodwill, start an armaments race and wreck the League—" He got to his feet. "Where's the subspace video? I want to see what Earth Headquarters has to say in today's bulletins."

The newsfax was sent from a local bureau a mere

fifty light-years away; only by straining his ambassa-dorial salary could Alex afford a receiver for programs sent all the way from Earth.

"I put it on the porch, dear," said Tanni. "That program the Hokas like so much—you know, *Tom Bracken of the Space Patrol*—it was on and they came to see it like they do every day."

Alex frowned at her. "I hope you didn't leave the circuits open, honey," he said. "You know the Hokas aren't supposed to have contact with anything too modern at this stage of their development."

"I locked it on that one channel," she reassured him. "They can only get the children's programs."

Alex sighed with relief and went out and wheeled in the video. The Hokas were just too blinking inventive, among their other faults. He wished Earth Headquarters hadn't been so quick about allowing them limited trade rights. A few unscrupulous traders could start furnishing them with stuff they shouldn't get for the next twenty years.

He tuned the video to EHQ and sat through an hour of official bulletins. But there was nothing of importance. Pornia was so far from Earth that a lethargic government couldn't appreciate the danger. But it was within a few light-years of Toka, and Alex was acutely aware of that fact. This was not the first time he had grumbled about the situation, to his wife or even to some of the Hokas. You'd think the human race's own history would have convinced it that militarism must be nipped in the bud, but—

He sighed, switched off the set, and yawned. Presently he and Tanni turned out the lights and went to bed.

❖   ❖   ❖

Alex was just failing off to sleep when there was small tap on the window. For a moment, he tried drowsily to ignore it, but it came again.

"Hist," whispered a Hoka voice through the opening.

Alex cursed, swiveled his eyes toward Tanni, and saw that she was already asleep. He signalled silence to the bear-like face which pressed its damp black nose the pane. "Just a minute," he murmured. "I'll be right out."

Growling to himself, he dressed clumsily in the dark and went out on the porch. One moon was up, almost full. In its bright glow he could see two Hokas waiting for him.

Surprise brought him up short, and his breath hissed between his teeth. Gone were the floppy boots, peak hats, and bell-covered motley of the local folk dress. The two that faced him had adorned their portly bodies with gray tunics, tight whipcord riding breeches, Sam Browne belts, jackboots, and goggled metal helmets. And holstered by the side of each was a—

"What are you doing with those," squeaked Alex. His heart tried to climb out of his mouth. "Where'd you get Holman raythrowers?"

They paid no attention. Solemnly, the larger Hoka saluted.

"Coordinator Jones," he said in the English which was rapidly becoming the world language of Toka, "the expedition is ready."

"What expedition?" cried Alex. "Look here, Buntu—"

"Sir," said the Hoka stiffly, "I am now Captain Jax Bennison of the Space Control, at your service." He clicked his heels and saluted again.

"Great jumping rockets!" exclaimed the other Hoka.

"Don't tell me the Coordinator didn't recognize you?"

"It's the moonlight, probably," said the first Hoka. "All clear and on green now, Coordinator?"

"I—I—" stammered Alex.

"Aye, aye!" repeated Jax Bennison crisply. "No time to lose, then. We lift gravs at 2330 hours. Follow us, sir."

The Hokas set rapidly off and Alex, his brain spinning, hurried after them. He didn't understand one part of this—but if it ever got back to Earth that he had allowed Holman raythrowers to get into the hands of aborigines— His brow beaded with cold sweat at the thought.

The Hokas led the way down narrow, cobbled streets between high-walled houses. The city was quiet, asleep it seemed. But the guards at the old defensive wall saluted and opened the gates for them. "Good hunting, Patrolmen," said one.

Outside, there was a broad empty field used for the infrequent spaceship landings. In the moonlight, Alex, saw that more than a hundred Hokas, uniformed like the two of them, were lined up at attention. But it was on the large shape behind them that his staggering mind focused.

"My courier boat!" he wailed. "What have you done to her?"

The once sleek shape of the *Tanni Girl* was now hacked and scarred. Holes had been cut the length of her sides and the muzzles of primitive gunpowder cannon projected beyond the air-seals. Her name had been painted out and the cognomen *Fearless* replaced it; below were the words *Space Patrol Ship Number One* and a large white star.

Alex made three long strides and caught up with Captain Jax Bennison, who was saluting an elderly

Hoka recognizable as a town official. But this one was now dressed in a blue tunic, gold braid, cutlass, at cocked hat.

"What's the idea?" barked Alex hysterically. "My ship—"

Jax pointed to the ornate shield with the legend *Space Patrol* that he wore on his breast.

"Sorry, sir," he answered, "but you know the rights of the Patrol. Patrolmen may requisition whatever is needed just by showing their badges."

"Who said so?" raged Alex.

"Tom Bracken of the Space Patrol, sir," said Jax. "He says it every day on the video."

Cocked-Hat saluted in his turn. "We knew that you, sir, as Supreme Coordinator, would approve," he said. "Fleet Admiral Ron Bronz at your command, sir."

"The danger is imminent, sir," added the second Hoka.

"The Malevonians are obviously preparing the great push, and yet the Patrol Fleet seems to be elsewhere. We could do nothing but organize our own branch of the Patrol to stop the enemy." He clicked heels. "Executive Officer Lon Meters at your command, sir."

Alex turned wildly to Admiral Ron Bronz. "What are you *doing?*" he spluttered.

"Admiral's inspection before the Patrol embarks," said the old Hoka. His cocked hat slipped down over his muzzle and he raised it with an irritated gesture. "Damn that tailor. Wouldn't surprise me if he was a Malevonian agent." His voice barked out over the waiting ranks of teddy bears. "Ten-SHUN! Inspection will proceed."

Solemnly, he and Captain Jax went down the line touching the nose of each spaceman to see that it was cold and moist. Alex groaned.

"All in good health, sir," said the admiral as returned. "All clear and on green." His cocked hat slipped down again. Alex found it strangely disconcerting to be addressing now a face and now a hat.

"But—but—but—" he stammered.

Lon Meters leaned over and said to Jax Bennison in a clearly audible whisper: "Something wrong with the Coordinator, Captain? You suppose the Malevonians have gotten control of his mind?"

"Of course not," said Jax. "They wouldn't dare. It's just his crusty way. He has a rough exterior but a heart of gold."

Admiral Bronz turned to Alex. "Well, sir, the men are ready," he reported. "Would you make a brief but touching speech before they take off?"

A hundred furry countenances turned expectantly to Alex where he stood in the moonlight. He raised a shaky voice: "This nonsense has got to stop!"

"That's right, sir," beamed Captain Jax. "We've got to stop the enemy."

"Go home to your wives and families!" screamed Alex, trying to rouse a sense of domestic duty. "Go home to your fireside brides!"

"Aye," shrilled the admiral. "When peace has come to the galaxy, we shall return to our homes."

"You've got your own work to do—" pleaded Alex.

"*Aye! Aye!*" The falsetto cheers seemed to shake the city walls. "We've got to stop the foe!"

"Form ranks!" barked Captain Jax. "Forward march!"

A hundred Hokas faced the boat and tramped toward its airlock. A hundred voices lifted in song.

> *"Off we go, into the vacuum yonder,*
> *Climbing high, into the black,*
> *Shaking out ee-vil with fire and thunder,*

> *Blasting down to the attack!*
> *All the wo-o-orlds watch us in wonder*
> *Till our mi-i-ission is done.*
> *We'll ride on high throughout the sky,*
> *For nothing can stop Patrol Ship*
>   *Number One!"*

"You encouraged them marvelously well, sir," said the admiral.

"Stop!" screamed Alex. He raced after the marching Hokas, trying to stem the tide.

"The Coordinator!" yelled Lon Meters in a burst of happiness. "The Coordinator himself has decided to come with us!"

Before Alex could catch his breath, he was caught up in the onward sweep. The press of a hundred solid little bodies forced him into the boat, up a companionway and onto the bridge. He heard the airlock clang shut behind him. There was no chance to open it again; all passages were jammed tight with shining-eyed Hokas.

Captain Jax strapped himself into the pilot chair while Alex was still gibbering. "Ready to blast," called a voice from the intercom. The engines growled.

"Ready to blast," echoed Captain Jax.

"Stop!" shrieked Alex, recognizing in panic what was about to happen. "Stop, I say!"

Nobody heard him. Captain Jax pulled the drive switch. Since he had not cut in the acceleration compensators, and Alex was not harnessed in place, the human was thrown back against a bulkhead and smashed into unconsciousness.

"Are you all right, sir?"

Fuzzily, with ringing head, Alex struggled back to

awareness. Through bleared eyes, he saw that he was alone on the bridge with Jax and Lon. They were bending anxiously over him.

"Here," said Jax, extending a flask. "Have a pull of Old Spaceman."

No matter what name it went under, Hoka liquor was potent stuff. Alex felt a measure of strength flow back into him with a gulp. He pulled his lanky frame up against the artificial gravity till he stood more or less erect. Then he glared.

"Sorry, sir," apologized the exec, Lon. "We didn't realize you were too busy planning our strategy to have prepared for takeoff."

Alex clenched his teeth. "Where are we?" he mumbled.

"Sir," replied the captain, "we don't know. After we went through the space warp, we lost orientation."

"Huh?" said Alex. "Went through the what?"

"The space warp, sir," explained Lon Meters.

"Oh," said Alex. For a moment the solemnity of the small Hoka was so convincing that he found himself wondering if the four years of astrogation courses he had taken had not perhaps been negligent in not mentioning this phenomenon.

"Well, then," said Captain Jax blandly, "you realize that we must be in a totally unfamiliar part of space. Maybe even in another universe. Observe." He pointed to the viewscreen and the black, starry sky it showed. Alex goggled. Some of the constellations had certainly changed, though not much.

The human's brain began to function once more; he could almost feel it sweating. Video programs never mentioned the elaborate mathematics of astrogation, so the Hokas must have assumed that you simply aimed your spaceship where you wanted it to go. Finding themselves unable to locate their position, they had leaped to the conclusion that a space warp—whatever that might be—had thrown them off course.

In fact, once they began taking the Tom Bracken program literally, everything else followed with a relentless kind of logic. The Pornian menace—they must have equated that with these Malevonians who, not content with mere rearmament, were apparently out to conquer the universe. They must have decided that the ostensible human plenipotentiary was really the Supreme Coordinator of the Space Patrol in disguise. Then they went ahead and organized their own unit and—and—

Oh, no!

"Where are we headed?" he asked.

"Sir?" said Lon Meters.

"Top secret," snapped Captain Jax quickly. "Exec Meters, close your eyes and put your hands over your ears." The other complied.

"We had this Pornia in mind, sir," resumed the captain. "It seems to be the local center of enemy operations. But now that we're lost—"

"Well—" Alex was slowly recovering his equilibrium. "Never mind. We're first going to have to figure out just where we are."

"That's what I thought we were going to have to do," said Captain Jax. "Exec Meters, you can open your eyes and ears. Do you think you can locate us, sir?"

A vision of the paper work involved in that little chore floated through Alex's head. As if it didn't ache enough already! "I think so," he groaned.

"Excellent, Coordinator," said Captain Jax. "You take over the chart room, and meanwhile the rest of us will maneuver the ship around and look for enemies."

"Oh, Lord," said Alex dismally. But there didn't seem to be much he could do about it; and even at trans-light velocities, interstellar space is so big that their chances of barging into a star or planet were negligible. As for the boat, these roboticized models all but handled themselves, which was the reason a few semi-trained Hokas had been able to get her under way.

"Of course," said Captain Jax, "the Malevonians may be any place. Perhaps even now we are in the heart of their stronghold. If—"

He was interrupted by a grizzled Hoka in an acid-stained smock who came indignantly into the bridge. "Sir," he squeaked, "you've got to do something about that chief engineer."

"Do what?" asked the captain.

"How should I know?" cried the newcomer, shaking his fists and dancing with rage. "Feed him to the bems. Make him walk the plank. Anything, just so he'll quit bothering me!"

"I don't believe you've met this man, sir," whispered Lon Meters to Alex. "Dr. Zarbovsky, our scientist. Quite mad, of course—but a genius."

"But if he's mad," said Alex, "then why—"

"Every Patrol ship has a mad scientist, sir, as you well know," said Lon firmly. "Tom Bracken's, for instance."

"How can I build a new-type disintegrator if the engineer won't let me have the busbars from the drive unit?" screamed Dr. Zarbovsky. "Answer me that!"

Alex stepped into the breach. "There should be extra busbars in the storeroom," he said diplomatically.

"In the storeroom," murmured Dr. Zarbovsky. "I never thought of that!" He hurried out again.

Jax and Lon looked awestruck at Alex. "What a brain!" breathed the exec.

"He wouldn't be Coordinator if he didn't have one," said Jax proudly.

"I wonder," whispered Lon, "I wonder if he's a mutant?"

"I'm getting out of here!" snarled Alex. He slammed the door behind him. The two Hoka officers looked affectionately in his direction.

"A crusty exterior," said Lon, "but a heart of gold. Eh, Jax?"

"On green, Lon," agreed the captain.

For the fortieth time, Alex's coffee cup leaped into the air and splashed on the floor as the boat's gravity beams ripped her through another sudden change of direction. Red-eyed from forty-eight hours with little sleep, he slammed his stylus down on the latest sheet of calculations and started to get up.

A burry voice grumbled over the intercom: "Engine rroom to brridge. Chief Engineerr MacTavish speaking. Wha' the hell d'ye think ye're doing? Can ye no keep the ship on a level coorse forr five minutes straight?"

"Sorry, Angus," replied Captain Jax soothingly. "We're dodging invisible space torpedoes."

Alex slumped back over the chart room desk, burying his face in his hands.

"Oh, no," he moaned. "Oh, no, no, no, no, no."

He lit a cigaret with trembling fingers, thinking that at least this lunatic ride would soon be over. Be brave, he told himself. Chin up and all that sort of thing. Just a few more hours.

Once he had pinpointed the boat in space, it had

not been hard to calculate a path to Pornia's sun. Now they were inside the Pornian System, moving at sub-light speed toward the only inhabited planet. The Hokas had naturally been enthusiastically in favor of going there to do battle.

Well, they'd land, and then he'd turn them over to the Pornians who, possessing a military force, could arrest them and return them to Toka. It was a dirty trick for him to play on his little friends, but he had no choice. You just couldn't allow this boatful of . . . of permanent children to go batting around the galaxy.

An obbligato of Hoka voices filtered to him over the intercom from the bridge.

"Rough section of space, this, captain."

"Space is like that, Lon. If the space tides don't get you, the radiation madness does. You dodge a meteor to find yourself trapped in a Sargasso of deadly space weed. And if you manage to battle your way out of that by some miracle, you emerge to find yourself blasting on all jets straight into the middle of the Malevonian fleet."

Alex closed his eyes and hung on to the coffee-stained calculation sheets—the data needed to land on Pornia. He thought bitterly that there might be a cupful of cosmic dust between them and the next star, but that was all that could be expected. . . .

"Then there's pirates—"

"Like that one bearing down on us now?"

"Don't be jet-happy, Lon. No pirate would dare attack a Patrol ship."

"Well, if he isn't a pirate, what's he doing with the skull and crossbones painted on his ship?"

"I don't see any skull and crossbones."

"Well, I can't see the skull either, but look at those red bloody crossbones on that white field."

"Great jumping comets, Lon, you're right! Attention, all gun crews! Attention, all gun crews! Stand by for battle!"

Struck by a sudden horrible suspicion, Alex flicked on the chart room's little viewscreen. Swimming in the nearby void was a long spaceship with a red cross large on its side.

"Stop!" roared Alex. "That's a hospital ship!"

He exploded out of the room and whizzed toward the bridge. Halfway there, he tripped over a small white-smocked figure.

"Damn interference!" squeaked Dr. Zarbovsky. "Can't let a mad scientist alone for a minute." Then, recognizing Alex's sprawled form: "Oh, sorry, sir. I was just coming to see you. Where can I get a one-farad condenser?"

"Go to the devil," raged Alex, picking himself up.

"But we don't have a devil on this ship," said Dr. Zarbovsky plaintively.

Alex was already running down the corridor. He burst into the bridge and skidded to a halt before the communications board.

"Do you wish to take over, sir?" asked Jax.

"I sure do," gasped Alex.

His fingers danced over the board as he sent a call to the other ship.

The image of a Pornian—two meters tall, snake-limbed, with a flat green face sticking out of a high gold-braided collar—formed on the screen. "What's up?" it demanded in the English of the spaceways. "Who are you?"

"Never mind that," said Alex impolitely. "Let me speak to your captain."

"Who are you?" repeated the Pornian in a stiff tone. "We are the Pornian Navy's hospital ship *Sudbriggan*.

Identify yourself, or else as aliens without passports you are liable to detention."

"Detention?" said Alex blankly. He hadn't realized the arrogance of the new militarist government had gone that far. "You're kidding!"

The Pornian's countenance turned chartreuse with anger. "Do you insult me?" he hissed. "You are under arrest. Stand by to be boarded."

Alex had a spine-chilling vision of himself explaining to Earth Headquarters just how he and a hundred of his wards came to be interned by the government of a notoriously touchy planet.

"Never mind," he said. "I was just about to leave."

Jumping up from the screen, he stepped over to the control panel. He was reaching for the main secondary-drive switch when a thunderous explosion rocked the *Fearless*. Alex felt himself hurled to the floor, his nose sideswiping a table on the way down.

He rose, wiping blood from his face, and glared at Captain Jax. "What happened now?" he yelled.

"Why, we opened fire," said the Hoka, pointing to the viewscreen. It showed a portion of the *Fearless*' exterior as well as the open sky. Smoke was whiffing into space from the cannon mouths. "We didn't get the pirate Malevonian, though," he added regretfully. "His force shield must already have been up."

If anybody, anywhere in the cosmos, has invented the legendary force screen, the Astrogation Improvement Authority of the Interbeing League will be very anxious to meet him, her, it, or xu. Alex took another horrified look at the Pornian ship. It was taking off sunward at full acceleration. The clumsy solid cannonballs had done no more than scratch its armored hull, but the captain had evidently had the fright of his life.

The image of an Earth Headquarters Cultural Development Board was replaced in Alex's unhappy mind by the picture of an Interbeing League court-room and one A. Jones on trial for armed assault. Since space piracy, being utterly impractical, had never occurred, perhaps the old laws about hanging pirates were still on the books. At the very least, no plenipotentiary who went around shooting up hospital ships could reasonably expect to keep his position. A certain dignity is demanded in such an office.

Out of the welter of thoughts there was only one that emerged with any clarity. And that was to catch the Pornian before he could officially report what had happened, explain, apologize, and ask him not to file charges.

"Full thrust ahead!" he bellowed, vaulting into the pilot chair and throwing down the grav-drive switch.

The Hokas whooped with joy.

"Trust us, Coordinator!" shouted Captain Jax. "They won't escape!"

—And the *Fearless* took off in pursuit.

The Lord High Admiral of the Pornian Navy thundered at the shaken, tentacled figure in the screen before him.

"What?"

"Help! Help!" cried the figure. "Hospital ship *Sudbriggan* reporting. There's a Space Patrol ship after me!"

"A what?" cried the Lord High Admiral.

"Space Patrol Ship Number One," choked the figure. It added breathlessly: "They've got a secret weapon."

"What do you mean, Space Patrol ship?" roared the Admiral. "There's no such thing as a Space Patrol."

"There is too!" shrieked the captain of the *Sudbriggan*. The Pornian Navy had not been in existence long enough to become well grounded in military courtesy. "And it's gaining."

Ferociously, the Lord High Admiral punched a button. The communications center of the huge dreadnaught answered him.

"Give me a long-range tracer," rapped the Admiral. "Find out what's behind this idiot."

Communications Center obliged.

"Fearless calling *Sudbriggan,"* gasped Alexander Jones into an unresponsive screen. "Come in, *Sudbriggan. Please* come in, *Sudbriggan!"*

The set flickered to life with the terrified figure of a Pornian who must be the exec of the hospital ship. He was waving his eye-stalks, too agitated to find English words.

"Get me your captain," said Alex. "I want your captain."

"N-n-no," stammered the officer. "We shall defend our captain to the l-last enlisted man."

"Then your Admiral," said Alex hoarsely. His contorted face looked more ferocious than he knew. "I must see your Admiral right away. This business has got to be stopped!"

"Eek," said the officer.

"I'm doing my best," pleaded Alex, "but if you don't get me through to your Admiral I can't answer for the consequences."

The Pornian paled at this bloodthirsty threat and switched off his receiver.

"Hey!" shouted Alex. "Come back there!"

"Never mind, Coordinator," said Captain Jax. "We're overhauling him."

The *Sudbriggan* was a glinting speck, lost among the stars, but a glance at the radar tracker told Alex that the courier boat was, indeed, gaining on the slower hospital ship. He mopped his brow in some relief. His chance of catching the other vessel in time to mollify its skipper and prevent a report looked pretty good after all. He began turning over in his mind the form his apology would take.

He had assumed that the *Sudbriggan* had taken off in a random sunward direction, and had no idea that the backbone of the Pornian Navy was close at hand. Consequently, the dreadnaught took him completely by surprise.

One minute, the viewscreen gleamed only with stars. Then all at once, looming up and growing with hideous speed, was the titanic figure of the space battleship, gun turrets glimmering ominously in the light of the distant sun.

"What is this farce?" demanded the Lord High Admiral angrily, looking at the boat in his tracer screen. He could make out the legend Space Patrol Ship Number One on its bow. What was it, and why was so minute a thing hurling itself so viciously on the great, and invincible super-dreadnaught?

He twined his boneless hands thoughtfully. Something occurred to him. What was it the captain of the *Sudbriggan* had said?

Secret weapon!

"Fire guns!" bawled the suddenly panic-stricken Admiral, clutching the intercom mike. "Fire torpedo! Fire One, fire Two, fire Three! Fire everything! Shoot that ship down before it hits us!"

Gun crews who have looked on their drills as a sort of pleasant exercise, are not at their peak when suddenly ordered without even the preamble of a battle alert to fire their weapons. Such an unexpected command breeds a certain amount of confusion. Nevertheless, they did their best.

Atomic explosions began to blossom about the hurtling *Fearless*, but in the vacuum of space a shell has to make a direct hit to do any significant harm. Therefore the guns gave way to the space torpedoes that leaped out at the enemy, each as big as the courier boat itself.

Now this was unfortunate. The torpedoes were equipped with the latest tracking devices to find their own targets. But it had been assumed that such targets would be destroyers, at the very least, since nothing smaller could possibly menace the new battleship. So simple preventive circuits had also been installed to keep them from homing on each other.

Thus when they reached the *Fearless* and matched velocities and accelerations, they didn't know what to do next. They trailed undecidedly after the Hoka ship, their computers clicking madly. One computer must have gone insane, for that torpedo blew itself up. The rest moved hesitantly toward their own ship.

The Admiral shivered in his quarters, gripping the arms of his chair and praying for a hit and regretting the day he had ever let the Racialist Party leaders talk him into figureheading the Navy. His wife had warned him against it and his wife always knew best. It was all very well strutting around in gold braid; but he might have suspected there would be a catch to it. And sure enough there was.

He might have known there was a real Space Patrol. He might have known a bloodthirsty race like the humans wouldn't really let a peaceful world like his own get away with a little rearming.

"Please," prayed the Admiral, rolling his eye-stalks toward the ceiling of his cabin. "Please. A direct hit. Just one."

"But I only want to apologize!" yelled Alex into the blank communicator screen, holding frantically onto the board while the *Fearless* rocked to the nearby explosions. "*Sudbriggan.* Dreadnaught. Anybody. It's all a mistake. I just want to apologize, dammit!"

"What's the old man up to?" Lon Meters asked Captain Jax as they both clung to their pilot chairs.

"I can't tell you," replied the captain with a knowing wink. "But I'll give you this much of a hint. Underneath that bluff exterior, the Coordinator's mighty shrewd. *Mighty* shrewd."

"Oh," said the exec. They nodded understandingly together.

All good things must come to an end; and the famous Space Patrol-Pornian battle was no exception. Aboard the enormous ship they opened a safety port to admit the fleeing *Sudbriggan.* It flashed inside, but before they could close the port again, the *Fearless*, moving too fast for Alex to stop her in time, had also entered.

If it had not been for the fantastic safety devices inside the dreadnaught, the episode would have ended then and there. But as it was, the absorber fields channeled the terrific kinetic energy of the two vessels into the dreadnaught's accumulators, and they lay inert in the belly of the monster. The port clanged to behind them.

The torpedoes decelerated as their circuits informed them that they were almost upon their mother craft. They milled about in space, their computers gibbering. One torpedo, perhaps equipped with a better-than-average "brain," went up and sniffed at the safety port, wagging its tail rather wistfully.

The *Sudbriggan* had been the first to enter. Its crew boiled from the airlock and scrambled toward the safety of the dreadnaught's interior. A few minutes later, Alex opened the lock of the *Fearless* and stuck his nose out. He jerked it hastily back as a raybeam shot past it and splattered on the hull of the Patrol boat. This was too much. After being shanghaied, kept up for two nights to make calculations, threatened with internment, and shot at, Alex finally lost his temper. He went storming back to the bridge.

"Give me a raythrower!" he roared.

"Hadn't you better get into a suit first, sir?" asked Lon Meters.

Alex did a double take. All along the main corridor, he could see the Hokas scrambling into things that looked like a cross between a spacesuit and a set of medieval armor. The exec was holding out one tailored more nearly to human proportions.

"What?" said Alex.

"Combat armor, sir," said Captain Jax proudly. "We used the ship's tools and made it out of the spare meteor plating in the hold."

Alex goggled. The labor in fashioning the suits must have been heartbreaking. Even given the ship's machine tools, the collapsed steel of meteor plating was almost unworkable. For a second he wavered between, admiration and a desire to blow his top at this latest outrage on his property. Then he remembered the near-singe his nose had taken, and began donning the armor without a word.

"Battle ax," said Captain Jax.

"Battle ax," repeated the exec, handing a wicked-looking double-bitted weapon to Alex.

"Raythrower," said the captain.

"Raythrower," repeated the exec, offering a gun.

Alex grabbed the Holman with his first real enthusiasm since this trip started. A smile was forming on his lips when he realized that the object was entirely too heavy to be what it appeared to be.

He inspected it. "What's this?" he demanded.

"The raythrower, sir?" Captain Jax looked a little crestfallen. "We had some trouble with them, Coordinator. We sent off our boxtops according to orders over the video, but when we got these, they wouldn't shoot."

"Sabotage," supplied Lon Meters.

"Exactly," said the captain. "So we fixed them up to fire regular bullets like the Western shooting irons. You see—"

He pressed the firing button on his imitation Holman, and a slug whanged off the low ceiling of the bridge. Alex ducked before remembering that his new clothes were bullet proof. He straightened, groaned as he looked at the clumsy weapon, and then, with a sigh, holstered it and clumped his way toward the airlock. At least his present equipment would protect him until he could get to some Pornian officer and explain the case—

But his last feeble intentions of legality were destroyed when he led his Hokas into the first corridor branching from the entry port. A barrage of rays from behind a hastily erected wall of office furniture made his armor glow and sparkle. He tingled with the shock of secondary radiation.

Plainly, the aliens weren't going to give him a chance to parley.

"That's enough!" he bellowed in a rage, his voice coming weirdly from the air holes in the top of his helmet. "Let's clean up the whole blinking ship!"

And he charged forward like a miniature tank, using the sheer mass of his armor to break through the barricade and send the defenders scooting before him in terror.

"The old man's finally got his dander tip," said the exec to the captain.

"Yep," answered Jax. "That he has. But let me tell you something, boy. Underneath that dander there's a heart of pure, eighteen-carat, solid gold!"

The true story of the cleaning up of the Pornian dreadnaught will never be adequately told, for words are insufficient to describe it.

For a century or more, no civilized entity had been seriously threatened by organized violence. On top of this fact was another: that the advanced military minds who designed this battleship would have tut-tutted in horror if they had been asked how the crew was to defend it against a boarding party. With icy politeness they would have pointed out that boarding vanished with wooden ships, and that no enemy vessel could approach within three thousand kilometers of this giant without being destroyed. Thus few of the crew had hand guns, and fewer still knew how to use them. So everywhere through the huge ship could be seen shrieking herds of tall Pornians fleeing before one or two small armored figures waving battle axes. It was like a host of Frankenstein dolls let loose in an enormous home for old ladies. Such of the crew of the dreadnaught as was not assailed—and after all, a hundred Hokas could reach only a fraction of the total acreage inside—stayed by its posts, shivering and hoping there would be no orders to counter-attack.

To be sure, there was one center of resistance. When the news reached the Admiral that the crew of the Space Patrol boat had effected an entrance, he gathered his personal staff around him on the bridge and resolved to die fighting. His followers unlimbered a mobile disintegrator, trained it on the doorway, and waited.

Meteor plating is good protection against hand guns. But it is about as useful as wet cardboard against the full power of a mobile disintegrator. Alex, leading a dozen Hokas around a bend in the main corridor, came full upon the bridge. The Pornians let off a panicky, ill-timed bolt which tore a hole through three floors above. Alex beat a hasty retreat, struggling to restrain the Hokas, who were all for rushing the gun.

"Look," he said grimly, when he finally had them settled down, "are Jax and Lon here?"

"Here, Coordinator."

"On green—I mean, aye, aye, sir."

"Well, look," said Alex. "That mobile unit isn't like a hand gun—that is, it doesn't have a self-contained power source. It gets its energy from a cable run directly to the ship's generators." As a former TISS man, Alex had of course been given training in the Solar Guard. "Now, what I want you to do is hunt around for the central power control room—it ought to be on this level—and pull every switch you find there. One of them should shut off the juice to that mobile."

The two little armored figures nodded their anonymous heads and toddled off down the corridor. Alex and the rest sat down to wait.

"Mighty smart, the old man," said Lon Meters as

they trudged along. "Imagine him knowing the way Malevonian ships are put together."

"There isn't much that goes on in the universe that the Coordinator of the Space Patrol doesn't know," replied Jax Bennison complacently. "Why, I imagine nobody will ever know how many spy rays the old man has in places, and how many undercover agents at work."

"Lonely life, though," said Lon sadly. "Can't trust anyone, the old man can't. The responsibility for the safety of all civilization rests on his shoulders." He paused, then went on: "Which of us do you think he's picked to take his place when his time comes?"

They had, by now, explored up and down several halls and looked into a number of luxurious apartments for the top officers of the dreadnaught. Now they came to a small door with a sign stencilled on it in the spatial English:

DANGER
DO NOT ENTER

"Ah-ha," said Lon.

"This'll be it," said Jax. He swung his battle ax at the lock, and the door—being unlocked—bounced open. They stepped inside.

"Yep," said Captain Jax, looking about him with satisfaction at the ranked masses of levers, wheels, buttons, and switches. "This is it, all right. Executive Meters, you take that side and I'll take this."

They started yanking levers.

Coughing, choking, sneezing, and gurgling, the Lord High Admiral of the Pornian Navy sloshed his way forward to surrender.

"My sword, sir," he said with what dignity he could summon up.

Alex accepted it.

"The ship, sir, is yours," coughed the Admiral. Then his official manner broke down "But if turning on the fire extinguisher sprinklers, the fumigation system, the leak-detector smoke system, the emergency radionic-heating system, the emergency refrigeration system, and directing the sewers into the deck-flushing system isn't a dirty way to fight, I'd like to know what is."

Alex ignored his resentment.

"The terms for your surrender are these," he began sternly.

"Yes, sir," said the Admiral in a meek voice.

"Your government will dismantle this dreadnaught and build no more ships of the line."

"Yes, sir," said the Admiral. "I, for one, will be happy to get back to civilian life—"

"You will disband the navy."

"Glad to, sir."

"You will inform Earth Headquarters of your decisions in these matters, but will not specify the reasons or mention this battle. That is classified information."

"Yes, sir."

"And you will inform the Racialist Party on Pornia that the Space Patrol, which owes allegiance to no race or system, but is dedicated to the upholding of law and order throughout the galaxy, takes a dim view of their government and demands another planet-wide election wherein other Pornian parties shall be given a fair chance to run for office."

The Admiral gulped.

"Well—I—yes, sir, I guess I can do that. Under the circumstances."

"Okay, fine," said Alex. Signalling the armored

figures around him to follow, he turned on his heel and went back toward the entry port.

When the *Fearless* was finally settled down on her return trip, Alex called the Hokas together and, speaking over the intercom, addressed them all.

"Gentlemen of the Space Patrol," he said crisply, "our mission is accomplished. Well done! But now I must inform you that there will be no more expeditions of the Patrol for an indefinite time."

"None?" asked Captain Jax in a wistful tone.

"None," said Alex, tossing the keys of the control panel in one hand and clamping firmly onto them as they landed back in his palm. "The Space Patrol is being disbanded as of now until such time as another threat to the galaxy brings us forth to scour the evildoer from the stars and the space between the stars."

There was a moment's sad quietude. Then the exec, Lon Meters, spoke up.

"But what's going to become of you, sir?" he asked sympathetically.

"That," said Alex, unable to disguise a slight quaver in his voice, "is what I am just about to find out."

He waved bravely to the assembled Hoka officers and dismissed them from the bridge and shut the door on them. The new long-range subspace communicator which the dreadnaught's technicians had installed for him glowed as his trembling fingers put in a call. While the Hoka at the switchboard in far-off Mixumaxu routed his beam, he licked dry lips and ran a shaky finger under his collar.

The figure of Tanni appeared on the screen. Her arms folded implacably as she recognized him.

"Well," she said, "and just where have you been?"

Weakly, Alexander Jones started to explain.

Interlude III

**Plenipotentiary of the
Interbeing League
Planet Toka**

HEADQUARTERS OFFICE   CITY OF MIXAMAXU

Interoffice No. X-73-Z-218-r-478-R

11/10/75

FROM: Alexander B. Jones, Plenipotentiary

TO: Adalbert Parr, C.C.C.

SUBJECT: Allegations concerning Tokan conduct with
   respect to reported interstellar piracy

REFERENCES: (a) EHQ-X-73-Z-218-r-261-RQ, (b)
   Proc. Gal. Psych. Assn., viii, 5, 221-296

ENCLOSURE: (a) CDS Acct. P-3547-291

1. Reply is hereby made to Ref. (a), your inquiry concerning small armed vessel somewhat unreliably reported to have committed piracy in this galactic section, said vessel having allegedly identified itself in English as belonging to a so-called "Space Patrol" and been asserted to bear a crew rumored to possess a slight resemblance to the Hokas under my care.

2. Since I hesitate to accuse Terrestrial diplomatic and intelligence officers of having uncritically swallowed the wild hoax of some intoxicated or possibly deranged Pornian outcase, I beg leave to confess myself at a loss to explain these statements.

3. As reference to the files will show, the Hokas are assigned to Class D, and are therefore by definition totally incapable of building a secondary-drive vessel, or operating one without trained assistance. As for the far-fetched hypothesis advanced—not, I am sure, by yourself—in Ref. (a), Par. 16, that a Hoka gang appropriated my courier boat, I can only point out that the mysterious damage which it suffered shortly prior to the time of the episode in question makes this most improbable, to put it mildly. (Expense account for repairs attached, Encl. (a).) To the additional rumor that there was, among these Hokoid individuals, a humanoid bearing a small similarity to myself, I offer either an indignant denial or the suggestion of erroneous testimony. After all, it is well known that one humanoid looks very much like another humanoid to the average non-humanoid. (Documentation in Ref (b).)

4. However, the entire question as concerns the planet Toka can be disposed of merely on a common-sense level. What reasonable person could seriously

entertain the notion that a mere handful of Class
D primitives aboard a mere courier boat could
conceivably overwhelm a dreadnaught armed (like
all dreadnaughts) to the teeth? I note that Ref.
(a), Par. 7, mentions that a certain Pornian Admiral
has been hospitalized for nervous overstrain
consequent to this by-no-means-proven episode.
Does that sound like the result of an encounter
of a ranking member of a Class A civilization with
my cheerful, friendly, innocent little Class D wards?
I leave the question to your judgment.

5. As noted in Par. 2 above, I do not pretend to
   understand the cause of these rumors, but I would
   suggest that either the Pornians were somewhat
   overwrought or else the affair is a case of mistaken
   identity, possibly involving some as yet unknown
   race.

ABJ/eek

**Foreign Ministry
of the
United Commonwealths**

Cultural Development Service
Earth Headquarters
Interoffice No. EHQ-X-73-Z-218-r-262
12/11/75

FROM: Adalbert Parr, C.C.C.
TO: A. Jones, Plenipotentiary, Mixumaxu, U.X.,
Brackneys Star III
SUBJECT: Reported activity in Pornian region
REFERENCES: (a) X-73-Z-218-r-478-R

1. Note has been taken of Ref. (a), and said reply to inquiries made is hereby judged satisfactory.
2. I should particularly like to commend you for the brilliant suggestion in Ref. (a), Par. 5. I have taken the matter up with higher echelons, who have in turn brought it to the attention of the League Council itself. A search for these aliens, who know English and possess a Space Patrol but have nevertheless remained undiscovered by us, is now under way.
3. Obviously, this is a matter of vital importance to the League. In view of the fact the aliens' action was, at least in its results, not so much piratical as pro-libertarian and anti-militaristic, I saw fit to expand your suggestion a trifle, and my own memorandum has received favorable consideration.

Therefore the League is acting on the tentative assumption that the aliens belong to an elder race of Great Galactics—that the Space Patrol is maintained by their Observers—and that our civilization would have much to learn from them if contact can somehow be established.

4. My own office has, accordingly, been commended for its zeal. Thus the entire Cultural Development Service benefits from your originality, which reflects great credit on you.

5. A copy of this letter will be placed in your 201 file.

AP/grd

The Adventure Of
The Misplaced Hound

Whitcomb Geoffrey was the very model of a modern major operative. Medium tall, stockily muscular, with cold gray eyes in a massively chiseled, expressionless face, he was quietly dressed in purple breeches and a crimson tunic whose slight bulge showed that he carried a Holman raythrower. His voice was crisp and hard as he said: "Under the laws of the Interbeing League, you are required to give every assistance to a field agent of the Interstellar Bureau of Investigation. Me."

Alexander Jones settled his lean length more comfortably behind the desk. His office seemed to crackle with Geoffrey's dynamic personality; he felt sure that the agent was inwardly scorning its easygoing sloppiness. "All right," he said. "But what brings you to Toka? This is still a backward planet, you know. Hasn't got very much to do with spatial traffic." Remembering the Space Patrol episode, he shuddered slightly and crossed his fingers.

"That's what you think!" snapped Geoffrey. "Let me explain."

"Certainly, if you wish," said Alex blandly.

"Thanks, I will," said the other man. He caught himself, bit his lip, and glared. It was plain that he thought Alex much too young for the exalted position of plenipotentiary. And in fact Alex's age was still, after nearly ten years in this job, well below the average for a ranking CDS official.

After a moment, Geoffrey went on: "The largest problem the IBI faces is interstellar dope smuggling, and the most dangerous gang in that business is—or was—operated by a group of renegade ppussjans from Ximba. Ever seen one, or a picture? They're small, slim fellows, cyno-centauroid type: four legs and two arms, spent years trying to track down this particular bunch of dream peddlers. We finally located their headquarters and got most of them. It was on a planet of Yamatsu's Star, about six light-years from here. But the leader, known as Number Ten—"

"Why not Number One?" asked Alex.

"Ppussjans count rank from the bottom up. Ten escaped, and has since been resuming his activities on a smaller scale, building up the ring again. We've *got* to catch him, or we'll soon be right back where we started.

"Casting around in this neighborhood with tracer beams, we caught a spaceship with a ppussjan and a load of nixl weed. The ppussjan confessed what he knew, which wasn't much, but still important. Ten himself is hiding out alone here on Toka—he picked it because it's backward and thinly populated. He's growing the weed and giving it to his confederates, who land here secretly at night. When the hunt for him has died down, he'll leave Toka, and space is so big that we might never catch him again."

"Well," said Alex, "didn't your prisoner tell you just where Ten is hiding?"

"No. He never saw his boss. He merely landed at a certain desolate spot on a large island and picked up the weed, which had been left there for him. Ten could be anywhere on the island. He doesn't have a boat of his own, so we can't track him down with metal detectors; and he's much too canny to come near a spaceship, if we should go to the rendezvous and wait for him."

"I see," said Alex. "And nixl is deadly stuff, isn't it? Hm-m-m. You have the coordinates of this rendezvous?"

He pushed a buzzer. A Hoka servant entered, in white robes, a turban, and a crimson cummerbund, to bow low and ask: "What does the sahib wish?"

"Bring me the big map of Toka, Rajat Singh," said Alex.

"He's been reading Kipling," said Alex apologetically. It did not seem to clear away his guest's puzzlement.

The coordinates intersected on a large island off the main continent. "Hm," said Alex, "England. Devonshire, to be precise."

"Huh?" Geoffrey pulled his jaw up with a click. An IBI agent is never surprised. "You and I will go there at once," he said firmly.

"Remember your duty, Jones!"

"Oh, all right. I'll go. But you understand," added the younger man diffidently, "there may be a little trouble with the Hokas themselves."

Geoffrey was amused. "We're used to that in the IBI," he said. "We're well-trained not to step on native toes."

Alex coughed, embarrassed. "Well, it's not exactly that—" he stumbled. "You see . . . well, it may be the other way around."

A frown darkened Geoffrey's brow. "They may hamper us, you mean?" he clipped. "Your function is to keep the natives non-hostile, Jones."

"No," said Alex unhappily. "What I'm afraid of is that the Hokas may try to help us. Believe me, Geoffrey, you've no idea of what can happen when Hokas take it into their heads to be helpful."

Geoffrey cleared his throat. He was obviously wondering whether or not to report Alex as incompetent. "All right," he said. "We'll divide up the work between us. I'll let you do all the native handling, and you let me do the detecting."

"Good enough," said Alex, but he still looked doubtful.

The green land swept away beneath them as they flew toward England in the plenipotentiary's runabout. Geoffrey was scowling. "It's urgent," he said. "When the spaceship we captured fails to show up with its cargo, the gang will know something's gone wrong and send a boat to pick up Ten. At least one of them must know exactly where on the island he's hiding. They'll have an excellent chance of sneaking him past any blockade we can set up." He took out a cigaret and puffed nervously. "Tell me, why is the place called England?"

"Well—" Alex drew a long breath. "Out of maybe a quarter million known intelligent species, the Hokas are unique. Only in the last few years have we really begun to probe their psychology. They're highly intelligent, unbelievably quick to learn, ebullient by nature . . . and fantastically literal-minded. They have difficulty distinguishing fact from fiction, and since fiction is so much more colorful, they don't usually bother. Oh, my servant back at the office doesn't consciously believe he's a mysterious East Indian; but his subconscious has gone overboard for the role, and he can easily rationalize anything that conflicts with his wacky assumptions." Alex frowned, in search of words. "The closest analogy I can make is that the Hokas are somewhat like small human children, plus having the physical and intellectual capabilities of human adults. It's a formidable combination."

"All right," said Geoffrey. "What's this got to do with England?"

"Well, we're still not sure just what is the best starting point for the development of civilization among the Hokas. How big a forward step should the present generation be asked to take? More important, what socio-economic forms are best adapted to their temperaments and so on? Among other experiments, about ten years ago the cultural mission decided to try a Victorian English setup, and chose this island for the scene of it. Our robofacs quickly produced steam engines, machine tools, and so on for them . . . of course, we omitted the more brutal features of the actual Victorian world. The Hokas quickly carried on from the start we'd given them. They consumed mountains of Victorian literature—"

"I see," nodded Geoffrey.

"You begin to see," said Alex a little grimly. "It's more complicated than that. When a Hoka starts out to imitate something, there are no half measures about it. For instance, the first place we're going to get the hunt organized is called London, and the office we'll contact is called Scotland Yard, and—well, I hope you can understand a nineteenth-century English accent, because that's all you'll hear."

Geoffrey gave a low whistle. "They're that serious about it, eh?"

"If not more so," said Alex. "Actually, the society in question has, as far as I know, succeeded very well—so well that, being busy elsewhere, I haven't had a chance to keep up with events in England. I've no idea what that Hoka logic will have done to the original concepts by now. Frankly, I'm scared!"

Geoffrey looked at him curiously and wondered whether the plenipotentiary might not perhaps be a little off-balance on the subject of his wards.

From the air, London was a large collection of peak-roofed buildings, split by winding cobbled streets, on the estuary of a broad river that could only be the Thames. Alex noticed that it was being remodeled to a Victorian pattern: Buckingham Palace, Parliament, and the Tower were already erected, and St. Paul's was halfway finished. An appropriate fog was darkening the streets, so that gas lamps had to be lit. He found Scotland Yard on his map and landed in the court, between big stone buildings. As he and Geoffrey climbed out, a Hoka bobby complete with blue uniform and bulging helmet saluted them with great deference.

" 'Umans!" he exclaimed. "H'I sye, sir, this must be a right big case, eh what? Are you working for 'Er Majesty, h'if h'I might myke so bold as ter awsk?"

"Well," said Alex, "not exactly." The thought of a Hoka Queen Victoria was somewhat appalling. "We want to see the chief inspector."

"Yes, sir!" said the teddy bear. "H'Inspector Lestrade is right down the 'all, sir, first door to yer left."

"Lestrade," murmured Geoffrey. "Where've I heard that name before?"

They mounted the steps and went down a gloomy corridor lit by flaring gas jets. The office door indicated had a sign on it in large letters:

FIRST BUNGLER

"Oh no!" said Alex under his breath.

He opened the door. A small Hoka in a wing-collared suit and ridiculously large horn-rimmed spectacles got up from behind the desk.

"The plenipotentiary!" he exclaimed in delight. "And another human! What is it, gentlemen? Has—" He paused, looked in sudden fright around the office, and lowered his voice to a whisper. "Has Professor Moriarty broken loose again?"

Alex introduced Geoffrey. They sat down and explained the situation. Geoffrey wound up with: "So I want you to organize your—CID, I imagine you call it—and help me track down this alien."

Lestrade shook his head sadly. "Sorry, gentlemen," he said. "We can't do that."

"Can't do it?" echoed Alex, shocked. "Why not?"

"It wouldn't do any good," said Lestrade, gloomily. "We wouldn't find anything. No, sir, in a case as serious as this, there's only one man who can lay such an arch-criminal by the heels. I refer, of course, to Mr. Sherlock Holmes."

"Oh, NO!" said Alex.

"I beg your pardon?" asked Lestrade.

"Nothing," said Alex, feverishly wiping his brow. "Look here—Lestrade—Mr. Geoffrey here is a representative of the most effective police force in the Galaxy. He—"

"Come now, sir," said Lestrade, with a pitying smile. "You surely don't pretend that he is the equal of Sherlock Holmes. Come, come, now!"

Geoffrey cleared his throat angrily, but Alex kicked his foot. It was highly illegal to interfere with an established cultural pattern, except by subtler means than argument. Geoffrey caught on and nodded as if it hurt him. "Of course," he said in a strangled voice. "I would be the last to compare myself with Mr. Holmes."

"Fine," said Lestrade, rubbing his stubby hands together. "Fine. I'll take you around to his apartment, gentlemen, and we can lay the problem before him. I trust he will find it interesting."

"So do I," said Alex, hollowly.

A hansom cab was clopping down the foggy streets and Lestrade hailed it. They got in, though Geoffrey cast a dubious look at the beaked, dinosaurian reptile which the Hokas called a horse, and went rapidly through the tangled lanes. Hokas were abroad on foot, the males mostly in frock coats and top hats, carrying tightly rolled umbrellas, the females in long dresses; but now and then a bobby, a red-coated soldier, or a kilted member of a Highland regiment could be seen. Geoffrey's lips moved silently.

Alex was beginning to catch on. Naturally, the literature given these—Englishmen—must have included the works of A. Conan Doyle, and he could see where the romantic Hoka nature would have gone wild over Sherlock Holmes. So they had to interpret everything literally; but who had they picked to be Holmes?

"It isn't easy being in the CID, gentlemen," said Lestrade. "We haven't much of a name hereabouts, y'know. Of course, Mr. Holmes always gives us the credit, but somehow word gets around." A tear trickled down his furry cheek.

They stopped before an apartment building in Baker Street and entered the hallway. A plump elderly female met them. "Good afternoon, Mrs. Hudson," said Lestrade. "Is Mr. Holmes in?"

"Indeed he is, sir," said Mrs. Hudson. "Go right up." Her awed eyes followed the humans as they mounted the stairs.

Through the door of 211-B came a horrible wail. Alex froze, ice running along his spine, and Geoffrey cursed and pulled out his raythrower. The scream sawed up an incredible scale, swooped down again, and died in a choked quivering. Geoffrey burst into the room, halted, and glared around.

The place was a mess. By the light of a fire burning in the hearth, Alex could see papers heaped to the ceiling, a dagger stuck in the mantel, a rack of test tubes and bottles, and a "V.R." punched in the wall with bullets. It was hard to say whether the chemical reek or the tobacco smoke was worse. A Hoka in dressing gown and slippers put down his violin and looked at them in surprise. Then he beamed and came forward to extend his hand.

"Mr. Jones!" he said. "This is a real pleasure. Do come in."

"Uh—that noise—" Geoffrey looked nervously around the room.

"Oh, that," said the Hoka, modestly. "I was just trying out a little piece of my own. Concerto in Very Flat for violin and cymbals. Somewhat experimental, don't y'know."

Alex studied the great detective. Holmes looked about like any other Hoka—perhaps he was a trifle leaner, though still portly by human standards. "Ah, Lestrade," he said. "And Watson—do you mind if I call you Watson, Mr. Jones? It seems more natural."

"Oh, not at all," said Alex, weakly. He thought the real Watson—no, dammit, the Hoka Watson!—must be somewhere else; and the natives' one-track minds—

"But we are ignoring our guest here, whom I perceive to be in Mr. Lestrade's branch of the profession," said Holmes, laying down his violin and taking out a big-bowled pipe.

IBI men do not start; but Geoffrey came as close to it as one of his bureau's operatives had ever done. He had no particular intention of maintaining an incognito, but no officer of the law likes to feel that his profession is written large upon him. "How do you know that?" he demanded.

Holmes' black nose bobbed. "Very simple, my dear sir," he said. "Humans are a great rarity here in London. When one arrives, thus, with the estimable Lestrade for company, the conclusion that the problem is one for the police and that you yourself, my dear sir, are in some way connected with the detection of criminals, becomes a very probable one. I am thinking of writing another little monograph— But sit down, gentlemen, sit down, and let me hear what this is all about."

Recovering what dignity they could, Alex and Geoffrey took the indicated chairs. Holmes himself dropped into an armchair so overstuffed that he almost disappeared from sight. The two humans found themselves confronting a short pair of legs beyond which a button nose twinkled and a pipe fumed.

"First," said Alex, pulling himself together, "let me introduce Mr.—"

"Tut-tut, Watson," said Holmes. "No need. I know the estimable Mr. Gregson by reputation, if not by sight."

"Geoffrey, dammit!" shouted the IBI man.

Holmes smiled gently. "Well, sir, if you wish to use an alias, there is no harm done. But between us, we may as well relax, eh?"

"H-h-how," stammered Alex, "do you know that he's named Gregson?"

"My dear Watson," said Holmes, "since he is a police officer, and Lestrade is already well known to me, who else could he be? I have heard excellent things of you, Mr. Gregson. If you continued to apply my methods, you will go far."

"Thank you," snarled Geoffrey.

Holmes made a bridge of his fingers. "Well, Mr. Gregson," he said, "let me hear your problem. And you, Watson, will no doubt want to take notes. You will find pencil and paper on the mantel."

Gritting his teeth, Alex got them while Geoffrey launched into the story, interrupted only briefly by Holmes' "Are you getting all this down, Watson?" or occasions when the great detective paused to repeat slowly something he himself had interjected so that Alex could copy it word for word.

When Geoffrey had finished, Holmes sat silent for a while, puffing on his pipe. "I must admit," he said finally, "that the case has its interesting aspects. I confess to being puzzled by the curious matter of the Hound."

"But I didn't mention any hound," said Geoffrey numbly.

"That is the curious matter," replied Holmes. "The area in which you believe this criminal to be hiding is Baskerville territory, and you didn't mention a

Hound once." He sighed and turned to the Scotland Yard Hoka. "Well, Lestrade," he went on, "I imagine we'd all better go down to Devonshire and you can arrange there for the search Gregson desires. I believe we can catch the 8:05 out of Paddington tomorrow morning."

"Oh, no," said Geoffrey, recovering some of his briskness. "We can fly down tonight."

Lestrade was shocked. "But I say," he exclaimed. "That just isn't done."

"Nonsense, Lestrade," said Holmes.

"Yes, Mr. Holmes," said Lestrade, meekly.

The village of St. Vitus-Where-He-Danced was a dozen thatch-roofed houses and shops, a church, a tavern, set down in the middle of rolling gray-green moors. Not far away, Alex could see a clump of trees which he was told surrounded Baskerville Hall. The inn had a big signboard announcing "The George and Dragon," with a picture of a Hoka in armor spearing some obscure monster. Entering the low-ceilinged tap-room, Alex's party were met by an overawed landlord and shown to clean, quiet rooms whose only drawback was the fact that the beds were built for one-meter Hokas.

By then it was night. Holmes was outside somewhere, bustling around and talking to the villagers, and Lestrade went directly to bed; but Alex and Geoffrey came back downstairs to the taproom. It was full of a noisy crowd of Hoka farmers and tradesmen, some talking in their squeaky voices, some playing darts, some clustering around the two humans. A square, elderly native introduced as Farmer Toowey joined them at their table.

"Ah, lad," he said, "it be turrible what yeou zee on

the moor o' nights." And he buried his nose in the pint mug which should have held beer but, true to an older tradition, brimmed with the fiery liquor this high-capacity race had drunk from time immemorial. Alex, warned by past experience, sipped more cautiously at his pint; but Geoffrey was sitting with a half-empty mug and a somewhat wild look in his eyes.

"You mean the Hound?" asked Alex.

"I du," said Farmer Toowey. "Black, 'tis, an' bigger nor any bullock. And they girt teeth! One chomp and yeou'm gone."

"Is that what happened to Sir Henry Baskerville?" queried Alex. "Nobody seems to know where he's been for a long time."

"Swall'd um whole," said Toowey, darkly, finishing his pint and calling for another one. "Ah, poor Sir Henry! He was a good man, he was. When we were giving out new names, like the human book taught us, he screamed and fought, for he knew there was a curse on the Baskervilles, but—"

"The dialect's slipping, Toowey," said another Hoka.

"I be zorry," said Toowey. "I be oold, and times I forget masel'."

Privately, Alex wondered what the real Devonshire had been like. The Hokas must have made this one up out of whole cloth.

Sherlock Holmes entered in high spirits and sat down with them. His beady black eyes glittered. "The game is afoot, Watson!" he said. "The Hound has been doing business as usual. Strange forms seen on the moors of late— I daresay it's our criminal, and we shall soon lay him by the heels."

"Ridic'lous," mumbled Geoffrey. "Ain't—isn't any Hound. We're affer dope smuggler, not some son of—YOWP!" A badly thrown dart whizzed by his ear.

"Do you have to do that?" he quavered.

"Ah, they William," chuckled Toowey. "Ee's a fair killer, un is."

Another dart zoomed over Geoffrey's head and stuck in the wall. The IBI man choked and slid under the table—whether for refuge or sleep, Alex didn't know.

"Tomorrow," said Holmes, "I shall measure this tavern. I always measure," he added in explanation. "Even when there seems to be no point in it."

The landlord's voice boomed over the racket. "Closing time, gentlemen. It is time!"

The door flew open and banged to again. A Hoka stood there, breathing hard. He was unusually fat, and completely muffled in a long black coat; his face seemed curiously expressionless, though his voice was shrill with panic.

"Sir Henry!" cried the landlord. "Yeou'm back, squire!"

"The Hound," wailed Baskerville. "The Hound is after me!"

"Yeou've na cause tu fee-ar naow, Sir Henry," said Farmer Toowey. " 'Tis Sheerlock Holmes unself coom own to track yan brute."

Baskerville shrank against the wall. "Holmes?" he whispered.

"And a man from the IBI," said Alex. "But we're really after a criminal lurking on the moors—"

Geoffrey lifted a tousled head over the table. "Isn't no Hound," he said. "I'm affer uh dirty ppussjan, I am. Isn't no Hound nowheres."

Baskerville leaped. "It's at the door!" he shrieked, wildly. Plunging across the room, he went through the window in a crash of glass.

"Quick, Watson!" Holmes sprang up, pulling out

his archaic revolver. "We'll see if there is a Hound or not!" He shoved through the panicky crowd and flung the door open.

The thing that crouched there, dimly seen by the firelight spilling out into darkness, was long and low and black, the body a vague shadow, a fearsome head dripping cold fire and snarling stiffly. It growled and took a step forward.

"Here naow!" The landlord plunged ahead, too outraged to be frightened. "Yeou can't coom in here. 'Tis closing time!" He thrust the Hound back with his foot and slammed the door.

"After him, Watson!" yelled Holmes. "Quick, Gregson!"

"Eek," said Geoffrey.

He must be too drunk to move, Alex thought. Alex himself had consumed just enough to dash after Holmes. They stood in the entrance, peering into darkness.

"Gone," said the human.

"We'll track him down!" Holmes paused to light his bull's-eye lantern, button his long coat, and jam his deerstalker cap more firmly down over his ears. "Follow me."

No one else stirred as Holmes and Alex went out into the night. It was pitchy outside. The Hokas had better night vision than humans and Holmes' furry hand closed on Alex's to lead him. "Confound these cobblestones!" said the detective. "No tracks whatsoever. Well, come along." They trotted from the village.

"Where are we going?" asked Alex.

"Out by the path to Baskerville Hall," replied Holmes sharply. "You would hardly expect to find the Hound anyplace else, would you, Watson?"

Properly rebuked, Alex lapsed into silence, which he didn't have the courage to break until, after what seemed an endless time, they came to a halt. "Where are we now?" he inquired of the night.

"About midway between the village and the Hall," replied the voice of Holmes, from near the level of Alex's waist. "Compose yourself, Watson, and wait while I examine the area for clues." Alex felt his hand released and heard the sound of Holmes moving away and rustling about on the ground. "Aha!"

"Find something?" asked the human, looking nervously around him.

"Indeed I have, Watson," answered Holmes. "A seafaring man with red hair and a peg leg has recently passed by here on his way to drown a sackful of kittens."

Alex blinked. "What?"

"A seafaring man—" Holmes began again, patiently.

"But—" stammered Alex. "But how can you tell that?"

"Childishly simple, my dear Watson," said Holmes. The light pointed to the ground. "Do you see this small chip of wood?"

"Y-yes, I guess so."

"By its grain and seasoning, and the type of wear it has had, it is obviously a piece which has broken off a peg leg. A touch of tar upon it shows that it belongs to a seafaring man. But what would a seafaring man be doing on the moors at night?"

"That's what I'd like to know," said Alex.

"We may take it," Holmes went on, "that only some unusual reason could force him out with the Hound running loose. But when we realize that he is a redheaded man with a terrific temper and a sackful of kittens with which he is totally unable to put up for another minute, it becomes obvious that he has sallied forth in a fit of exasperation to drown them."

Alex's brain, already spinning somewhat dizzily under the effect of the Hoka liquor, clutched frantically at this explanation, in an attempt to sort it out. But it seemed to slip through his fingers.

"What's all that got to do with the Hound, or the criminal we're after?" he asked weakly.

"Nothing, Watson," reproved Holmes sternly. "Why should it have?"

Baffled, Alex gave up.

Holmes poked around for a few more minutes, then spoke again. "If the Hound is truly dangerous, it should be sidling around to overwhelm us in the darkness. It should be along very shortly. Hah!" he rubbed his hands together. "Excellent!"

"I suppose it is," said Alex, feebly.

"You stay here, Watson," said Holmes, "and I will move on down the path a ways. If you see the creature, whistle." His lantern went out and the sound of his footsteps moved away.

Time seemed to stretch on interminably. Alex stood alone in the darkness, with the chill of the moor creeping into his bones as the liquor died within him, and wondered why he had ever let himself in for this in the first place. What would Tanni say? What earthly use would he be even if the Hound should appear? With his merely human night vision, he could let the beast stroll past within arm's reach and never know it. Of course, he could probably hear it. . . .

Come to think of it, what kind of noise would a monster make when walking? Would it be a *pad-pad*, or a sort of *shuffle-shuffle-shuffle* like the sound on the path to his left?

The sound—*Yipe!*

The night was suddenly shattered. An enormous section of the blackness reared up and smashed into him with the solidity and impact of a brick wall. He went spinning down into the star-streaked oblivion of unconsciousness.

When he opened his eyes again, it was to sunlight streaming through the leaded windows of his room. His head was pounding, and he remembered some fantastic nightmare in which—hah!

Relief washing over him, he sank back into bed. Of course. He must have gotten roaring drunk last night and dreamt the whole weird business. His head was splitting. He put his hands up to it.

They touched a thick bandage.

Alex sat up as if pulled on a string. The two chairs which had been arranged to extend the bed for him went clattering to the floor. "Holmes!" he shouted. "Geoffrey!"

His door opened and the individuals in question entered, followed by Farmer Toowey. Holmes was fully dressed, fuming away on his pipe; Geoffrey looked red-eyed and haggard. "What happened?" asked Alex, wildly.

"You didn't whistle," said Holmes reproachfully.

"Aye, that yeou di'n't," put in the farmer. "When they boor yeou in, tha face were white nor a sheet, laike. Fair horrible it were, the look on tha face, lad."

"Then it wasn't a dream!" said Alex, shuddering.

"I—er—I saw you go out after the monster," said Geoffrey, looking guilty. "I tried to follow you, but I couldn't get moving for some reason." He felt gingerly of his own head.

"I saw a black shape attack you, Watson," added Holmes.

"I think it was the Hound, even though that luminous face wasn't there. I shot at it but missed, and it fled over the moors. I couldn't pursue it with you lying there, so I carried you back. It's late afternoon now—you slept well, Watson!"

"It must have been the ppussjan," said Geoffrey with something of his old manner. "We're going to scour the moors for him today."

"No, Gregson," said Holmes. "I am convinced it was the Hound."

"Bah!" said Geoffrey. "That thing last night was only—was only—well, it was not a ppussjan. Some local animal, no doubt."

"Aye," nodded Farmer Toowey. "The Hound un were, that."

"Not the Hound!" yelled Geoffrey. "The ppussjan, do you hear? The Hound is pure superstition. There isn't any such animal."

Holmes wagged his finger. "Temper, temper, Gregson," he said.

"*And stop calling me Gregson!*" Geoffrey clutched his temples. "Oh, my head—!"

"My dear young friend," said Holmes patiently, "it will repay you to study my methods if you wish to advance in your profession. While you and Lestrade were out organizing a futile search party, I was studying the terrain and gathering clues. A clue is the detective's best friend, Gregson. I have five hundred measurements, six plaster casts of footprints, several threads torn from Sir Henry's coat by a splinter last night, and numerous other items. At a conservative estimate, I have gathered five pounds of clues."

"Listen." Geoffrey spoke with dreadful preciseness. "We're here to track down a dope smuggler, Holmes.

A desperate criminal. We are not interested in country superstitions."

"I am, Gregson," smiled Holmes.

With an inarticulate snarl, Geoffrey turned and whirled out of the room. He was shaking. Holmes looked after him and tut-tutted. Then, turning: "Well, Watson, how do you feel now?"

Alex got carefully out of bed. "Not too bad," he admitted. "I've got a thumping headache, but an athetrine tablet will take care of it."

"Oh, that reminds me—" While Alex dressed, Holmes took a small flat case out of his pocket. When Alex looked that way again, Holmes was injecting himself with a hypodermic syringe.

"Hey!" cried the human. "What's that?"

"Morphine, Watson," said Holmes. "A seven percent solution. It stimulates the mind, I've found."

"Morphine!" Alex cried. Here was an IBI man currently present for the purpose of running down a dope smuggler and one of his Hokas had just produced— "OH, NO!"

Holmes leaned over and whispered in some embarrassment: "Well, actually, Watson, you're right. It's really just distilled water. I've written off for morphine several times, but they never send me any. So—well, one has one's position to keep up, you know."

"Oh," Alex feebly mopped his brow. "Of course."

While he stowed away a man-sized dinner, Holmes climbed up on the roof and lowered himself down the chimney in search of possible clues. He emerged black but cheerful. "Nothing, Watson," he reported. "But we must be thorough." Then, briskly: "Now come. We've work to do."

"Where?" asked Alex. "With the search party?"

"Oh, no. They will only alarm some harmless wild animals, I fear. We are going exploring elsewhere. Farmer Toowey here has kindly agreed to assist us."

"S'archin', laike," nodded the old Hoka.

As they emerged into the sunlight, Alex saw the search party, a hundred or so local yokels who had gathered under Lestrade's direction with clubs, pitchforks and flails to beat the bush for the Hound— or for the ppussjan, if it came to that. One enthusiastic farmer drove a huge "horse"-drawn reaping machine. Geoffrey was scurrying up and down the line, screaming as he tried to bring some order into it. Alex felt sorry for him.

They struck out down the path across the moor. "First we're off to Baskerville Hall," said Holmes. "There's something deucedly odd about Sir Henry Baskerville. He disappears for weeks, and then reappears last night, terrified by his ancestral curse, only to dash out onto the very moor which it is prowling. Where has he been in the interim, Watson? Where is he now?"

"Hm—yes," agreed Alex. "This Hound business and the ppussjan—do you think that there could be some connection between the two?"

"Never reason before you have all the facts, Watson," said Holmes. "It is the cardinal sin of all young police officers such as our impetuous friend Gregson."

Alex couldn't help agreeing. Geoffrey was so intent on his main assignment that he just didn't take time to consider the environment; to him, this planet was only a backdrop for his search. Of course, he was probably a cool head ordinarily, but Sherlock Holmes could unseat anyone's sanity.

Alex remembered that he was unarmed. Geoffrey

had a raythrower, but this party only had Holmes' revolver and Toowey's gnarled staff. He gulped and tried to dismiss thoughts of the thing that had slugged him last night. "A nice day," he remarked to Holmes.

"It is, is it not? However," said Holmes, brightening up, "some of the most bloodcurdling crimes have been committed on fine days. There was, for example, the Case of the Dismembered Bishop—I don't believe I have ever told you about it, Watson. Do you have your notebook to hand?"

"Why, no," said Alex, somewhat startled.

"A pity," said Holmes. "I could have told you not only about the Dismembered Bishop, but about the Leaping Caterpillar, the Strange Case of the Case of Scotch, and the Great Ghastly Case—all very interesting problems. How is your memory?" he asked suddenly.

"Why—good, I guess," said Alex.

"Then I will tell you about the Case of the Leaping Caterpillar, which is the shortest of the lot," commenced Holmes. "It was considerably before your time, Watson. I was just beginning to attract attention with my work; and one day there was a knock on the door and in came the strangest—"

"Here be Baskerville Hall, laike," said Farmer Toowey.

An imposing Tudoresque pile loomed behind its screen of trees. They went up to the door and knocked. It opened and a corpulent Hoka in butler's black regarded them with frosty eyes. "Tradesmen's entrance in the rear," he said.

"Hey!" cried Alex.

The butler took cognizance of his humanness and became respectful. "I beg your pardon, sir," he said.

"I am somewhat near-sighted and— I am sorry, sir, but Sir Henry is not at home."

"Where is he, then?" asked Holmes, sharply.

"In his grave, sir," said the butler, sepulchrally.

"Huh?" said Alex.

"His grave?" barked Holmes. "Quick, man! Where is he buried?"

"In the belly of the Hound, sir. If you will pardon the expression."

"Aye, aye," nodded Farmer Toowey. "Yan Hound, ee be a hungry un, ee be."

A few questions elicited the information that Sir Henry, a bachelor, had disappeared one day several weeks ago while walking on the moors, and had not been heard from since. The butler was surprised to learn that he had been seen only last night, and brightened visibly. "I hope he comes back soon, sir," he said. "I wish to give notice. Much as I admire Sir Henry, I cannot continue to serve an employer who may at any moment be devoured by monsters."

"Well," said Holmes, pulling out a tape measure, "to work, Watson."

"Oh, no, you don't!" This time Alex asserted himself. He couldn't see waiting around all night while Holmes measured this monstrosity of a mansion. "We've got a ppussjan to catch, remember?"

"Just a little measurement," begged Holmes.

"No!"

"Not even one?"

"All right." Jones relented at the wistful tone. "Just one."

Holmes beamed and, with a few deft motions, measured the butler.

"I must say, Watson, that you can be quite tyrannical at times," he said. Then, returning to Hoka normal:

"Still, without my Boswell, where would I be?" He set off at a brisk trot, his furry legs twinkling in the late sunlight. Alex and Toowey stretched themselves to catch up.

They were well out on the moor again when the detective stopped and, his nose twitching with eagerness, leaned over a small bush from which one broken limb trailed on the ground. "What's that?" asked Alex.

"A broken bush, Watson," said Holmes snappishly. "Surely even you can see that."

"I know. But what about it?"

"Come, Watson," said Holmes, sternly. "Does not this broken bush convey some message to you? You know my methods. Apply them."

Alex felt a sudden wave of sympathy for the original Dr. Watson. Up until now he had never realized the devilish cruelty inherent in that simple command to apply the Holmesian methods. Apply them—how? He stared fiercely at the bush, which continued to ignore him, without being able to deduce more than that it was (a) a bush and (b) broken.

"Uh—a high wind?" he asked hesitantly.

"Ridiculous, Watson," retorted Holmes. "The broken limb is green; doubtless it was snapped last night by something large passing by in haste. Yes, Watson, this confirms my suspicions. The Hound has passed this way on its way to its lair, and the branch points us the direction."

"They be tu Grimpen Mire, a be," said Farmer Toowey dubiously. "Yan mire be impassable, un be."

"Obviously it is not, if the Hound is there," said Holmes. "Where it can go, we can follow. Come, Watson!" And he trotted off, his small body bristling with excitement.

They went through the brush for some minutes until they came to a wide boggy stretch with a large signboard in front of it.

GRIMPEN MIRE
FOUR MILES SQUARE
DANGER!!!!!!

"Watch closely, Watson," said Holmes. "The creature has obviously leaped from tussock to tussock. We will follow his path, watching for trampled grass or broken twigs. Now, then!" And bounding past the boundary sign, Holmes landed on a little patch of turf, from which he immediately soared to another one.

Alex hesitated, gulped, and followed him. It was not easy to progress in jumps of a meter or more, and Holmes, bouncing from spot to spot, soon pulled away. Farmer Toowey cursed and grunted behind Alex. "Eigh, ma oold boons can't tyke the leaping na moor, they can't," he muttered when they paused to rest. "If we'd knowed the Mire were tu be zo much swink, we'd never a builted un, book or no book."

"You made it yourselves?" asked Alex. "It's artificial?"

"Aye, lad, that un be. 'Twas in the book, Grimpen Mire, an' un swall'd many a man doon, un did. Many brave hee-arts lie asleep in un deep." He added apologetically: "Ow-ers be no zo grimly, though un tried hard. Ow-ers, yeou oonly get tha feet muddy, a-crossing o' 't. Zo we stay well away fran it, yeou understand."

Alex sighed.

The sun was almost under the hills now, and long shadows swept down the moor. Alex looked back, but could not make out any sign of Hall, village, or search party. A lonesome spot—not exactly the best place to meet a demoniac Hound, or even a ppussjan. Glancing ahead, he could not discern Holmes either, and he put on more speed.

An island—more accurately, a large hill—rose above the quaking mud. Alex and Toowey reached it with a final leap. They broke through a wall of trees and brush screening its stony crest. Here grew a wide thick patch of purple flowers. Alex halted, looked at them, and muttered an oath. He'd seen those blossoms depicted often enough in news articles.

"Nixl weed," he said. "So this is the ppussjan hideout!"

Dusk came swiftly as the sun disappeared. Alex remembered again that he was unarmed and strained wildly through the gathering dimness. "Holmes!" he called. "Holmes! I say, where are you, old fellow?" He snapped his fingers and swore. *Damn! Now I'm doing it!*

A roar came from beyond the hilltop. Jones leaped back. A tree stabbed him with a sharp branch. Whirling around, he struck out at the assailant. "Ouch!" he yelled. "Heavens to Betsy!" he added, though not in precisely those words.

The roar lifted again, a bass bellow that rumbled down to a savage snarling. Alex clutched at Farmer Toowey's smock. "What's that?" he gasped. "What's happening to Holmes?"

"Might be Hound's got un," offered Toowey, stolidly. "We hears un eatin', laike."

Alex dismissed the bloodthirsty notion with a frantic gesture. "Don't be ridiculous," he said.

"Ridiculous I may be," said Toowey stubbornly, "but they girt Hound be hungry, for zartin sure."

Alex's fear-tautened ears caught a new sound— footsteps from over the hill. "It's—coming this way," he hissed.

Toowey muttered something that sounded like "dessert."

Setting his teeth, Alex plunged forward. He topped the hill and sprang, striking a small solid body and crashing to earth. "I say, Watson," came Holmes' dry, testy voice, "this really won't do at all. I have told you a hundred times that such impetuosity ruins more good police officers than any other fault in the catalogue."

"Holmes!" Alex picked himself up, breathing hard. "My God, Holmes, it's you! But that other noise—the bellowing—?"

"That," said Holmes, "was Sir Henry Baskerville when I took the gag out of his mouth. Now come along, gentlemen, and see what I have found."

Alex and Toowey followed him through the nixl patch and down the rocky slope beyond it. Holmes drew aside a bush and revealed a yawning blackness. "I thought the Hound would shelter in a burrow," he said, "and assumed he would camouflage its entrance. So I merely checked the bushes. Do come in, Watson, and relax."

Alex crawled after Holmes. The tunnel widened into an artificial cave, about two meters high and three square, lined with a spray-plastic—not too bad a place. By the vague light of Holmes' bull's-eye, Alex saw a small cot, a cookstove, a radio transceiver, and a few luxuries. The latter, apparently, included a middle-aged Hoka in the tattered remnants of a once-fine tweed suit. He had been fat, from the way his skin hung about him, but was woefully thin and dirty now. It hadn't hurt his voice, though—he was still swearing in a loud bass unusual for the species, as he stripped the last of his bonds from him.

"Damned impertinence," he said. "Man isn't even safe on his own grounds any more. And the rascal

had the infernal nerve to take over the family legend—
my ancestral curse, dammit!"

"Calm down, Sir Henry," said Holmes. "You're safe
now."

"I'm going to write to my M.P.," mumbled the real
Baskerville. "I'll tell him a thing or two, I will. There'll
be questions asked in the House of Commons, egad!"

Alex sat down on the cot and peered through the
gloom. "What happened to you, Sir Henry?" he asked.

"Damned monster accosted me right on my own
moor," said the Hoka, indignantly. "Drew a gun on
me, he did. Forced me into his noisome hole. Had
the unmitigated gall to take a mask of my face. Since
then he's kept me on bread and water. Not even fresh
bread, by Godfrey! It—it isn't British! I've been tied
up in this hole for weeks. The only exercise I got
was harvesting his blinking weed for him. When he
went away, he'd tie me up and gag me—" Sir Henry
drew, an outraged breath. "So help me, he gagged
me *with my own school tie!*"

"Kept as slave and possibly hostage," commented
Holmes. "Hm. Yes, we're dealing with a desperate
fellow. But Watson, see here what I have to show
you." He reached into a box and pulled out a limp,
black object with an air of triumph. "What do you
think of this, Watson?"

Alex stretched it out: a plastimask of a fanged
monstrous head, grinning like a toothpaste ad. When
he held it in shadow, he saw the luminous spots on
it. The Hound's head!

"Holmes!" he cried. "The Hound is the—the—"

"Ppussjan," supplied Holmes.

"How do you do?" said a new voice, politely.

Whirling around, Holmes, Alex, Toowey, and Sir
Henry managed, in the narrow space, to tie themselves

in knots. When they had gotten untangled, they looked down the barrel of a raythrower. Behind it was figure muffled shapelessly in a great, trailing black coat, but with the head of Sir Henry above it.

"Number Ten!" gulped Alex.

"Exactly," said the ppussjan. His voice had a Hoka squeakiness, but the tone was cold. "Fortunately, I got back from scouting around before you could lay an ambush for me. It was pathetic, watching that search party. The last I saw of them, they were headed for Northumberland."

"They'll find you," said Alex, with a dry voice. "You don't dare hurt us."

"Don't I?" asked the ppussjan, brightly.

"I zuppoze yeou du, at that," said Toowey.

Alex realized sickly that if the ppussjan's hideout had been good up to now, it would probably be good until his gang arrived to rescue him. In any case, he, Alexander Braithwaite Jones, wouldn't be around to see.

But that was impossible. Such things didn't happen to him. He was League plenipotentiary to Toka, not a character in some improbable melodrama, waiting to be shot. He—

A sudden wild thought tossed out of his spinning brain: "Look here, Ten, if you ray us you'll sear all your equipment here too." He had to try again; no audible sounds had come out the first time.

"Why, thanks," said the ppussjan. "I'll set the gun to narrow-beam." Its muzzle never wavered as he adjusted the focusing stud. "Now," he asked, "have you any prayers to say?"

"I—" Toowey licked his lips. "Wull yeou alloo me to zay one poem all t' way through? It have given me gree-at coomfort, it have."

"Go ahead, then."

"By the shores of Gitchee Gumee—"

Alex knelt too—and one long human leg reached out and his foot crashed down on Holmes' lantern. His own body followed, hugging the floor as total darkness whelmed the cave. The raybeam sizzled over him—but, being narrow, missed and splatted the farther wall.

"Yoiks!" shouted Sir Henry, throwing himself at the invisible ppussjan. He tripped over Alex and went rolling to the floor. Alex got out from underneath, clutched at something, and slugged hard. The other slugged back.

"Take that!" roared Alex. "And that!"

"Oh, no!" said Sherlock Holmes in the darkness. "Not again, Watson!"

They whirled, colliding with each other, and groped toward the sounds of fighting. Alex clutched at an arm. "Friend or ppussjan?" he bellowed.

A raybeam scorched by him for answer. He fell to the floor, grabbing for the ppussjan's skinny legs. Holmes climbed over him to attack the enemy. The ppussjan fired once more, wildly, then Holmes got his gun hand and clung. Farmer Toowey yelled a Hoka battle cry, whirled his staff over his head, and clubbed Sir Henry.

Holmes wrenched the ppussjan's raythrower loose. It clattered to the floor. The ppussjan twisted in Alex's grasp, pulling his leg free. Alex got hold of his coat. The ppussjan slipped out of it and went skidding across the floor, fumbling for the gun. Alex fought the heavy coat for some seconds before realizing that it was empty.

Holmes was there at the same time as Number Ten, snatching the raythrower from the ppussjan's grasp. Ten clawed out, caught a smooth solid object falling from Holmes' pocket, and snarled in triumph. Backing,, away, he collided with Alex. "Oops, sorry," said Alex, and went on groping around the floor.

The ppussjan found the light switch and snapped it. The radiance caught a tangle of three Hokas and one human. He pointed his weapon. "All right!" he screeched. "I've got you now!"

"Give that back!" said Holmes indignantly, drawing his revolver.

The ppussjan looked down at his own hand. It was clutching Sherlock Holmes' pipe.

Whitcomb Geoffrey staggered into the George and Dragon and grabbed the wall for support. He was gaunt and unshaven. His clothes were in rags. His hair was full of burrs. His shoes were full of mud. Every now and then he twitched, and his lips moved. A night and half a day trying to superintend a Hoka search party was too much for any man, even an IBI man.

Alexander Jones, Sherlock Holmes, Farmer Toowey, and Sir Henry Baskerville looked sympathetically up from the high tea which the landlord was serving them. The ppussjan looked up too, but with less amiability. His vulpine face sported a large black eye, and his four-legged body was lashed to a chair with Sir Henry's old school tie. His wrists were bound with Sir Henry's regimental colors.

"I say, Gregson, you've had rather a thin time of it, haven't you?" asked Holmes. "Do come have a spot of tea."

"Whee-ar's the s'arch party, lad?" asked Farmer Toowey.

"When I left them," said Geoffrey, dully, "they were

resisting arrest at Potteringham Castle. The earl objected to their dragging his duckpond."

"Wull, wull, lad, the-all ull be back soon, laike," said Toowey, gently.

Geoffrey's bloodshot eyes fell on Number Ten. He was too tired to say more than: "So you got him after all."

"Oh, yes," said Alex. "Want to take him back to Headquarters?"

With the first real spirit he had shown since he had come in, Geoffrey sighed. "Take him back?" he breathed. "I can actually leave this planet?"

He collapsed into a chair. Sherlock Holmes refilled his pipe and leaned his short furry form back into his own seat.

"This has been an interesting little case," he said. "In some ways it reminds me of the Adventure of the Two Fried Eggs, and I think, my dear Watson, that it may be of some small value to your little chronicles. Have you your notebook ready? . . . Good. For your benefit, Gregson, I shall explain my deductions, for you are in many ways a promising man who could profit by instruction."

Geoffrey's lips started moving again.

"I have already explained the discrepancies of Sir Henry's appearance in the tavern," went on Holmes implacably. "I also thought that the recent renewed activity of the Hound, which time-wise fitted in so well with the ppussjan's arrival, might well be traceable to our criminal. Indeed, he probably picked this hideout because it did have such a legend. If the natives were frightened of the Hound, you see, they would be less likely to venture abroad and interfere with Number Ten's activities; and anything they did notice would be attributed to the Hound and dismissed by those outsiders who did not take the superstition seriously. Sir Henry's disappearance was, of course, part of this program of terrorization; but also, the ppussjan needed a Hoka face. He would have to appear in the local villages from time to time, you see, to purchase food and to find out whether or not he was being hunted by your bureau, Gregson. Watson has been good enough to explain to me the process by which your civilization can cast a mask in spray-plastic. The ppussjan's overcoat is an ingenious, adaptable garment; by a quick adjustment, it can be made to seem either like the body of a monster, or, if he walks on his hind legs, the covering of a somewhat stout Hoka. Thus, the ppussjan could be himself, or Sir Henry Baskerville, or the Hound of the Baskervilles, just as it suited him."

"Clever fella," murmured Sir Henry. "But dashed impudent, don't y'know. That sort of thing just isn't done. It isn't playing the game."

"The ppussjan must have picked up a rumor about our descent," continued Holmes. "An aircraft makes quite a local sensation. He had to investigate and see if flyers were after him and, if so, how hot they might be on his trail. He broke into the tavern in the Sir Henry disguise, learned enough for his purposes, and went out the window. Then he appeared again in the Hound form. This was an attempt to divert our attention from himself and send us scampering off after a non-existent Hound—as, indeed, Lestrade's search party was primarily doing when last heard from. When we pursued him that night, he tried to do away with the good Watson, but fortunately I drove him off in time. Thereafter he skulked about, spying on the search party, until finally he returned to his lair. But I was already there, waiting to trap him."

That, thought Alex, was glossing the facts a trifle. However—

Holmes elevated his black nose in the air and blew a huge cloud of nonchalant smoke. "And so," he said smugly, "ends the Adventure of the Misplaced Hound."

Alex looked at him. Damn it—the worst of the business was that Holmes was right. He'd been right all along. In his own Hoka fashion, he had done a truly magnificent job of detection. Honesty swept Alex off his and he spoke without thinking.

"Holmes—by the Lord Harry, Holmes," he said, "this—this is sheer genius."

No sooner were the words out of his lips than he realized what he had done. But it was too late now—too late to avoid the answer that Holmes must inevitably give. Alex clutched his hands together and braced his tired body, resolved to see the thing through like a man. Sherlock Holmes smiled, took his pipe from between his teeth, and opened his mouth. Through a great, thundering mist, Alexander Jones heard THE WORDS.

"Not at all. *Elementary, my dear Watson!*"

Interlude IV

Plenipotentiary of the Interbeing League
Planet Toka

HEADQUARTERS OFFICE   CITY OF MIXUMAXU

2/3/85

Mr. Hardman Terwilliger
2011 Maori Towers
League City, N.Z., Sol III

Dear Hardman,

  Good to hear from you—and many thanks for the booties. They're just the right size, says Tanni, though since this is now our third offspring, I maintain with some authority that human babies come in pretty

145

standardized lots. How are your own kids, and Dory? Give them our regards. Congratulations on your promotional transfer to the CDS inspection office. Any chance of your being the next inspector who'll come to review my progress? No, I guess not—your job will be mostly Earthside, evaluating the reports of poor devils like me. It was decent of you to write unofficially, concerning that complaint about my alleged religious intolerance. I do hate sweating out governmentalese for our mutual Great White Father, Parr. It's one reason why I sometimes think of resigning, in spite of a long stay here on Toka. The Hokas themselves, of course, are another reason or fifty.

No one who hasn't spent time with these furry little demons of mine seems to realize their capabilities. Between you and me and the circular file, I believe the Testing Section goofed dramatically when they pegged this race for a mere Stage D, back in the beginning. They failed to take into account the paralyzing effect of a geological era (?) of armed competition with the Slissii. Now that that damper has been taken off—but come to think of it, I doubt if you know what happened to the Slissii. You'll need the information in your new post, but rather than send you through a decade's worth of reports, here's the gist of it.

They're an odd race. In general temperament and character, they are everything the Hokas are not, cold, calculating, xenophobic, as if nature had struck a needed balance between good and evil on this planet. (Though that, of course, is a purely anthropomorphic value judgment. I daresay the Slissii are kind to their own families.) Early in the game it became clear that we could never make an agreement with them that they'd respect; man has to deal with Hokas on this planet, or no one. But since I could supply my own wards, the Five and a Half Cities, with gunpowder weapons—an inducement, among others, which helped get all the rest of the Hoka nations to accept ward status—the Slissii tribes were totally defeated in a few years.

Meanwhile, their aristocrats had been studying the galactic situation for all they were worth. By the time their last confederation surrendered to the Hoka . . . well, let's face it, to the United States Cavalry and the Royal Canadian Mounted Police . . . they knew what to do. So they were to be Injuns? All right. They became Noble Savages. They wrote pamphlets about the Vanishing Tokan. A very bad novel by one of them, *The Last of the Reptiles,* became a planet-wide best seller. They invented rain dances and charged admission. They wrung tears from the Hoka leaders and, against my strongest advice, some of the best oil lands on this world for reservations.

Soon they were all hog-rich, and presently their leaders weaseled a Class A rating out of the Testing Section. I have some evidence that they cheated outrageously on the tests, but for Pete's sake, don't check up on that! We're well rid of them. You see, as Class A's they can go anywhere they wish, so now practically the entire species is playboying it through the known galaxy, with sidelines in crooked stock, card-sharping and so on.

Don't conclude from this that they are more intelligent than the Hokas. I suspect it's actually the other way around, though the leaping Hoka imagination obscures the fact. Damn it. I've been given an impossible job! A Hoka is *not* a miniature human being, and all my attempts to make him one have blown up in my face.

Which brings me to this complaint of religious discrimination made against me by the Bedrock Fundamentalist Church. You're damn well right I refused their missionaries permission to operate on Toka. This is not intolerance. Any faith that wants to proselytize here is welcome, and many have done so; but there are certain reasonable restrictions which must be observed.

Can you imagine what would happen if I admitted a band of preachers who not only read from the Old Testament—and won't give our local rabbis a chance to explain the details—but hand out illustrated biographies of Oliver Cromwell?

Heigh-ho. Earthman's Burden and all that sort of thing. It's late now, and I have a big day ahead of me, so I'll close. We're being threatened with a spate of piracy, and tomorrow I have to investigate a Venetian claim that Captain Nemo had been sinking their gondolas.

> All the best,
> Alex

Yo Ho Hoka!

Alexander Jones was in trouble again. His lean form strode through narrow, cobbled streets between half-timbered houses, automatically dodging horse-drawn carriages. The "horses" were dinosaurian monstrosities, but otherwise Plymouth was a faithful small-scale copy of what the Hokas thought its original had been, circa 1800 A.D. in Earth's England. (This *England* was not to be confused with the Tokan Great Britain, which had been brought up to a Victorian level of civilization.)

The natives who thronged the streets made a respectful way for him, closing in again behind. He heard the awed whispers: "Bli'me, it's the Pleni-potentiary 'imself! . . . Look thar, Alf, ye'll allus remember ye saw the great Jones wid yer own blinkin' eyes. . . . Wonder wot e's after? . . . Prob'ly Affairs of State. . . . Yus, ye can see that on the poor lad, it's mykin' 'im old afore 'is time . . ." These citizens were variously dressed: cocked hats, tailcoats, knee breeches; burly dock wallopers in carefully tattered work clothes; red-coated musketeers; long skirts on the females; and no few males in striped jerseys and bell-bottomed trousers, for Plymouth was a major base of His Majesty's Navy.

Now and then Alex's lips moved. "Old Boney," he muttered. "I keep telling them and telling them there isn't any Napoleon on this planet, but they won't believe me! Damn Old Boney! Blast these history books!"

He turned in at the Crown and Anchor, went through a noisy bar where Hokas sat puffing churchwardens and lying about their exploits with many deep-sea oaths, and proceeded up a narrow stair. The room which he had engaged was clean, though the furniture was inconvenient for a human with twice the Hoka height and half the breadth of beam. Tanni looked up at him from a crudely printed newspaper with horror in her eyes. She had left the children with their nurse, to accompany him here.

"Alex!" she cried. "Listen to this, dear. They're getting violent—killing each other!" She read from the *Gazette*, "Today the notorious highwayman Dick Turpin was hanged on Tyburn Hill—"

"Oh, that," said Alex, relieved. "Turpin gets hanged every Thursday. It's wonderful sport for all."

"But—"

"Didn't you know? You can't hurt a Hoka by hanging him. Their neck musculature is too strong in proportion to their weight. If hanging hurt Dick Turpin, the police would never do it. They're proud of him."

"Proud!"

"Well, he's part of this eighteenth-century pattern

they're trying so hard to follow, isn't he?" Alex sat down and ran a hand through his hair. He was sometimes surprised that it hadn't turned gray yet.

"Poor dear," said Tanni sympathetically. "How did it go?" They had flown here only today from Mixumaxu, and she was still a little puzzled as to the nature of their mission.

"I couldn't get any sense out of the Admiralty Office at all," said Alex. "They kept babbling about old Boney. I can't convince them that these pirates represent a real menace."

"How did it ever happen, darling? I thought the imposed cultural patterns were always modified so as to exclude violence."

"Oh, yes, yes . . . but some dimwit out in space learned how the Hokas go for Earth fiction and smuggled some historical novels into this sector. Pirates, forsooth!" Alex grinned bitterly. "You can imagine what the idea of swaggering around with a cutlass and a Jolly Roger could do to a Hoka. The first I heard, there were a couple of dozen ships turned pirate, off to the Spanish Main . . . wherever on Toka they've decided *that* is! So far no trouble, but they're probably fixing to attack some place like the Bermuda we've established."

"Criminals?" Tanni frowned, finding it hard to believe of her little friends.

"Oh, no. Just . . . irresponsible. Not really realizing it'll mean bloodshed. They'll be awfully sorry later. But that'll be too late for us, sweetheart." Alex looked gloomily at the floor. "Once Headquarters learns I've permitted a war-pattern to evolve on this planet, I'll be out on my ear and blacklisted from here to the Lesser Magellanic Cloud. My only chance is to stop the business before it blows up."

"Oh, dear," said Tanni inadequately. "Can't they understand? I'd like to give those bureaucrats back home a piece of—"

"Never mind. You have to have iron-bound regulations to run a civilization the size of ours. It's results that count. Nobody cares much how I get them, but get them I must." Alex got up and began rummaging in their trunk.

"What are you looking for?" asked Tanni.

"That green beard . . . the one I wore to the Count of Monte Cristo's masquerade ball last week . . . thought it'd come in handy." Alex tossed articles of apparel every which way, and Tanni sighed. "You see, I've already been to the Admiralty in my proper *persona*, and they wouldn't order out the fleet to catch those pirates—said the routine patrols were adequate. Going over their heads, through Parliament and the King, would take too long. . . . Ah, here!" He emerged with a hideous green beard, fully half a meter in length.

"I'll go direct to Lord Nelson, who's in town," he went on. "It's best to do it incognito, to avoid offending the Admiralty; this beard is disguise enough, not being included in the Hokas' Jones-Gestalt. Once alone with him, I'll reveal myself and explain the situation. He's pretty level-headed, I'm told, and will act on his own responsibility." He put the beard to his chin and the warmth of his body stuck it as fast as a natural growth—more so, for the synthetic fibers could not be cut or burned.

Tanni shuddered at the loathsome sight. "How do you get it off?" she asked.

"Spirits of ammonia. All right, I'm on my way again." Alex stooped to kiss her and wondered why she shrank away. "Wait around till I get back. It may take a while."

The foliage flapped around his chest as he went downstairs. "Scuttle my hatches!" said someone. "What is it?"

"Seaweed," theorized another. "He's been too long underwater."

Alex reached the dock and stared over the tangle of rigging and tall masts which lay beyond. The Hokas had built quite a sizable navy in expectation of imminent Napoleonic invasion, and HMS *Intolerable* lay almost side by side with *Incorrigible* and *Pinafore*. Their mermaid figureheads gleamed gilt in the light of the lowering sun—that is, Alex assumed the fishtailed Hoka females to be mermaids, though the four mammaries were so prominent as to suggest ramming was still standard naval practice. He couldn't see where the *Victory* was. Casting about for assistance, he spotted a patrol of sailors swinging along with a burly little Hoka in the lead. "Ahoy!" he yelled.

The patrol stepped smartly up to him, neat in their English Navy uniforms. "Tell me," said Alex, "how do I get out to the flagship? I must see Admiral Lord Nelson at once."

"Stow my top-hamper!" squeaked the leader. "You can't see the Admiral, mate. 'Tain't proper for a common seaman to speak to the Admiral unless spoken to first."

"No doubt," said Alex. "But I'm not a common seaman."

"Aye, that you are, mate," replied the other cheerfully. "Pressed right and proper as a common seaman, or me name's not Billy Bosun."

"No, no, you don't understand—" Alex was beginning, when the meaning filtered through to him. *"Pressed?"*

"Taken by the press gang of Billy Bosun for His Majesty's frigate *Incompatible*," said the Hoka. "And a fair bit of luck for you, mate. The worst hell-ship afloat, not counting the *Bounty*, and we sail on patrol in two hours. Toss the prisoner into the gig, men."

"No! Wait!" yelled Alex, frantically trying to pull his beard loose. "Let me explain! You don't know who I am. You can't—".

As he himself had remarked, the Hoka musculature is amazingly strong. He landed on his head in the bottom of the gig and went out like a light.

"Pressed man to speak with you, Cap'n Yardly," said Billy Bosun, ushering Alex into the captain's cabin.

The human blinked in the light from the cabin portholes and tried to brace himself against the rolling of the ship. He had been locked in the forward hold all night, during which time HMS *Incompatible* had left Great Britain far behind. He had gotten over a headache and a tendency to seasickness, but was wild with the thought that every minute was, taking him farther from Tanni and his desperately urgent mission. He stared at the blue-coated, cocked-hatted Hoka who sat behind a desk facing him, and opened his mouth to speak; but the other beat him to it.

"Does, does he?" growled Captain Yardly. The fur bristled on his neck. "Thinks he signed on for a pleasure cruise, no doubt! We'll teach him different, b'gad, won't we, Bosun?"

"Aye, sir," said Billy, stiffly.

"Wait, Captain Yardly!" cried Alex. "Let me just have a word with you in private—"

"Private, eh? Private, damme!" exploded the Hoka. "There's no such thing as privacy aboard a King's ship. Ain't that right, Bosun?"

"Aye, aye, sir."

"But if you'll just listen to me for a moment—" wailed Alex.

"Listen, b'gad! I don't listen to men, do I, Bosun?"

"Aye, aye, sir."

"Nothing in the articles of war that makes it my duty to listen! My duty's to flog, b'gad; keelhaul, damme; drive the mutinous dogs till they drop. Stap my vitals, eh, Bosun?" Captain Yardly snorted with indignation.

"Aye, aye, sir."

Alex took a firm grip on his temper. He reminded himself that there was no use arguing with a Hoka once he had decided to play a certain role. The only way to handle him was to act along. Alex forced his face into a meek expression.

"Sorry, Captain," he said. "The truth is, I've come to confess that I'm not what I appear to be."

"Well, that's different!" huffed the officer. "Nothing against my listening to a man's confession as long as I flog him afterwards anyway."

Alex gulped, and quickly continued: "The truth is, Captain, this green beard of mine is false. You probably think I'm one of these outworlders you see occasionally, but without it, you'd recognize me at once. I'll bet you can't guess who I really am."

"Done!" roared the captain.

"Huh?" said Alex.

"I wager I can guess who you are. Your name's Greenbeard."

"No—no—"

"Said so yourself."

"No, I said—"

"SILENCE!" thundered the captain. "You've lost your wager. No carping, damme. It's not done. Not sporting at all. I'm appointing you first mate, Mr. Greenbeard, in accordance with regulations—"

"Regulations?" stammered Alex. "What regulations?"

"Pressed man always appointed first mate," snorted Captain Yardly, "in spite of his well-known sympathy for the crew. Got sympathy for the crew, haven't you?"

"Well . . . I suppose so . . ." stammered Alex, weakly— "I mean . . . what kind of first mate would I be— No, wait, I'm all mixed up. I mean—"

"No back talk, if you please!" interrupted the Hoka. "Step lively and drive her smartly, Mr. Greenbeard. We're headed 'round the Horn and I want no malingerers aboard."

"The Horn?" goggled Alex.

"You heard me, Mr. Greenbeard."

"But—" protested Alex, wildly, as Billy Bosun started pulling him by main force out of the cabin. "How . . . how long a voyage is this supposed to be?"

The captain's face dropped suddenly into an unhappy embarrassed expression.

"That depends," he said morosely, "on which way we go."

And he turned and vanished through a connecting door into the inner cabin. His voice came back, somewhat muffled: "Clap on all sail, Mr. Greenbeard, and call me if the weather freshens."

The words were followed by what sounded like a sob of desperation.

Giving up further argument as a bad job, Alex went back on deck. A stiff breeze drove the *Incompatible* merrily over a sea which sparkled blue, to the sound of creaking boards and whining rigging. The crew moved industriously about their tasks, and Alex hoped he wouldn't be needed to direct them. He could pilot a spaceship between the stars, but the jungle of lines overhead baffled him.

Probably he wasn't essential, though. He was simply part of the pattern which the Hokas followed so loyally. In the same way, all that talk about gruesome punishment must be just talk—the Navy felt it was expected of them. Which was, however, small consolation, since the same blind devotion would keep the ship out here for as long as the orders said. Without this eternally cursed beard, Alex could easily take command and get back to shore; but he couldn't get rid of the beard until he was ashore. He had a sense of futility.

As he walked along the deck, his eyes lit on a completely incongruous figure leaning on one of the deck guns. This was a Hoka in shirt and trousers of coarse cloth, leather leggings, a chain-mail coat, a shaggy cape, a conical helmet with huge upcurving horns and an interminable sword. A pair of very large and obviously fake yellow mustaches drooped from underneath his nose. He looked mournful.

Alex drew up to the anachronism, realizing he must be from the Viking-culture area in the north and wondering how he had gotten here. "Hello," he said. "My name's Jo—" He stopped; it was useless to assert his identity until he got that triply damned spinach off his face—"Greenbeard."

"Pleased to meet yü," said the viking in a high-pitched singsong. "Ay ban Olaf Button-nose from Sveden. Have yü ever been to Constantinople?"

"Well—no," said Alex, taken somewhat aback.

"Ay vas afraid yü hadn't," said Olaf, with two large tears running down into his mustache. "Nobody has. Ay come sout' and signed on here, hoping ve vould touch at Constantinople, and ve never do."

"Why did you want to—" began Alex, fascinated.

"To yoin the Varangian Guard, of course," said Olaf. "Riches, loot, beautiful vimmen, lusty battles, ha, Odin." He shed two more tears.

"But—" Alex felt a twinge of compassion. "I'm afraid, Olaf, that there isn't any Constantinople on this planet."

"How do yü know, if yü never been there?"

"Why, because—" Alex found the conversation showing the usual Hoka tendency to get out of hand. He gritted his teeth.

"Now, look, Olaf, if I *had* been there, I'd be able to tell you where it was, wouldn't I?"

"Ay hope yü vould," said Olaf, pessimistically.

"But since I *haven't* been there, I can't tell you where it is, can I?"

"Exactly," said Olaf. "Yü don't know. That's yust what Ay vas telling yü."

"No, no, *no!*" yelled Alex. "You don't get the point—"

At this moment, the door to the captain's cabin banged open and Yardly himself came popping out on deck.

"Avast and lay forrad!" he bellowed. "All hands to the yards! Aloft and stand by to come about! We're standing in to round the Horn."

There was a stampeding rush, a roar, and Alex found himself alone. Everybody else had gone into the rigging, including the helmsman and captain. Alex turned hesitantly to one of the masts, changed his mind and ran to the bows. But there was no land in sight.

He scratched his head and returned amidships. Presently everyone came down again, the crew growling among themselves. Captain Yardly slunk by Alex, avoiding his eyes and muttering something about "slight error—happen to anyone—" and disappeared back into his cabin.

Olaf returned, accompanied by Billy Bosun. "Wrong again," said the viking gloomily.

"Rot me for a corposant's ghost, if the crew'll take much more o' this," added Billy.

"Take more of what?" inquired Alex.

"The captain trying to round the Horn, sir," said Billy. "Terrible hard it is, sir."

"Are they afraid of the weather?" asked Alex.

"Weather, sir?" replied Billy. "Why, the weather's supposed to be uncommon good around the Horn."

Alex goggled at him. "Then what's so hard about rounding it?"

"Why, nothing's hard about *rounding* it," said Billy. "It's *finding* it that's so hard, sir. Few ships can boast they've rounded the Horn without losing at least part of their crew from old age first."

"But doesn't everybody know where it is?"

"Why, bless you, sir, of course everybody knows it doesn't move around. But we do. And where are we?"

"Where are we?" echoed Alex, thunderstruck.

"Aye, sir, that's the question. In the old days, if we were here we'd be about one day's sail out of Plymouth on the southwest current."

"But that's where we are."

"Oh, no, sir," said Billy. "We're in the Antarctic Ocean. That's why the captain thought he was close to the Horn. That is, unless he's moved us since."

Alex gave a wordless cry, turned, and fled to the captain's cabin. Inside it, Yardly sat at a desk mounded high with sheets of calculations. There was a tortured look on his furry face. On the bulkhead behind him was an enormous map of Toka crisscrossed with jagged pencil lines.

"Ah, Mr. Greenbeard," he said in a quavering voice as he looked up. "Congratulate me. I've just moved us three thousand miles. A little matter of figuring declination in degrees east instead of degrees west." He glanced anxiously at Alex. "That sounds right, doesn't it?"

"Ulp!" said Alex.

In the following four days, the human gradually came to understand. In earlier times, native ships had found their way around the planet's oceans by a familiarity with the currents and prevailing winds, but with the technology of 1800 had come the science of navigation and since then no Hoka would be caught dead using the old-fashioned methods. With the new, some were successful and some were not. Lord Nelson, it was said, was an excellent navigator. So was Commodore Hornblower. Others had their difficulties. Captain Yardly's was that while he never failed to take a proper sight with his sextant, he invariably mistrusted the reading he got and was inclined to shift his figures around until they looked more like what he thought they should be. Also, he had a passion for even numbers, and was always rounding off his quantities to more agreeable amounts.

Under this handicap, the physical ship sailed serenely to her destination, guided by a non-navigating crew who automatically did the proper things in the old fashion at the proper time. But the hypothetical ship of Captain Yardly's mathematical labors traversed a wild and wonderful path on the map, at one time so far at sea that there was not enough fresh water for them to make land alive, at another time perched high and dry on the western plains of Toka's largest continent. It was not strange that the captain had a haunted look.

All of which was very unsettling to the crew who, however willing to give him the benefit of the doubt, were finding it somewhat of a strain even on their elastic imaginations to be told they were in the tropics one moment and skirting the south polar ice cap the next. Their nerves were on edge. Moreover, Alex discovered, the consensus among them was that the captain was becoming too obsessed with his navigation to pay proper attention to the running of the ship. No one had been hanged for several weeks, and there hadn't been a keel-hauling for over a month. Many a Hoka standing on the sun-blistered deck cast longing glances at the cool water overside and wished he would be keelhauled (which was merely fun on a planet without barnacles). There was much fo'c'sle talk about what act could be committed dastardly enough to rate the punishment.

"If you want a swim, why don't you just fall overboard?" asked Alex of Billy Bosun on the fourth day.

The Hoka's beady eyes lit up, and then saddened again. "No, sir," he said wistfully. "It's contrary to the articles of war, sir. Everybody knows British sailors can't swim a stroke."

"Oh, well," said Alex, helpfully. "If you've got

scruples—" He picked up the boatswain and tossed him over the rail. Billy splashed into the sea with a howl of delight.

"Shiver my timbers!" he roared gleefully, threshing around alongside and blowing spouts of water into the air. "I'm murdered! Help! Man overboard!"

The crew came boiling up on deck. Small furry bodies began to go sailing into the sea, yelling something about rescue. The second mate started to lower a boat, decided to pitch the nearest sailor into the ocean instead, and followed him.

"Heave to!" yelled Alex, panic-stricken. "Man—er—men overboard! Bring her about!"

The helmsman spun the wheel and the ship pivoted into the wind's eye with a rattle of canvas. Whooping, he overbalanced, and fell. His joyously lamenting voice joined the chorus already resounding below.

The door to the captain's cabin flew open. Yardly rushed out. "Avast!" he cried. "Belay! What's about, here?" He headed for the rail and stared downward.

"We're drowning!" the crew informed him, playing tag.

"Belay that!" shouted the captain. "Avast drowning immediately. Call yourselves British seamen, do you? Mutinous dogs, I call you. Treacherous, mutinous dogs! Quarrelsome, treacherous, mutinous dogs! Careless, quarrel—"

He looked so hot and unhappy in his blue coat and cocked hat that Alex impulsively picked him up and threw him over the side.

He hit the water and came up spouting and shaking his fist. "Mister Greenbeard!" he thundered. "You'll hang for this. This is mutiny!"

❖   ❖   ❖

"But we don't have to hang him, do we?" protested Alex.

"Blast my bones, Cap'n Greenbeard," said Billy, "but Yardly was a-going to hang you."

"Ay don't see how yü can avoid it," said Olaf, emptying sea water out of his scabbard. "Ve ban pirates now."

"Pirates!" yelped Alex.

"What else is left for us, Cap'n?" asked Billy. "We've mutinied, ain't we? The British Navy'll never rest till ve're hunted down."

"Oh well," said Alex, wearily. If hanging the ex-captain was considered part of the pattern, he might as well play along. He turned to the two seamen holding Yardly. "String him up."

They put a noose around Yardly's neck and politely stepped back. He took a pace forward and surveyed the crew, then scowled blackly and folded his arms.

"Treacherous, ungrateful swine!" he said. "Don't suppose that you will escape punishment for this foul crime. As there is a divine as well as a Hoka justice—"

Alex found a bollard and seated himself on it with a sigh. Yardly gave every indication of being good for an hour of dying speech. The human relaxed and let the words flow in one ear and out the other. A sailor scribbled busily, taking it all down for later publication in a broadside.

"—this causeless mutiny—plotted in secret— ringleaders did not escape my eye—some loyal hearts and true poisoned by men of evil—forgive you personally, but cannot—sully the British flag— cannot meet my eye—in the words of that great man—"

"Oh, no!" said Alex involuntarily, but Billy was already giving the captain the pitch on his boatswain's whistle.

> *"Oh, my name it is Sam Hall, it is Sam Hall*
> *Yes, my name it is Sam Hall, it is Sam*
> *Hall. . . ."*

Like most Hokas, the captain had a rather pleasant tenor, Alex reflected, but why did they all have to sing "Sam Hall" before being hanged?

> *"Now up the rope, I go, up I go. . . ."*

Alex winced. The song came to an end. Yardly wandered off on a sentimental side issue, informed the crew that he had had a good home and loving parents, who little suspected he would come to this, spoke a few touching words concerning his little golden-furred daughter ashore, wound up by damning them all for a pack of black-hearted scoundrels, and in a firm voice ordered the men on the end of the rope to do their duty.

The Hokas struck up a short-haul chanty, and to the tune of "Haul Away, Joe" Yardly mounted to the yard-arm. The crew paled and fainted enthusiastically as for five minutes he put on a spirited performance of realistic twitches, groans, and death rattles—effective enough to make Alex turn somewhat the same shade as his beard. He was never sure whether or not something at this stage had gone wrong and the Hoka on the rope was actually being strangled. Finally, however, Yardly hung limp. Billy Bosun cut him down and brought him to the captain's cabin, where Alex signed him up under the name of Black Tom Yardly and sent him forward of the mast.

Thus left in charge of a ship which he had only the foggiest notion of how to run, and a crew gleefully looking forward to a piratical existence, Alex put his head in his hands and tried to sort out matters.

He was regretting the mutiny already. Whatever had possessed him to throw the captain of a British frigate overboard? He might have known such a proceeding would lead to trouble. There was no doubt Yardly had been praying for an excuse to get out of his navigational duties. But what could Alex have done once his misguided impulse had sent Yardly into the ocean? If he had meekly surrendered, Yardly would probably have hanged him . . . and Alex did not have a Hoka's neck muscles. He gulped at the thought. He could imagine the puzzlement of the crew once they had cut him down and he didn't get up and walk away. But what good is a puzzled Hoka to a dead plenipotentiary? None whatsoever.

Moreover, not only was he in this pickle, but five days had gone by. Tanni would be frantically flying around the world looking for him, but the chance of her passing over this speck in the ocean was infinitesimal. It would take at least another five days to get back to Plymouth, and hell might pop in Bermuda meanwhile. Or he might be seized in the harbor if someone blabbed and strung up as a mutineer before he could get this green horror off his chin.

On the other hand—

Slowly, Alex got up and went over to the map on the bulkhead. The Hokas had been quick to adopt

Terrestrial place names, but there had, of course, been nothing they could do about the geographical dissimilarity of Toka and Earth. The West Indies here were only some 500 nautical miles from Great Britain; HMS *Incompatible* was almost upon them now, and the pirate headquarters at Tortuga could hardly be more than a day's sail away. It shouldn't be too hard to find and the buccaneer fleet would welcome a new recruit. Maybe he could find some ammonia there. Otherwise he could try to forestall the raid, or sabotage it, or something.

He stood for several minutes considering this. It was dangerous, to be sure. Cannon, pistols, and cutlasses, mixed with Hoka physical energy and mental impulsiveness, were nothing a man wanted close to him. But every other possibility looked even more hopeless.

He went to the door and called Olaf. "Tell me," he said, "do you think you can steer this ship in the old-fashioned way?"

"To be sure Ay can," said the Viking, "Ay'm old-fashion myself."

"True," agreed Alex. "Well, then, I'm going to appoint you first mate."

"Ay don't know about that, now," interrupted Olaf, doubtfully. "Ay don't know if it ban right."

"Of course," said Alex, hastily, "you won't be a regular first mate. You'll be a Varangian first mate."

"Of course Ay will!" exclaimed Olaf, brightening. "Ay hadn't t'ought of that. Ay'll steer for Constantinople."

"Well—er—remember we don't know where Constantinople is," said Alex. "I think we'd better put in at Tortuga first for information."

Olaf's face fell. "Oh," he said sadly.

"Later on we can look for Constantinople."

"Ay suppose so."

Seldom had Alex felt so much like a heel.

They came slipping into the bay of Tortuga about
sunset of the following day, flying the skull-and-
crossbones which was kept in the flag chest of every
ship just in case. The island, fronded with tropical
trees, rose steeply over an anchorage cluttered with
a score of armed vessels; beyond, the beach was
littered with thatch huts, roaring bonfires, and
swaggering pirates. As their anchor rattled down,
someone whooped from the crow's nest of the nearest
vessel: "Ahoy, mates. Ye're just in time. We sail for
Bermuda tomorry."

Alex shivered, the green beard and the thickening
dusk concealing his unbuccaneerish reaction. To the
eagerly swarming crew, he said: "You'll stay aboard
till further orders."

"What?" cried Black Tom Yardly, outraged. "We're
not to broach a cask with our brethren of the coast?
We're not to fight bloody duels, if you'll pardon the
language, and wallow in pieces of eight and—"

"Later," said Alex. "Secret mission, you know. You
can break out our own grog, bosun." That satisfied
them, and they lowered the captain's gig for him and
Olaf to go ashore in. As he was rowed away from
the *Incompatible*, Alex heard someone start a song
about a life on the ocean wave, in competition with
someone else who, for lack of further knowledge,
was endlessly repeating, "Yo-ho-ho—and a bottle of
rum—" *They're happy*, thought Alex.

"What yü ban going to do now?" inquired Olaf.

"I wish I knew," said Alex, forlornly. The little Viking,
with his skepticism about the whole pirate pattern,
was the only one he could trust at all, and even to

Olaf he dared not confide his real hopes. Such as they were.

Landing, they walked through a roaring, drunken crowd of Hokas trying to look as villainous as possible with the help of pistols, knives, cutlasses, daggers, sashes, earrings, and nose-rings. The Jolly Roger flew over a long hut within which the Captains of the Coast must be meeting; outside squatted a sentry who was trying to drink rum but not succeeding very well because he would not let go of the dagger in his teeth.

"Avast and belay there!" shrilled this freebooter, lurching erect and drawing his cutlass as Alex's bejungled face came out of the gloom. "Halt and be run through!"

Alex hesitated. His sea-stained tunic and trousers didn't look very piratical, he was forced to admit, and the cutlass and floppy boots he had added simply kept tripping him up. "I'm a captain too," he said. "I want to confer with my . . . er . . . confreres."

The sentry staggered toward him, waving a menacing blade. Alex, who had not the faintest idea of how to use a sword, backed up. "So!" sneered the Hoka. "So ye'll not stand up like a man, eh? I was tol' t' run anybody through what came near, and damme, I will!"

"Oh, shut up," said Olaf wearily. His own sword snaked out, knocking the pirate's loose. That worthy tried to close in with his dagger, but Olaf pushed him over and sat on him. "Ay'll hold him here, skipper," said the Viking. Hopefully, to his squirming victim: "Do know the vay to Constantinople?"

Alex opened the door and walked in, not without trepidation. The hut was lit by guttering candles stuck in empty bottles, to show a rowdy group of individuals seated around a long table. One of them, with a patch over his eye, glared up. "Who goes?" he challenged.

"Captain Greenbeard of the *Incompatible*," said Alex firmly. "I just got in."

"Oh, well, siddown, mate," said the pirate. "I'm Cap'n One-eye, and these here is Henry Morgan and Flint and Long John Silver and Hook and Anne Bonney and our admiral La Fontaine, and—" someone clapped a hand over his mouth.

"Who's this?" squeaked La Fontaine from under his cocked hat. Twenty pairs of Hoka eyes swiveled from him to Alex and back again.

"Why, scupper and gut me!" growled another, who had a hook taped to the end of his hand. "Don't ye know Cap'n Greenbeard?"

"Of course not!" said La Fontaine. "How could I know a Cap'n Greenbeard when there ain't any such man? Not in any of the books, there ain't. I'll wager he's John Paul Jones in disguise."

"I resent that!" boomed a short Hoka, bouncing to his feet. "Cap'n Greenbeard's my cousin!" And he stroked the black, glossy, but obviously artificial beard on his chin.

"Blast me, nobody can say that about a friend of Anne Bonney," added the female pirate. She was brilliantly bedecked in jewels, horse pistols, and a long gown which she had valiantly tried to give a low-cut bodice. A quadrimammarian Hoka needed two bodices, one above the other, and she had them.

"Oh, very well," grumbled La Fontaine. "Have a drink, cap'n, and help us plan this raid."

Alex accepted a tumbler of the fiery native distillation. The Hokas' fantastic capacity for beverage alcohol he was well aware of, but he hoped to go slow and, in view of the long head start the others had, stay halfway sober. Maybe he could master the situation somehow. "Thanks," he said. "Have one yourself."

"Don't mind if I do, mate," said La Fontaine amiably, tossing off another half liter. "Hic!"

"Is there any spirits of ammonia here?" asked Alex.

One-eye shifted his patch around to the other orb and looked surprised. "Not that I know of, mate," he said. "Should be some in Bermuda, though. Ye want it for polishing up treasure before burying it?"

"Let's come to order!" piped Long John Silver, pounding his crutch on the table. His left leg was strapped up against his thigh. "By the Great Horn Spoon, we have to make some plans if we're going to sail tomorrow."

"I, er, don't think we should start that soon," said Alex.

"So!" cried La Fontaine triumphantly. "A coward, is it? Rip my mainto'gallantstuns'l if I think ye're fit to be a Captain o' the Coast. Hic!"

Alex thought fast. "Shiver my timbers!" he roared back. "A coward, am I? I'll have your liver for breakfast for that, La Fontaine! What d'ye take me for, a puling clerk? Stow me for a—a—sea chest if I think a whitefaced stick like yourself is fit to be admiral over the likes of us. Why," he added, cunningly, "You haven't even got a beard."

"Whuzzat got to do with it?" asked La Fontaine muzzily, falling into the trap.

"What kind of admiral is it that hasn't got a hair to his chin?" demanded Alex, and saw the point strike home to the Hokas about him.

"Admirals don't have to have beards," protested La Fontaine.

"Why, hang, draw, and quarter me!" interrupted Captain Flint. "Of course admirals have to have beards. I thought everybody knew that." A murmur of assent went up around the table.

"You're right," said Anne Bonney. "Everybody knows that. There's only two here fit to command the fleet: Cap'n Blackbeard and Cap'n Greenbeard."

"Captain Blackbeard will do very well," said Alex graciously.

The little Hoka got to his feet. "Bilge me," he quavered, "if I ever been so touched in m'life before. Bung me through the middle with a boarding pike if it ain't right noble of you, Cap'n Greenbeard. But amongst us all, I can't take an unfair advantage. Much as I'd be proud to admiral the fleet, your beard is a good three inches longer'n mine. I therefore resigns in your favor."

"But—" stammered Alex, who had expected anything but this.

"That's fantastic!" objected La Fontaine, tearfully. "You can't pick a man by his beard—I mean—it isn't— you just can't!"

"La Fontaine!" roared Hook, pounding the table. "This here council o' pirate captains is following the time-honored procedure o' the Brethren o' the Coast. If you wanted to be elected admiral, you should ha' put on a beard afore you came to meeting. I hereby declares the election over."

At this last and cruelest cut, La Fontaine fell speechless. "Drawer!" shouted Henry Morgan. "Flagons all around to drink to the success of our venture."

Alex accepted his warily. He was getting the germ of an idea. There was no chance of postponing the raid as he had hoped; he knew his Hokas too well. But perhaps he could blunt the attack by removing its leadership, both himself and La Fontaine. . . . He reached over and clapped the ex-chief on the shoulder. "No hard feelings, mate," he said. "Come, drink a bumper with me, and you can be admiral next time."

La Fontaine nodded, happy again, and threw another down his gullet. "I like a man who drinks like that!" shouted Alex "Drawer, fill his flagon again! Come on, mate, drink up. There's more where that came from."

"Split my mizzenmast!" put in Hook. "But that's a neat way o' turning it, Admiral! 'More where that came from.' Neat as a furled sail. True, too."

"Oh, well," said Alex, bashfully.

"Here, drawer, fill up for Admiral Greenbeard," cried Hook. "That's right. Drink deep, me hearty. More where this came from. Haw!"

"Ulp!" gulped Alex. Somehow he got it down past shriveling tonsils. "Hoo-oo-oo!"

"Sore throat?" asked Anne Bonney solicitously.

"More where that came from," bellowed Hook. "Fill up!"

Alex handed his goblet to La Fontaine. "Take it, mate," he said generously. "Drink my health."

"Whoops!" said the ex-admiral, tossed it off, and passed out.

"Yo, heave ho," said Billy Bosun. "Up you come, mate."

They hoisted the limp figure of La Fontaine over the rail of the *Incompatible*. Alex, leaning heavily on Olaf, directed operations.

"Lock 'm in m' cabin," he wheezed. "Hois' anchor and set sail for Bermuda." He stared toward a sinking moon. Toka seemed suddenly to have acquired an extra satellite. "Secret mission, y' know. Fi-ifteen men on a dead-ead man's chest—"

"Sling a hammock on deck for the captain," ordered Billy. "He doesn't seem to be feeling so well."

"Yo-ho-ho and a bottle of rum," warbled Alex.

"Aye, aye, sir," said Billy, and handed him one.

"Woof!" groaned Alex and collapsed. The night sky began majestically revolving around him. Shadowy sails reached out to catch the offshore breeze. The *Incompatible* moved slowly from the harbor. Alex did not see this. . . .

Bright sunlight awakened him. He lay in his hammock until the worst was over, and then tried to sort things out. The ship was heeling to a steady wind and the sounds of sail-flap, rigging-thrum, plank-creak and crew-talk buzzed around him. Rising, he saw that they were alone in the great circle of the horizon. In the waist, the starboard watch were sitting about telling each other blood-curdling tales of their piratical exploits. Black Tom Yardly, as usual, was outdoing all the rest.

Alex accepted breakfast from the cook, lit the captain's pipe in lieu of a cigaret, and considered his situation. It could be worse. He'd gotten away with La Fontaine, and they should be in Bermuda shortly after sunset. There would be time to warn it and organize its defenses; and the pirates, lacking both their accustomed and their new admiral, would perhaps botch the attack completely. He beamed and called to his first mate. "Mr. Button-nose!"

Olaf approached. "Ay give yü good morning," he said gravely.

"Oh? Well, the same to you, Olaf," replied Alex. There was a certain air of old world courtesy about the small Viking which seemed to be infectious. "What kind of speed are we making?"

"About ten dragon's teeth," said Olaf.

"Dragon's teeth?" repeated Alex, bewildered.

"Knots, yü would say. Ay don't like to call them knots, myself. It don't sound Varangian."

"Fine, fine," smiled Alex. "We should be there in no time."

"Vell, yes," said Olaf, "only Ay suppose ve must heave to, now."

"Heave to?" cried Alex. "What for?"

"So yü can have a conference vit' the other captains," said Olaf, pointing astern. Alex spun on his heel and stared along the creamy wake of the *Incompatible*. There were sails lifting over the horizon. The pirate fleet!

"My God!" he exclaimed, turning white. "Pile on all sail!" Olaf looked at him surprised. "Pile on all sail!"

Olaf shook his round head. "Veil, Ay suppose yü know best," he said tiredly, and went off to give the necessary orders.

The *Incompatible* leaped forward, but the other ships still crept up on her. Alex swallowed. Olaf returned from heaving the log.

"Twelve dragon's teeth," he informed Alex reproachfully.

It was not a pleasant day for Admiral Greenbeard. In spite of almost losing his masts, he could not distance the freebooters, and the gap continued to narrow. Toward sunset, the other ships had almost surrounded him. The islands of Bermuda were becoming visible, and as darkness began to fall the whole fleet rounded the headland north of Bermuda City Bay. Lights twinkled on the shore, and the Hokas crowding the shrouds set up a lusty cheer. Resignedly, Alex ordered his crew to heave to. The other craft did likewise, and they all lay still.

Alex waited, chewing his fingernails. When an hour had passed and nothing happened except sailors hailing each other, he hunted up Olaf. "What do you think they're waiting for?" he asked nervously.

The bear-like face leaned forward out of shadow. "Ay don't t'ink," said Olaf. "Ay know. They're vaiting for yü to signal the captains aboard your flagship. The qvestion is, what are yü waiting for?"

"Me? Summon *them?*" said Alex. "But they were chasing us!"

"Ay vould not call it shasing," said Olaf. "Since yü ban admiral, they vould not vant to pass yü up."

"No, no, Olaf." Alex lowered his voice to a whisper. "Listen, I was trying to escape from them."

"Yü vere? Then yü should have said so," declared Olaf strongly. "Ay ban having a terrible time—yust terrible—to keep from running avay from them vit' all sails set."

"But why did you think they were following us?" raved Alex.

"Vy, what should they be doing?" demanded Olaf. "Yü ban admiral. Naturally, ven we leave for Bermuda, they're going to follow yü."

Speechless, Alex collapsed on a bollard. After a while he stirred feebly.

"Signal all captains to report aboard for conference," he said in a weak voice.

"Gut and smoke me!" thundered Captain Hook, as the chiefs crowded around a table arranged on the poop. "Slice me up for hors d'oeuvres, but you're a broom-at-the-mast sailor, Admiral Greenbeard. We had to clap on all canvas to keep you in sight."

"Oh, well," said Alex, modestly.

"Blast my powder magazine if I ever seen anything like it. There you was, flying through the water like a bloody gull; and at the same time I could have laid me oath you was holding the ship back as hard as you could."

"Little sailing trick. . . ." murmured Alex.

"Blind me!" marveled Hook. "Well, to business. Who's to lead the attack on the fort, Admiral?"

"Fort?" echoed Alex blankly.

"You knows how it is," said Hook. "They got cannon mounted on that fort which juts out into the bay. We'll have to sail past and give 'em a broadside to put 'em out of action. Then we can land and sack the town before Lord Nelson, blast his frogs and facings, shows up."

"Oh," said Alex. He was thinking with the swiftness of a badly frightened man. Once actual fighting started, Hokas would be getting killed—which, quite apart from any natural sympathy, meant the end of his tenure as plenipotentiary. If he himself wasn't knocked off in the battle. "Well. . . ." he began slowly. "I have another plan."

"Hull and sink me!" said Long John Silver. "A plan?"

"Yes, a plan. We can't get by that fort without getting hurt. But one small boat can slip in easily enough, unobserved."

"Stab me!" murmured Captain Kidd in awe. "Why, that's sheer genius."

"My mate and I will go ashore," went on Alex. "I have a scheme to capture the mayor and make him order the fort evacuated." Actually, his thoughts extended no further than warning the town and getting this noxious vegetation off his face. "Wait till I signal you from the jetty with lanterns how you're to arrive. One if by land and two if by sea."

"Won't go, Admiral," said Anne Bonney. She waved into the darkness, from which came the impatient grumbling of the crews. "The men won't brook delay. We can't hold 'em here more than a couple of hours. Then we'll have to attack or face a mutiny."

Alex sighed. His last hope of avoiding a fight altogether, by making the fleet wait indefinitely, seemed to have gone glimmering. "All right," he agreed hollowly. "Sail in and land the men. Don't fire on the fort, though, unless it shoots first, because I may be able to empty it, the way I suggested."

"Scupper and split me, but you're a brave man," said Hook. "Chop me up for shark bait if I think we could ha' done anything without you."

"Thanks," gritted Alex. This last was the unkindest cut of all.

The other Hokas nodded and mumbled agreement. Hero worship shone in their round black eyes.

"I moves we drinks to the Admiral's health," boomed Flint. "Steward! Fetch the flagons for—"

"I'd better leave right away," said Alex hurriedly.

"Nonsense!" said Henry Morgan. "Who ever heard of a pirate doing anything sober?"

"Psssh!" said Alex, rapping on the window of the mayor's residence. Muffled noises came from the garden behind, where Olaf had tied up the guards who would never have permitted a green-bearded stranger to approach.

The window opened and the mayor, an exceedingly fat Hoka, pompous in ruffles and ribbons, looked out, square into the nauseous tangle of hair beyond.

"Eek!" he said.

"Hic!" replied Alex, holding on to the sill while the official mansion waltzed around him.

"Help!" cried the mayor. "Sea monsters attacking! Drum up the guard! Man the battlements. Stow the belaying pins!"

He was quite obviously preparing to launch his not inconsiderable weight from the window at Alex, when a familiar golden head appeared over his shoulder.

"Alex!" gasped Tanni. "Where have you been?"

"Pressed pirate," said Alex, reeling. "Admiral Greenbeard. Help me in. Hic!"

"Drunk again," said Tanni resignedly, grabbing his collar as he scrambled over the sill. She loved her husband; she had been scouring the planet is search of him, had come here as a forlorn hope; but it is hard to shed joyful tears over a green beard quaking with hiccups.

"Mayor Bermuda," mumbled Alex. "British gen'leman. En'ertain th' lady. Ge' me anti-alco—anti-alco—alkyho—yo-ho-ho an' a bo'le o' rum—"

Tanni left him struggling with the word and went off after a soberpill. Alex got it down and shuddered back to normal.

"Whoof!" he exclaimed. "That's better. . . . Tanni, we're in one hell of a spot. Pirates—"

"The pirates," she said firmly, "can wait until you get that thing off your face." She extended a bottle of ammonia and a wad of cotton.

Thankfully, Alex removed the horror and gave them the story. He finished with: "They're too worked up to listen to me now, even in my character of plenipotentiary. They'll be landing any minute. But if we don't offer resistance, there'll at least be no bloodshed. Let them have the loot if they must."

"Come, come," said the mayor. "It's out of the question. Out of the question entirely."

"But they outnumber your garrison!" spluttered Alex.

"Beastly fellows," agreed the mayor happily, lighting a cigar.

"You can't possibly fight them off. The only thing to do is surrender."

"Surrender? But we're British!" explained the mayor patiently.

"Damn it, I order you to surrender!"

"Impossible," said the mayor doggedly. "Absolutely impossible. Contrary to Colonial Office Regulations."

"But you're bound to lose."

"Gallantly," pointed out the mayor.

"This is stupid!"

"Naturally," said the mayor, mildly. "We're muddling through. Muddle rather well, if I do say so myself."

Alex groaned. Tanni clenched her fists. The mayor turned to the door. "I'd better have the soldiers informed," he said.

"No . . . wait!" Alex leaped to his feet. Something had come back to him. *Chop me up for shark bait if I think we could ha' done anything without you.* And the others had agreed . . . and once a Hoka got an idea in his head, you couldn't blast it loose. . . . His hope was wild and frail, but there was nothing to lose. "I've got a plan."

"A plan?" The mayor looked dubious.

Alex saw his error. "No, no," he said hastily. "I mean a ruse."

"Oh, a *ruse!*" The mayor's eyes sparkled with pleasure. "Excellent. Superb. Just the sort of thing for this situation. What is it, my dear plenipotentiary?"

"Let them land unopposed," said Alex. "They'll head for your palace here, of course, first."

"Unopposed?" asked the mayor. "But I just explained—"

Alex pulled out his cutlass and flourished it. "When they get here, I'll oppose them."

"One man against twenty shiploads of pirates?"

Alex drew himself up haughtily. "Do you imply that I, your plenipotentiary, can't stop twenty ships?"

"Oh, no," said the mayor. "Not at all. By all means, my dear sir. Now, if you'll excuse me, I must have the town crier inform the people. They'd never forgive me if they missed such a spectacle." He bustled away.

"Darling!" Tanni grabbed his arm. "You're crazy. We don't have so much as a raythrower—they'll kill you!"

"I hope not," said Alex, bleakly. He stuck his head out the window. "Come in, Olaf. I'll need your help."

The corsair fleet moved in under the silent guns of the fort and dropped anchor at the quay. Whooping, shouting, and brandishing their weapons, the crews stormed ashore and rushed up the main street toward the mayor's palace. They were mildly taken aback to see the way lined with townsfolk excitedly watching and making bets on the outcome, but hastened on roaring bloodthirsty threats.

The palace lay inside a walled garden whose gate stood open. Nearby, the redcoats of the garrison were lined up at attention. Olaf watched them gloweringly: it was his assignment to keep any of them from shooting. Overhead, great lanterns threw a restless yellow light on the scene.

"Fillet and smoke me, but there's our admiral!" shouted Captain Hook as the tall green-bearded figure with drawn cutlass stepped through the gateway. "Three cheers for Admiral Greenbeard!"

"Hip, hip, hooray!" Echoes beat against the distant rumble of surf. The little round pirates swarmed closer, drawing to a disorderly halt as they neared their chief.

"Aha, me hearties!" cried Alex. "This is a great day, for the Brethren of the Coast. I've got none less than

Alexander Jones, the plenipotentiary of Toka, here, and I'm about to spit him like a squab!" He paused. "What, no cheers?"

The pirates shuffled their feet.

"What?" bellowed Alex. "Speak up, you swabs. What's wrong?"

"Stab me!" mumbled Hook. "But it don't seem right to spit the plenipotentiary. After all he done for this planet."

Alex felt touched, but redoubled the ferocity of his glare.

"If it's glory you're after, Admiral," contributed Captain Kidd, "blast me if I'd waste time on the plenipotentiary. There's no glory to be gained by spitting him. Why, he's so feeble, they say he has to have a special chair to carry him around."

This description of the one small luxury Alex had purchased after three years of saving—a robot chair for his office—so infuriated him that he lost his temper completely.

"Is that so?" he yelled. "Well, it just happens that he's challenged me to a duel to the death, and I'm not going to back out. And you scuts will stay there and watch me kill him and like it!"

"No, I won't have it," cried a soldier, raising his musket. Olaf took it away from him, tied it into a knot, and gave it back.

Alex ducked inside the portal, where Tanni and the mayor waited in the garden, still muttering furiously to himself.

"What's wrong now, dear?" asked Tanni, whitefaced.

"Blankety-blanks," snarled Alex. "For two cents I'd kill myself, and then see how they'd like it!" He stamped over to a large brass urn that had been placed in readiness.

"*En garde!*" he roared, fetching it a lusty swipe with his cutlass. "Take that!"

The gathered pirates jumped nervously. Billy Bosun tried to go through the gateway to see what was happening, but Olaf picked him up and threw him over the heads of Henry Morgan and One-eye. "Private matter," said the Viking imperturbably.

Viciously, Alex battered the clamoring urn with his blade, meanwhile yelling imprecations. "Don't try to get away! Stand and fight like a man! Aha! Take that, me hearty!"

Hammering away, he fumbled in his pocket with his free hand and brought out some ammonia-soaked cotton. The beard came loose and he gave it to Tanni, who was dabbing him with ketchup here and there, as he shouted in a slightly lower pitch.

"Is that so? Take that yourself! And that, Greenbeard! Didn't know, did you" —he thrust his clean-shaven face around the edge of the gate— "that I was on the fencing team as a boy?"

Impulsively, the pirates cheered.

"As well," said Alex, circling back out of view and belaboring the urn, "as having my letter in track and swimming. I could have made the basketball team too, if I'd wanted. Take that!"

Hurriedly, he stuck the beard back on and signaled for more ketchup.

"Bum and blister me," be swore, backing a little ways out of the gate and scowling horribly at the buccaneers, "but you've a tricky way about you, Jones. But it won't save you. The minute I trap you in a corner I'll rip you up for bait. Take that!" He stepped out of sight again. "Ouch!" he cried in the lower voice.

The pirates looked sad. "It don't seem right,"

muttered Long John Silver. "It just never come to me, like, that people might get hurt."

Captain Hook winced at the din.

"Aye," he said, shakily. "What've we gotten ourselves into, mates?"

"Don't be too cocky, Greenbeard!" cried Alex, appearing with a bare chin and lunging while Tanni struck the urn. "Actually, I've got muscles of steel. Take that! And that! And that!"

Vanishing again, he fetched the urn three ringing blows, dropped his cutlass, and clapped the beard back onto his face, giving vent to a spine-freezing scream.

"You got me!" he yammered. Clasping ketchup-soaked hands over his heart, he reeled across the gateway, stopping before the terrified visage of the pirates.

"Oh," he groaned. "I'm done for, mates. Spitted in fair and equal combat. Who'd ha' thought the plenipotentiary was such a fighter? Goodby, mates. Clear sailing. Anchors aweigh. Don't look for my body. Just let me crawl off and die in peace."

"Goodby," wept Anne Bonney, waving a handkerchief at him. The whole buccaneer band was dissolving into tears.

Alex staggered out of sight, removed his beard, and breathed heavily for a while. Then he picked up his cutlass and strode slowly out the gate and looked over his erstwhile followers.

"Well, well," he said scornfully. "What have we here? Pirates?"

There was a pause.

"Mercy, sir!" wept Captain Hook, failing to his knees before the conqueror of the terrible, the invincible, the indispensable Greenbeard, "We was just having our bit of fun, sir."

"We didn't mean nothing," pleaded Flint.

" 'Specially to get nobody hurt," added Billy Bosun.

"Silence!" commanded Alex. "Do you give up?" There was no need to wait for an answer. "Very well. Mister Mayor, you will have these miscreants hanged at dawn. Then put them on their ships and let them go. And" —he scowled at the pirates— "see that you all behave yourselves hereafter!"

"Y-y-y-es sir," said Black Tom Yardly.

Alex felt someone shyly plucking at his sleeve. He looked around, and saw it was the mayor.

"Oh . . . I don't know." The mayor looked up at him. Wistfulness edged his tone. "They weren't so bad, now were they, sir? I think we owe 'em a vote of thanks, damme. These colonial outposts get infernally dull."

"Why, thank'ee, mayor," said Anne Bonney. "We'll come sack you any time."

Alex interrupted hastily. Piracy seemed to have become an incurable disease, but if you can't change a Hoka's ways, you can at least make him listen to reason . . . on his own terms.

"Now hear this," he decreed loudly. "I'm going to temper justice with mercy. The Brethren of the Coast may sack Bermuda once a year, but there must be no bloodshed—"

"Why should there be?" asked the mayor, surprised.

"—and the loot must be returned undamaged."

"Slice and kipper me!" exclaimed Captain Hook indignantly. "Of course it'll be returned, sir. What d'ye think we are—thieves?"

Festivities lasted through all the next day, for the pirates, of course, had to sail away into the sunset. Standing on a terrace of the palace garden, his arm about Tanni and the mayor nearby, Alex watched their masts slip over the horizon.

"I've got just one problem left," he said. "Olaf. The poor fellow is still hanging around, trying to find someone who knows the way to Constantinople. I wish I could help."

"Why, that's easy, sir," said the mayor. "Constantinople's only about fifty miles due south of here."

"What?" exclaimed Alex. "No, you're crazy. That's the Kingdom of Natchalu."

"It was," nodded the mayor. "Right up till last month it was. But the queen is a lusty wench, if you'll pardon the expression, madam, and was finding life rather dull until a trader sold her some books which mentioned a, hm," the mayor coughed delicately, "lady named Theodora. They're still getting reorganized, but it's going fast and—"

Alex set off at a run. He rounded the corner of the house and the setting sun blazed in his, eyes. It gilded the helmet and byrnie of Olaf Button-nose, where he leaned on his sword, gazing out to sea.

"Olaf!" cried Alex.

The Hoka Viking turned slowly to regard the human. In the sunset, above the droop of his long blond mustaches, his face seemed to hold a certain Varangian indomitability.

Interlude V

Plenipotentiary of the
Interbeing League
Planet Toka

HEADQUARTERS OFFICE   CITY OF MIXUMAXU

7/6/86

Mr. Adalbert Parr
Chief Cultural Commissioner
EHQ of CDS
League City, N.Z., Sol III

Dear Mr. Parr :

Thank you for your personal letter of the 10th ult., inquiring about second-hand reports that I contemplate resigning my office. I will answer your questions just as informally and off the record, as I have not yet reached any definite decision.

I realize that what you are pleased to term my "unmatchable knowledge of the race based on years of experience" would be hard to duplicate; and I realize what damage might be done to Hoka society by someone lacking such qualifications. Were the matter as simple as this, I would certainly remain at my post; for I care for the little fellows as if they were my own children.

But I have been increasingly nagged by a very basic doubt—a doubt of the value, even the rightness, of the Service's very *raison d'être*. Is it possible that our problem of "civilizing backward planets" is only a subtler form of the old, discredited imperialism of Earth's brutal past? Have I merely been turning my wards into second-rate humans, instead of first-rate Hokas? I don't know. In spite of all our pretentious psychocultural tests, I doubt if anyone really knows.

But leaving this aside, there is also a personal horn to my dilemma. Ordinary human flesh and nerves can only stand so much. I am tired of becoming Mr. Chips or Tarzan on a minute's notice. There are wild moments in which I see myself lighting a huge bonfire of all the books on this planet, and dancing before it. Yet, paradoxically, I find growing within myself a kind of Hokaishness—an awful sort of addiction to these childlike heroisms.

Am I in danger of losing my humanness? I did not realize what years of Tokan liquor had done to me until, on a recent vacation trip to Gelkar, I absentmindedly drank off an entire pitcher of martinis, taking it merely for a tall tumbler of the local mineral water. Consciously, I remain myself— most of the time—I think—but is my subconscious becoming an alcoholic? On the same trip, I was sight-seeing in Callipygia City, when a visiting Klkr'n arachnoid took me for a Gelkarite policeman; and I have grown so used to falling into different roles that I confidently directed him to some place I myself had never heard of before; and when I left for home two days later, the poor chap was still missing.

At one time, as you know, I had high hopes of bringing the Hokas, practically single-handed, to a sane, sober, and civilized condition where their talents could fully serve the Interbeing League. But I see now, quite apart from all my doubts mentioned above, that the task is too big. And I do have my own family, as well as my sanity, to consider.

Therefore I welcome the arrival of Inspector Brassard, whom I have been notified to expect soon. If he can give the situation here a clean bill of health, I shall very probably step aside for a new man with a new viewpoint to try his luck on the Hokas.

Yours truly, Alexander Jones.

The Tiddlywink Warriors

The whole trouble began with Jorkins Brassard, Cultural Development Inspector from Earth Headquarters. Or perhaps you should blame the bureaucratic tradition in general. But a rigid set of rules is necessary if the League is to civilize some thousands of new planets in a gradual and humane fashion. Therefore the blame goes back to the inventors of gravity control and the faster-than-light secondary drive. However, if they had not done what they did, history would have been different and Alexander Jones would never have been born. This is getting us nowhere, so we shall leave the onus on the well-meaning but dogmatic head of Jorkins Brassard.

His tour of the frontier worlds had brought him, complete with military escort, to Toka, where he landed in Mixumaxu. The subspace radio had announced his coming, and preparations consonant with his exalted rank had been made.

Emerging from his ship, Brassard blinked in the hot sunshine. He was a balding red-faced man, sweaty in dress uniform, with a promising pot belly that he yanked in whenever he remembered it. A score of crisp young marines followed. They paused on the gangway and stared in most unmilitary stupefaction. They had not been expecting a double column of knights in full armor, mounted on dinosaurian monstrosities, sitting rigid with lances aloft except when someone broke formation to oil himself.

A group of Hokas trotted up and surrounded the Earthmen as these came slowly down to the field. This bunch wore scarlet coats, purple capes, blue trousers with gold frogging, jack-boots with spurs, cocked hats and ceremonial swords. They were preceded by a Scottish bagpipe corps.

Their leader bowed so his black nose almost touched the ground. "Welcome to Toka, sirs," he squeaked in fluent English.

"Uh . . . thank you . . . but who are these?" Brassard waved at me knights.

"Those are your honor guard, sir," beamed the chief. His breast glittered blindingly with medals. "There was some argument over who should have the privilege. It nearly came to a fight between the United States Cavalry and the Varangian Guard. But then King Arthur allied himself with the Black Watch and overawed the others."

"I see," murmured Brassard faintly. "But who are you?"

"Sir!" The Hoka drew himself up with a touch of hauteur. "We're the Secret Service, of course. Now, if you please, sir, we'll take you to His Excellency."

It was a slow ride through the old city's narrow streets, under peaked tile roofs and between cheering crowds, to the metal and plastic tower of the League Office. The vehicle was a perfectly good electric groundcar, but protocol seemed to demand it should be drawn by the reptilian "horses." Brassard and his men sighed with relief when they had got past a native sentry in full Samurai costume and into the cool interior of the new building.

Alex met them in the reception room. After the formalities, he apologized. "I'm afraid my wife isn't here, Inspector. We'll have to bach it. But I have an excellent Hoka chef—hired him away from Louis XIV."

"Oh," said Brassard. Recovering himself: "Doesn't matter. Just here to check up. Routine. I'll want to see your records, visit a few spots, make a report to EHQ." He sighed and sipped the aperitif which a Hoka in full footman's livery had just handed him. "Earthman's burden. Not easy. Sure you understand."

"Of course," said Alex, and wondered if it would be mutual.

Tanni Jones was a loyal wife, as well as a blonde and beautiful one, but she had declared that one more official function would unfunction her. Alex sympathized and suggested they send the children to the Hoka London to watch Parliament; he had hopes of government careers for them, and this was an unparalleled education in how not to conduct such business. "And maybe you'd like to take a flitter and run outsystem."

"Yes." Tanni smoothed her dress over her hips and winced. "I've been meaning to go to Gelkar anyway, the reconditioning center."

"What off Earth for?" demanded Alex.

"Do you realize I've put on three kilos?" she answered "None of my clothes will fit me any longer. I can get a ten-day treatment there."

Alex could see no difference in her, but had been married long enough not to admit that. She did have a slight tendency to plumpness and fought it bitterly.

"All right," he agreed, and went on to instruct her in the handling of a spaceship: run on normal gravs until well out of the system, than switch to secondary for the two-day voyage to Gelkar, and always trust your autopilot no matter what your senses tell you. She had flown before, but Alex had firm prejudices.

He saw her off and went back to prepare for Brassard's arrival.

The bureaucrat went through his files first, a dull business. They had been at it for a day, and it was four days after Tanni's departure, when the news of catastrophe came.

Alex was sitting and smoking in a heap of papers, listening to acrid criticism of his methods. "Not done at all. You know very well census figures should be under P for Population. Cross-reference. Regulations." At that, he was getting off lightly.

The Secret Service chief came into the office on the run, tangled with his sword, and skidded across the floor. Somehow he got his head jammed into the waste-basket. Alex dragooned Brassard into pulling on the legs while he held the container. The Hoka emerged with a pop and looked wildly about him.

"Sabotage!" he hissed.

The beady eyes glittered suspiciously at Brassard. "Has he been cleared?"

The inspector huffed. "Of course I've been cleared."

The chief scratched his head. "But have the people who cleared you been cleared?" he asked.

"Never mind," sighed Alex. "I'll vouch for him."

The chief looked under the desk, opened a few cabinet drawers, and checked under the tenth-story window. Then he came back and drew Alex's ear down to his muzzle. Cupping his hands, he whispered hoarsely: "Visio call for you, sir."

"Oh." Alex was hardened, after a dozen years on Toka. "Excuse me, Mr. Brassard." He went out, took a gravshaft to the fifth level, and tuned in the buzzing subspatial transceiver.

Tanni's face swam into the screen. It was streaked with dirt, her long golden hair was tangled, and tears furrowed the dust. In the background, against the flitter control panel, Alex saw a squat non-human figure with what appeared to be a weapon.

"Oh, Alex!" wailed Tanni.

His initial horror lessened when he realized she was unhurt. And at least the boat's communicator was working. "What happened?"

"I . . . I've crashed," she said.

Alex gaped. "Where?"

"On Telko—"

"How in space did that happen?" he yelped.

"I tried to . . . cut in past the sun to build up speed!" she sniffled. "I came too close, and it was either fall in toward Telko or overload the cooling system—"

Alex snorted indignantly. "How many tines have I told you to lay off that close-orbit stunt? Women astrogators!"

Tanni wiped her eyes. "I tried to land for another start," she went on shakily. "Northern peninsula . . . b-but you know I c-c-can't land without a GCA beam."

Alex glowered. "How badly is it damaged?"

"Th-the flitter? I don't know. It just w-w-won't fly."

"Well," grumbled Alex. "Broadcast a signal so I can find you. I'll get you in the courier boat."

"Yes . . ." whispered Tanni. "And come quick, darling."

His fears stirred anew. "Is something really wrong?"

"The—the natives."

"Are they threatening you?" shouted Alex. His heart popped into his mouth. The natives of Telko had not molested the few visitors to their planet so far, but they were known to be warlike.

"No-o-o-o!" wailed Tanni. "Worse!"

"Worse!"

"They think I'm a—a—goddess, or a mascot, or something."

"Well," he asked slowly, "what's wrong with that?"

"But they keep feeding me and feeding me. They won't let me eat the boat supplies. They almost stuff their own food down my mouth. It was all I could do to be allowed to come here and call you."

"Oh . . . that's all right," said Alex with a shudder of relief. "Telkan food has vitamin deficiencies, but a few days of it won't hurt you."

"But there's something in it! High calories or something. I'm putting on kilos and kilos. Alex, you've got to come right away!"

"You ought to be glad it's not poisoned," said the man unfeelingly. Most of him was turned to the worried planning of a rescue expedition. A few raythrowers would get rid of the Telks if they'd not listen to reason, but it could be a ticklish operation.

Tanni burst into tears and softened his heart. "It's all right, dear," he said soothingly. "Remember, Inspector Brassard is here with a military escort. We'll pull you out in a couple of days at most."

The Telk in the background laid an impatient hand on her shoulder. She gulped and blew a trembling kiss. Then she was led out of sight.

❖   ❖   ❖

It was ridiculous, really. Telko was in the same planetary system as Toka, being the next world sunward. But Alex, on speaking terms with the natives of planets a thousand light-years removed, had never been there and knew almost nothing about it. Nobody did.

The reason, though, was simple. Telko was a hot, cloudy world with a voracious life, terrestroid to only six points of classification. That meant you wouldn't be killed outright by eating its food, but you would suffer from the complete lack of Vitamins A, B, C, and E.

Furthermore, the natives were an unpromising lot. On their single continent, they had only one language, its dialects mutually comprehensible; but they were split into thousands of tribes with wildly different cultures. One point all the Telks had in common: they loved battle. It was instinctive, a hangover from ages when they had fought wild beasts barehanded. Unless he could take something sharp-edged at least once a month and go out and kill somebody, a Telk pined away.

So, after a few scientific studies, they were left alone. They were certainly not a race among whom you'd want to park your wife.

Alex came into the office at full speed. Brassard looked up from a sheaf of reports and asked querulously: "What's this about the Heisenberg Uncertainty Principle?"

"Tanni—" panted Alex.

"Don't interrupt me! I want to know. Important to get serious xenological survey of original autochthonous cultures. How else can we know best course for natives? Here I—don't interrupt, I say!—I have report from xenologist. Tried to study untouched Hoka village. Took statistics, asked questions, standard approved methods. Comes back babbling about impossibility of getting results due to Heisenberg Uncertainty Principle. What's the explanation?"

Alex braced himself. He was beginning to understand Brassard's mind. It was worthy of a Hoka, except for lacking the Hoka *joie de vivre.* "The fellow should have known better," he said between his teeth. "I warned him."

"But what happened?"

"What would you expect? Here you had a Hoka tribe whose first exposure to human culture was a xenologist. You know how they go overboard for anything new. They started asking *him* questions about tribal customs and sex practices. They followed him around and took notes. They decided his watch was an ancestral totem and— Oh, never mind. Now they're making nuisances of themselves all over the planet. Will you listen to me for a change?"

Rapidly, Alex outlined the situation.

Brassard drummed impatiently on the desk top. "Well," he asked, when the younger man had run down, "what d'you want, hey?"

"Your help, of course! We've got to go rescue my wife!"

"Sorry. Inspector not permitted to use force on any natives unless directly threatened. Colonial Office Regulations, Vol. XXXVIII, Sec. 12, Par. 3-b."

"Then I'll go!" screamed Alex. "I'll rescue her myself!"

Brassard pressed the buzzer. "Rescue?" he barked. "What d'you mean, rescue? No charging in there with modern weapons and decimating the natives, Jones."

"B-b-but they won't give her up otherwise!"

"Then we'll send a commission. Yes, commission.

That's what we'll send. Have one out there in a month. Two months at the latest. Long as I'm inspector in charge of this region there'll be no exposing of Class W planets to any weapons above Class 6."

A couple of Brassard's men appeared in the doorway in response to the buzzer. "Not sure I trust you, Jones," said the bureaucrat. "Have to sequester your sidearms. Better remove secondary-drive units from your boats, too, so you can't go outsystem for mercenary soldiers."

"But those vitamin deficiencies," pleaded Alex. "In two months she'll have scurvy and—and weigh three hundred kilos—"

"Sorry," said Brassard. "Earthman's burden. I'm not unreasonable, though. Go to Telko yourself if you like and see what you can do. I'll push hard for commission to negotiate if you fail."

Alex wavered, rebellion hot within him. But there were two strong marines in the doorway. Also— In his mind's eye he saw a picture of his lovely wife, captive, sadly stuffing herself and putting on weight. But right beside it, his mind's eye was placing another vision of Tanni growing thin and wan on his meager ensign's pension, which was all he would have if he got broken from his present job rather than resigning with honors.

Maybe he should rely on the government after all. But if the commission failed, Tanni was doomed . . . assuming she hadn't already gone out of her head from watching herself balloon and done something desperate. No!

Class 6 weapons—Wait, simple gunpowder was Class 5, wasn't it? He could round up some Hokas to help. The cowboys of the Western plains? No, it would take weeks to gather enough of them . . . *Hey!*

Very formally, Alexander Jones applied in triplicate for permission to attempt a rescue with Tokan auxiliaries. Equally formally, Jorkins Brassard stamped his OK. Then the plenipotentiary went out to the spacefield, where a sympathetic but rule-bound marine turned his emasculated courier boat over to him and watched it dwindle eastward in the sky.

Alex had not specified what auxiliaries he would use.

Toka had one desert. Once outworld traders had discovered what a market there was here for second-rate historical novels, it was inevitable that this desert would be populated by Arabs and the French Foreign Legion.

Alex landed outside Sidi Bel Abbès, a cluster of flat-roofed mud huts in an oasis. A kilometer or so beyond it lay the main Legion outpost, the Tricolor drooping over its walls. Everywhere else was rock and sand, glimmering under a brilliant sun.

A few portly figures in kaftan and burnoose watched him as he hurried through the streets. Once he collided with one of the brontosaurian beasts locally supposed to be a camel. He was rather dazed, both by the crisis and the hypno he had taken en route— all available information on Telko. A knowledge of its dialects swirled through his head, mixed with technical dissertations on the biochemistry and its rapid action (that must be why Tanni was getting fat so fast) and a recording of a bloodthirsty folk song.

Arriving at the civil governor's mansion, he was led at once to that worthy. It was cool and dim in the office, but the Hoka stuck firmly by his sun helmet. He had also glued spiked mustaches and a goatee to his face.

"*Ah, M'sieur L'Ambassadeur!*" he cried, rising with

a sweeping gesture that knocked a vase off his desk. *"Quel honneur! Bienvenu!"*

"Hoog whah hogoo—" panted Alex. "Damn! I mean, how do you do. Look, M. LaFontanelle, I've got troubles."

"Tiens!" The governor waved his arm nonchalantly and upset a floor lamp. "Something has occurred, then?" Like nearly all Hokas, he spoke good English, but as a Frenchman considered it his duty to throw in an accent.

"My wife—" began Alex, and stopped. The fewer beings told about Tanni's humiliating plight, the better; it would be enough to raise the Legion.

"Ah," said the governor, drawing a sharp breath. "Your lady?"

"She—er—well, I guess I better not talk about it," stumbled Alex.

"But of course!" cried LaFontanelle, raising his hands in horror. "My poor friend! It is *La Légion Etrangère* you wish, *hein?*"

Startled at such prescience, Alex could only nod. "Come with me," said the governor, laying a furry hand on his. There were tears in the black button eyes. Dazedly, Alex permitted himself to be led out toward the fortress.

He had been here before, to make sure that the Legion and the Arab Hokas were not killing each other. They weren't; there was no grudge between them, in fact, a brisk trade, though they felt obliged to exchange occasional shots. But the Arabs preferred to skulk behind sand dunes and be highlighted against the setting sun on camelback, while the French— true to the tradition of Legionnaire marksmanship— never fired at less than 500 meters; and their black powder rifles, though producing the loud report and

heavy smoke prized by Hokas, had an extreme range
of about half that.

Guards in blue tunic, white breeches, red sash
and kepi presented arms as the governor and the
plenipotentiary hurried in through the gates. Beyond
lay a dusty courtyard littered with adobe buildings.
Toward the largest of these Alex was conducted,
and found himself standing before the desk of the
elderly commandant. "Here you are, *mon vieux,*"
said LaFontanelle.

"*Qu'est-que-c'est-que-ca?*" rattled the commandant.

"*La Femme*—" said the governor.

"*Non!*" The officer's jaw dropped.

"*Mais oui.*"

"*Avec un autre—un plus jeune—*"

"*On ne le dit pas, cependant. . . .*" said the governor,
nodding knowingly. The other Hoka nodded also and
took out a printed form.

"Brassard!" muttered Alex between clenched jaws.

"*Ah, Brassard son nom-de-guerre.*" The commandant
wrote it down. "If you will sign here—" Alex scribbled
his name without stopping to think. The commandant
beamed, leaned across the desk and shook the human's
hand. "Congratulations, *mon brave,*" he burbled. "You
are now a Legionnaire. Report to Sergeant LeBrute."

"What?" yelped Alex, coming out of his daze. "What
did you say?"

The commandant rubbed his hands and smiled in
a fatherly fashion. "You are joining the Foreign Legion
to forget."

"What do you mean?" shouted Alex. "I can't join
the French Foreign Legion! I'm the League Plenipotentiary!"

"He tests us," nodded the governor of the commandant. "Ah, my friend, one knows how to preserve a

secret. One understands you wish to forget. Ah, the frailty of woman." He sighed. "A word, a glance, and their heart is turned. No, Private Brassard, your secret is safe with me."

"And with *la Légion*," said the Hoka behind the desk. "Fear not, Private Brassard. What you were before entering is a secret that you may bury with you. The Legion asks no questions. The Legion will release you to no one," he turned his head. "Sergeant LeBrute!"

The door opened and a burly little Hoka came in.

"Wait!" cried Alex desperately, the sudden awful realization sweeping over him that he had slipped into another of those situations that beset his path on Toka like pools of quicksand. "You can't do this to me! I tell you, I belong to Earth!"

"Once, perhaps," replied the commandant. "Now you belong to La Belle France. It matters not what you were before joining. . . . Another *bleu*, Sergeant LeBrute. Take it out."

"*Cochon!*" bawled the sergeant, trying hard to get a sadistic rasp into his squeaky voice. "*Nom d'un chameau!* Come along now!" And with the usual Hoka strength, so greatly disproportionate to their size, he clamped hold of Alex's collar and dragged him easily out as the human kicked and struggled and screamed for justice.

The governor twirled his mustache and wiped a tear from his eye.

"Ah," he said. "How well he pretends. *Un brave.* But underneath, his heart is breaking for the wife who has deceived him."

"*Naturellement,*" replied the commandant.

They got out a bottle marked *Chablis*, poured, and raised glasses solemnly.

❖   ❖   ❖

"Remain there, *bleu misérable!*" said Sergeant LeBrute, tossing Alex onto a hard cot and stamping out.

The man sat up and looked around. He was in some kind of barracks, with several Legionnaires sitting about. None of them looked very surprised; they must get some odd types here, even for this planet.

"Bit of a brute, that Sergeant LeBrute," observed an Oxford accent. Alex turned to see an aristocratic-mannered Hoka on the adjoining cot, who continued: "Allow me to introduce myself. Cecil Fotheringay-Phipp Alewyn Smith. You'll find the Legion isn't such a bad spot, old man. Of course, they march you till you drop, the food is terrible, the Arabs torture you to death if they catch you, the officers and non-coms are sadistic beasts, and you associate with the scum of the earth—but on the whole, it's not a bad life."

"Oh?" said Alex, feebly. He knew from his survey that it was mostly just talk: Hokas who had read P. C. Wren thought it was expected of them, but were much too kindly to put it into practice. Still, soldiering here could be rugged, and there was Tanni—

"No, indeed," went on the English Hoka. "Our platoon, for example, is fairly representative. Right next to you on the other side is Rastignon, whom we playfully call the Murderer."

Alex jumped and became aware of the other Hoka, sitting and sharpening his bayonet on a whetstone. "I am, too!" he squeaked, and by the usual native courtesy his whopper was taken at face value.

"Next to him," went on Smith, "is LeRat, a scum of the Paris sewers type. Next to him is Alf Sniggs, a scum of the London sewers type. That mysterious fella playing with ink and paper at the table is Le Forgeur. Beyond him, that enormously strong and brutal-looking chap is Giuseppe Fortissimo." To the untrained eye, he was indistinguishable from the other round-bellied ursinoids. "Over in the corner—"

The Hoka he was pointing at looked up and suddenly broke into song. "My name is John Wellington Wells, I'm a dealer in magic and spells—"

"Mad, poor fellow," sighed Smith. "We call him Les Ciseaux, or in English, The Scissors. That sullen chap beside him is Kurt Wilhelm Schwartzmann von und zu Griffentaffel, a typical Prussian beast. At least, he would be typical if he weren't the only one on Toka."

The Legionnaire in question leaped onto his feet, clicked his heels and shouted: "*Achtung!*" He wore the standard uniform, but had added a monocle.

Alex shook his head, dazedly. "How does a Prussian beast get into the French Foreign Legion?" he asked in a numb voice.

"*Ach!*" sighed von und zu Griffentaffel. "It vas *schrecklich*. I had read about Bismark, *verstehen Sie?* I vanted to machen all der odder *deutsche* Hokas into ein *Landswehr*. Nobody listened." He took off his monocle to let a tear fall from his eye. "Vot good iss it to be ein Prussian beast mit spiked helmet und all, ven effery time I shouten '*Achtung!*' efferybody else chust clicken der beer steins und singen '*In München steht ein Hofbräuhaus*'? I am ein failure." He collapsed into tears.

Alex sighed and got back to his own troubles. "Look here, Smith," he said, "my wife—"

"Tut, tut, old chap," interrupted the Hoka. "No need to tell your story. In the Legion, one doesn't ask. A code of sorts, don't y'know."

"But you don't understand! My wife—"

"Of course, of course," said Smith. "A word is

sufficient. Wives. Women. The ladies. Gentlemen, the Queen!" He stood up suddenly, raised his hand as if to propose a toast, caught himself, and sat down. "What am I doing?" he asked shakily. "Excuse me, old boy. You arouse old memories."

Alex slumped. He was getting nowhere.

That evening he was issued a uniform and told by Sergeant LeBrute, with many oaths, to put it on. Since it was meant for a Hoka and Alex was rather tall and lanky, even for a human, the effect can be imagined. He spent an unhappy night, and the next morning— after breakfast, which was coffee and French bread— his platoon was called out at a gruesome hour for a work detail.

He gulped when he saw what it was. His sleek courier boat was now the property of the Legion, and had been hauled into the fortress grounds. Nobody knew how to fly it, or cared. But the commandant was interested in its temperature-regulating coils.

It seemed that Sidi Bel Abbès did a lively trade in beer with the Arabs. These Hokas had heard vaguely that Bedouins don't drink, and abstained from the 180-proof rotgut the French fondly consumed as wine. But no Hoka could imagine life without alcohol, so they settled for homebrew beer. The daily consumption of this by the average Bedouin was awesome. The commandant decided to use the boat's coils in fermenting the mixture. Great vats of it were installed, and hundreds of bottles put in the hold for later use.

"*Bleus misérables!* Idler! *Cochon! Chameau! Vache! Hommard!*" Sergeant LeBrute scurried up and down, shouting curses at the platoon. Now and then he kicked them. This did not hurt a well-padded Hoka, but Alex was built differently. In any event, a man does not enjoy turning his own spaceboat into a brewery. He spent a seething day and returned exhausted to his barracks at the end of it.

As darkness fell, he lay on his cot and brooded. This was ridiculous. And poor Tanni! But how the devil was he going to get out of it?

His eyes wandered about the lantern-lit room, where the Legionnaires sat telling enormous lies about the heat and thirst they had suffered in the desert, and the girls in the Casbah. He could get no help from them; they were enjoying their roles too much . . . No—wait! An idea struck him.

He hurried over to the table where Le Forgeur was copying a fifty-franc note with considerable skill. "Er—pardon me," he said.

" 'Allo," said the Hoka, amiably.

"Er—look—you couldn't possibly whip me up a discharge from the Legion, could you?"

"A discharge?" echoed Le Forgeur, looking up in astonishment. "*Mais, mon ami*, there are no discharges in the Legion. One deserts."

"One does?"

"*Exactement*. And if one is caught, one is sent to the penal battalion."

"Ulp!" said Alex.

Le Forgeur got up, alight with the quick heady enthusiasm of his race. "Is it that you intend perhaps to desert?" he cried. "*Alors*, I will accompany you."

"Huh?" said Alex. "You?"

A friendly hand fell on his arm. "If you're going to desert, old man," said Smith, "you'll need the help of an old hand who knows the desert. I'll come too. No, no thanks, I insist."

"*Ach*, to see Alt Heidelberg again!" said von und zu Griffentaffel. "I vill come mit."

"*Buono! Bravo!*" shouted Giuseppe Fortissimo. "Napoli! Vesuvio! Ice cream! La Scala!" And he broke into opera at the top of his lungs: "*Sì, fuggiam da queste mura . . . !*"

"Oh, no!" moaned Alex, as they all crowded around him.

"This way," whispered Alex.

He led the file of Hokas toward the shadowy form of his courier boat.

"Quiet now," he cautioned, opening the airlock.

"*Bleus misérables!*" shrilled a voice, splitting the night, and the rotund figure of Sergeant LeBrute popped up to confront him. "Aha! *Deserting!*"

Alex swallowed his heart and thought fast.

"No, no, mon . . . er . . . sergeant," he said. "Secret mission—I mean patrol. Yes, that's it. We're a patrol—out to get lost!"

"A lost patrol!" cried LeBrute. Even in the dark, Alex could see his eyes shine with sudden excitement. "Ah, *mes enfants*, you will need Sergeant LeBrute to guide you."

"B-but—" stammered Alex.

"*Silence! C'est un fait accompli.* I, Sergeant LeBrute, am now in command. *En avant, marche!*"

"Into the boat," supplemented Alex, hurriedly.

"Into the *bâteau*," agreed the noncom.

One by one, they crowded in.

Well . . . he had got his auxiliaries, though not precisely in the way he had planned. Alex set the autopilot for Telko and ran spaceward at full acceleration. The Hokas were too preoccupied with

staring out at the stars and speculating on their
mission to give much trouble. Alex had a chance
to review his hypnotically acquired knowledge.

The trouble was, the northern peninsula on which
Tanni had crashed was completely unknown. Cut off
from the rest of the continent by a rugged mountain
range, it had developed its own cultures, whatever
they might be; all you could be sure of was (a) the
language; (b) the technology, primitive iron-working,
and agriculture; and (c) a state of continuous warfare.
Well, he'd have to play by ear. The platoon had its
rifles, such as they were. And his anachronistic charges
had recently led Alex to develop skill with sword,
bow and lance, if it came to that.

He called to mind the Telk physiognomy. An average
male was a bit taller than a Hoka and even broader,
one mass of muscle under a green skin, nude except
for assorted cutlery. He had four powerful arms, and
his stocky bowlegs ended in prehensile-toed feet
which could serve as hands. The head was round,
hairless, bat-eared, with small yellow eyes protected
by bony ridges, mouth and nose contained in a porcine
snout. Formidable characters, but—

At top acceleration, with gravitic fields to protect
against pressure, the boat reached Telko in a few hours.
Alex dove beneath the cloud layer to find himself
under a gloomy sky and over a sullen, tideless ocean.
When he located the single continent, he followed
its jungled shores to the peninsula, and there he picked
up Tanni's broadcast signal and homed on it.

The peninsula was a stony waste, thinly covered
with scrub brush and tilled fields. The mountains
ran out into steep hills. At their foot, Alex saw a flash
of metal and swooped low. The flitter stood there,
its drive-cones smashed. It was inside the thick earth

walls of a village whose rounded huts resembled igloos more than anything else. There was no sign of life, but he thought it best not to land within the settlement at once. He might get shot full of arrows.

Casting about, he saw a large ruined structure some two kilometers south, on a hilltop—a similar village, but wrecked and deserted in some war or other. It would do for a base. He set the boat down behind its walls and cut the engines.

The lost patrol poured out with glad cries. They were in a courtyard overgrown with native plants, mostly tubers. A warm dry wind blew upon them, and the eternal clouds lay moodily overhead. It looked like a good situation. Alex was somewhat startled, therefore, when he emerged to see Sergeant LeBrute prowling about with a worried expression. The platoon was posted on the wall facing the other village, rifles ready.

"What's wrong?" asked the human.

The sergeant spat. "Name of a name of a name of a name of a—uh—"

"Name?" suggested Alex.

"*Merci.* Name!" finished the sergeant. "But we will never from here emerge alive, *bleu.*"

Alex did a double take. This was no attitude to find in those he expected to overcome the Telks.

"Nonsense!" he replied. "Why, we'll walk right out of here—"

"*Bleu misérable!*" stormed LeBrute. "Do you contradict me? This is Zinderneuf—the fort which perishes to the last man!"

"But—but—"

"*Silence, cochon!*" LeBrute turned away. "Rastignon, Sniggs, you are detailed to the kitchen. Prepare these plants for eating."

"Wait—" screeched Alex, remembering Tanni's experience and seeing the Hokas and himself, grossly overweight, rolling around on the earth like helpless basketballs. "The . . . the Arabs have poisoned the fort's food supply. Use the stores in the galley of the boat."

He sighed with relief when the sergeant conceded the point, and went back himself to try calling Tanni. Somewhat to his surprise, the communicator responded and her distracted face looked out at him. He noticed that it had grown fuller.

"Alex!" she gasped. "Where are you?"

"I'm here," said Alex. "I mean, I'm on Telko. I just landed in this old ruin up the hill. I've got some Legionnaires with me— But how are you?"

"I—" she choked back a sob. "I'm still eating."

"How much do you weigh now?"

"Don't ask me that!" she shrieked.

"Well . . . you're in the flitter again, I see."

"Yes. But—Alex, you came just at the right moment. The Telks won't let me go without fighting like devils. But they have a new war on now. The hill tribes are invading and the village warriors are out to fight them. I've been left here in the flitter, nobody but the females to guard me. If you hurry—"

"I'll see," said Alex, dubiously. "Sit tight, sweetheart."

He rushed outside, his brain humming.

"*Mes amis!*" he shouted. "Join me! We must hasten! The Arabs have got Cigarette, the daughter of the Legion, locked up over there. We've just time to rescue her!"

Hoka faces fell. But to Alex's dismay, not one of them moved.

"What are you waiting for?" he demanded. "Come on!"

"*Hélas!*" sobbed Sergeant LeBrute.

"*Hélas?*" asked Alex.

"*Oui, hélas,*" said Rastignon the murderer in a choked voice. "*La pauvre petite. Quel dommage* that one so young and beautiful should perish while *les soldats de la Légion* stand helplessly by."

"Helpless!" squeaked Alex.

"*Oui,*" said Sergeant LeBrute. "Helpless. Our duty is to defend this post to the last man. We may not abandon it. Cigarette is a child of the Legion. She will understand. She will die thinking of La Belle France and singing the Marseillaise."

"The hell she will!" snarled Alex, grabbing his rifle. "All right, I'll go alone."

"Halt!" ordered Sergeant LeBrute, aiming at him. "*Ne pas bouger!*"

"What do you mean, *ne pas bouger?*" cried Alex. "I certainly won't *ne pas bouger*. I—"

"*Silence, bleu!*" bellowed LeBrute. "It is your duty to die like the rest of us on the wall of Zinderneuf. If you attempt a rescue of Cigarette, I will order the platoon to open fire on you."

"At less than 500 meters?" asked Alex.

LeBrute put down his rifle and scratched his head. Taking a perhaps unfair advantage of his confusion, the human made a dash for the wall.

But he barely got one leg over it when a roar from the hills petrified him. Out of a nearby defile poured a good two thousand battling creatures. The village Telks were in grim retreat, and the hillmen after them. In moments, the fight had spilled across the plain and there was no hope of escaping Zinderneuf.

Alex goggled. He had never seen a combat like this. Not a sword or a spear in sight. The natives were fighting with—Yipe!—eggbeaters, scissors, tennis balls, pipes, spoons and mousetraps!

After a while, the man began to understand.

The eggbeaters, a defensive weapon like the medieval pike, had sharp blades on the end of a three-meter shaft, turned by a crank. The scissors were for clipping off an enemy's head or hand. Only a four-armed Telk could have wielded such monstrosities. The mousetraps were oversized affairs, big enough to catch a bear, thrown in the path of an advancing army. The spoons were enormous ladles, dipped into pots of corrosive acid which was splattered at the foe. The rubber-like balls held needles which must be poisoned, and were sent bouncing into opposing ranks by Telks with carefully developed calluses on their hands. The pipes were of Gargantuan dimensions, smoked by certain warriors who blew great greasy clouds; a flaw of the wind gave Alex a whiff and sent him from the wall, coughing, weeping and swearing. Their "tobacco" must be some noxious weed to which the pipemen had cultivated an immunity.

And he was supposed to rescue Tanni from this!

"They collide!" shouted Le Forgeur. "They come together with force of the extreme and slaughter indescribable!"

"Whoops!" said Alf Sniggs. "H'I sye, they ain't 'arf fightin', are they?"

"Buck up, old chap," advised Smith. "Remember the playing fields of Eton."

"Well," yelled Alex, desperately, "Come on, then!"

Smith raised his eyebrows. "But these *aren't* the playing fields of Eton," he pointed out.

Helplessly, Alex watched the battle surge past his stronghold. There was another corps among the villagers, who now formed a rearguard while the rest streamed inside their walls. These Telks spat something into their horny hands and spunged them at the foe-objects which even the raging hillmen avoided. One skittered over the ramparts of Zinderneuf, and Alex got a close look at it: a small metal disk with sharp edges that glistened with some poison.

He buried his face in his hands. "Oh, no," he groaned. "Oh, no, not tiddlywinks!"

By littering the ground with these missiles, the villagers covered their retreat and got safely home. The great wooden gates slammed shut as the enemy poured up. Spoonmen made it discouraging to walk about under the walls, and the invaders withdrew sullenly, dragging their casualties along.

Carried away by enthusiasm, Smith hopped up and gave three cheers for the defenders; then, remembering his British sportsmanship, he politely added three cheers for the attackers.

They heard him. Snouted faces turned around, yellow eyes glistened balefully, a harsh war cry lifted—and as one, the barbarians charged at this new object.

"Aux armes!" yelled LeBrute, gleefully. *"Formez vos bataillons! Marchons! Un pour tous et tous pour un!"*

Rifles cracked as the Telks swarmed close. Alex saw a number of direct hits. Only—they didn't do any damage! A punctured Telk was bowled over, but picked himself up and resumed his advance. That damned rapid biochemistry—blood clotted almost instantly—black powder rifles just weren't any good here!

For a moment, shears gleamed before him as a warrior mounted the wall. Then Giuseppe Fortissimo pushed him off. Doggedly, the Telk climbed up again, to be pushed off again. This might have gone on indefinitely, but the charge spent itself and the hillmen drew back, grumbling. They might not be seriously hurt by bullets, but the shock was painful.

For a moment, Telk and Hoka glared at each other. There was a hurried conference among the barbarian leaders, and one native was sent forward. He walked on his hands with feet in the air and a scrap of cloth in his mouth.

LeBrute looked puzzled. "Name of an adequate little red wine," he muttered. "What is it he does, that one?"

"Parley, old bean," guessed Smith astutely. "Must be their idea of a flag of truce, don't y'know . . . shows he's completely disarmed."

"Ah, so!" Sergeant LeBrute sprang up on the wall. His round, furry face looked down on the envoy, who stood upright.

"Eh bien?" snapped Sergeant LeBrute.

"Hoog, whag, waag!" said the Telk.

"Qu'est-ce que vous dîtes?"

"Waag ah hoog wha hoog."

"Jamais! Nous sommes soldats de la Légion!"

"Wugh wugh wahaag!"

"Cochon! Nous n'avons pas peur. Nous ne savons pas ce que c'est que la peur!"

"Whog!"

"Vache!"

"One has to give the devil his due," whispered Smith to Alex. "A sadistic oaf, our sergeant, but he has courage. I'll wager it's not often that someone has stood up to that Telk and told him off in just those words."

Alex climbed up beside the Hoka noncom. This was getting nowhere. He broke in, speaking Telkan, and LeBrute spat a final *"Chameau!"* and stood aside.

The conversation was brief and to the point. His Most Heathen Majesty, Illustrious King-Emperor of Whaa, Magnificent Duke of Hoog-Guggl, Incomparable Lord of the Marsh Marches, Warrior of the Order of Wug, Protector of the Gods, Hereditary Head-snipper of the Tribes of Gung and Wuh, Earl of the High Whaag, Commander of Skuggwah, the Very-Invincible-And-Much-To-Be-Feared-Whose-Tread-Shakes-The-Earth-And-Whose-Burps-Are-Thunder-In-The-Hills, Hooglah Hooglah Hooglah Gungwhoo Whog Hooglah XVII, offered alliance to the furbearing strangers against the impious village of Gundersnath which had not only refused him his rightful tribute, but had demanded tribute from *him*. In exchange for what petty but perhaps amusing assistance they might give, the furbearing stranger would get a small share of the loot. If they refused this generous offer of His Most Heathen Majesty, half of them would be hanged without mercy, and the rest beheaded without reprieve. A reply was requested at their earliest convenience.

Alex, describing himself as Ambassador Plenipotentiary and Extraordinary of the Most Terrible and Carnivorous Empire Of Earth, accepted, on condition that he should have the hairless, two-armed female held prisoner by the admittedly vile and unspeakable Gundersnathians. This was agreed, and the envoy walked off on his hands.

"Bien!" snapped Sergeant LeBrute. "What was said?"

Alex explained. "It's our only chance to get at that village," he added.

"Non!" cried the Hoka. "Have I not told you, we are here to defend this fortress *à l'outrance?"*

"Oh, but this is different," said Alex, hastily. "We'll be making a sally."

"*Bleu misérable!*" screamed LeBrute. "Have you the impudence to give advice to your sergeant?"

"Yes," said Alex.

"Excellent!" said LeBrute. "What courage! I shall recommend you for a decoration. Let us sally, therefore, at once." And he leaped off the wall and started toward the hillmen, crying, "*Marchons! Vive la France!*"

The rest followed. Alex dashed back into the boat to call Tanni and give her the word. It would be slaughter if he tried to land directly; nor was a vessel this size maneuverable enough to be used as a weapon in itself, say to knock enemy soldiers off the walls. But if his allies could storm the village—

A rank smell assailed his nose. He heard a seething behind the after bulkhead. Flinging it open, he was horrified to see the vats of green beer foaming and boiling. The entire engine room was one vast mass of suds.

"Oh, no," whimpered Alex.

That Telkan biochemistry again. Airborne yeasts—?

He tested the engines nervously, finding them unharmed behind their insulation. Despite her fears for him, Tanni was somewhat hurt at the briefness of her husband's message. But she did not have to speak from a cabin filled with the odor of 500 liters of sour beer.

Hooglah Hooglah Hooglah Gungwhoo Whog Hooglah XVII was not optimistic. He had tried another charge and seen it reel back from the walls of Gundersnath. The village was amply provisioned, but the hillmen had no supplies and could not live off this barren country. Anyhow, the fiery Telk temperament did not include the patience for a siege.

As night fell, the army camped around the settlement, their fires twinkling through the dense gloom, and sang defiant songs to drown out the jeers therefrom. Alex listened to one because it had a rather pleasant little melody.

> *"Ha, carrion birds*
> *shall batten on them—*
> *belly gashes,*
> *guts and blood! Eggbeaters howl;*
> *heads shall roll;*
> *the foe shall tread*
> *on tiddlywinks!"*

The king paced murkily before his own fire. Its red light shimmered off the scissors of his guards. A dozen assorted knives rattled at his waist. The Legionnaires sat nearby, smoking vicious cigarets—that much was authentically French—and yarning about their desperate adventures in the trackless Sahara. Alex paced side by side with the king, even more worried than he. The effect was like a tall palm walking next to a stumpy cactus.

"Had we but some long-range weapon," grumbled the Telk. " 'Tis their spoonmen and tiddlywinkers up on the walls which will not let us near enough to bash in the gates. Were I not the mightiest butcher the world had known, I'd give up and go kill somebody else. I may do it anyway."

Alex gulped. "Our rifles—" he suggested.

"Bah!" said the king. " 'Tis a good idea, having weapons which shoot from afar, but yours only make holes a cub would laugh at. It takes a broad cutting edge, see you, to lay those wights out."

Alex considered introducing the longbow. But no—it would take days to make enough, nor would a Telk submit to the intensive training required—nor did he and Tanni have that much time.

John Wellington Wells, alias Las Ciseaux, pushed back his kepi and said plaintively: "Ah, for some wine!"

"An excellent idea, *mon brave*," answered Sergeant LeBrute. "Rastignon, Sniggs, Fortissimo, fetch us the old and rare."

"Pardon, Sergeant," said Le Forgeur, unhappily. "But there is no wine."

"No wine!"

The Legionnaires looked thunderstruck. Too late, Alex remembered that he had left Toka without a supply of the potent liquor which was so much a part of everyday Hoka life.

"We are wineless!" sobbed LeRat. "It is the end of the universe."

"No—wait—" Alex spoke hurriedly, before they should get completely demoralized. "We do have some beer on the boat, you know."

"*Bière?*" snorted LeBrute. His moist black nose wrinkled.

"It's better than nothing."

"*Ach, Bier!*" sighed von und zu Griffentaffel ecstatically. "*Alt Heidelberg! Ach, du lieber Augustine—*"

The other Hokas, shouting above his song, agreed with Alex and sent a party to get some flasks. When it arrived, King Hooglah snatched a bottle, sniffed it, sipped, and threw it away in disgust. "Not poisonous," he growled.

The bottle hit the ground and exploded, scattering shrapnel. Alex dove for the dirt. When he looked up, the Hokas were calmly gulping their own ration.

"It is of a nothing," said LeBrute reassuringly. "It is but that here the fermentation is so rapidly proceeding. Be of good courage, Private Brassard."

"Brassard!" Alex jumped with blood in his eye. He had endured being railroaded into the Legion, making his boat a brewery, crossing space, fighting aliens . . . but to call him Brassard was beyond endurance. Snatching a bottle, he lifted it to break LeBrute's head.

Just in time, he stopped himself. Shaken, the flask jetted a stream of evil-smelling foam over his tunic. But—

"Your Majesty!" he croaked. "Your Majesty!"

In the gray dawn of Telko, Hooglah's army attacked again.

It came in a solid wave, howling, brandishing its weapons. Pouring down the slope and across the plain, demoniac, their feet shaking the earth like the ponderous unstoppable advance of the incoming tide, the hill warriors rushed at the defenders.

But in front of them was a line of special troops, to the number of a hundred. Each member held a tightly corked beer bottle in each of his upper hands, and had a bag full of them into which his lower hands could dip. And each wooden cork had a knife blade driven into it by the tang.

At the head of the assault charged King Hooglah with his guards. There, too, was the French Foreign Legion—Alex could not hold them back, and something forbade him to linger in the rear when his Hokas were going to war.

Up on the walls, now, he could see the Gundersnath garrison. The wind was at his back, so there were no pipemen; but spoons waved ominously over bubbling pots, and tiddlywinks were already bouncing to meet him.

Alex sweated and tried not to swallow his tongue. He had seen what those edges, whetted and venomous, could do. But beyond the enemy, he saw the metallic gleam of the flitter holding Tanni.

They were almost at the stronghold when Hooglah roared a battle cry and lifted his eggbeater in signal. Alex stole a glance behind him.

He saw the beermen shake their flasks, brace them against the upper shoulders, and take aim, all in one motion. He did not see the corks come out—those traveled nearly as fast as a rifle bullet—but he saw the silver jet of liquid and foam that arrowed from the mouths of the bottles and sprayed across the foe.

The knife blades whistled among the defenders. They did not make fatal wounds, but were enough to put a Telk *hors de combat* for a few hours. Spoonmen and tiddlywinkers dropped. Their line grew ragged.

"Once more into the breach, dear friends!" squeaked Smith.

"*Allons, enfants!*" cried LeBrute, popping away with his rifle. He ignored a gob of acid spattering within centimeters of him. Hokas did not lack courage. "*Aux armes! Marchons! Voilà!*"

"*Donnerwetter!*" cheered von und zu Griffentaffel. "*Vorwärts! Drang nach Osten!*" He broke into *Die Beiden Grenadiere*, in competition with Guiseppe Fortissimo who was singing *Di quella pira*, complete with high C's.

Again the cosmos exploded. And again. And again. The beermen stood like machines, grabbing out bottles, shaking, aiming, firing, sweeping the walls clean. And meanwhile a hundred of their comrades were battering down the gates.

As the invaders swarmed through, Alex found himself whirled off with his Hokas. He glimpsed snatches of the fight, Telk against Telk with what they considered conventional weapons. In spite of all the activity, there were surprisingly few casualties. A fair number were hopping about scratching frantically with all four arms where the ladled acid had got to them, but they seemed too tough for serious damage. Near the flitter, a hill Telk with oversize shears was energetically trying to cut a village Telk in half. He was not succeeding, the victim's six flailing limbs knocking the blades aside as fast as they approached.

The excitement of the battle carried Alex away as he clubbed his rifle and led the Hokas toward the flitter.

"Sally on!" he cried.

"*Chargeons!*" agreed LeBrute, slamming a Telk into the air.

"And a left!" whooped Alex. "And a right! Let 'em have it! Yea, team! Brrrackety-ax, co-ax, co—oh, hello, dear. We've come to rescue you." He hung on the airlock of the flitter and gasped for breath.

"Alex!" cried Tanni, emerging. She had definitely put on weight, but not to any serious extent as yet. So far she had just achieved a look of pleasantly bouncy plumpness. Her tunic and skirt, however, were already strained to the bursting point and had begun to give at the seams in discreet places.

"Back, now!" said Alex. "Return to the boat!" He added quickly: "The lost patrol has accomplished its mission. Now we must get the secret papers back to headquarters."

The Hokas formed a square about Tanni and slugged their way to the gate. There they halted.

The flight was ending, more and more Gundersnath Telks standing on their hands and waving their feet in the air. But it was urgent to escape, lest King Hooglah turn on his allies.

Nevertheless, the ground for half a kilometer outside was strewn with tiddlywinks.

The Legionnaires milled nervously. "What are you waiting for?" bawled Alex. He was still half berserk.

"Out there, *mon vieux*—" LeBrute pointed.

"We have shoes on, what?" ventured Smith. "They may protect us. Then again, they may not. What say, eh, what, what, what?"

Alex swept Tanni into his arms and led a dash. His voice lifted in a howl:

"Damn the tiddlywinks! Full speed ahead!"

A bright and cheerful sun shone on the parade ground of the Foreign Legion at Sidi Bel Abbès, and on the troops drawn up in dress uniform. The Lost Patrol stood in front, Sergeant LeBrute almost bursting his buttons with pride. The entire platoon was being awarded the Croix de Guerre, and he had the Legion of Honor.

Jorkins Brassard hovered unhappily about. He had enforced the regulations about weapons, but there were also regulations about needlessly exposing wards of the League to danger. Alex bore no special grudge; still, with the inspector under his thumb, he could be sure of a glowing report to Earth Headquarters.

Near Tanni and her husband, the Hoka governor twirled his mustaches diffidently.

"How can Madame forgive me?" he asked. "For my . . . indelicate assumption, *c'est à dire.*"

"You're forgiven," said Tanni graciously.

Alex ducked as a button popped off LeBrute's tunic.

"I am so sorry," went on the governor. "*Naturelle-ment,* one has torn up the enlistment papers—" He stammered in embarrassment.

"That's all right," said Alex, not to be outdone.

"I would never have leaped to such an erroneous conclusion," said LaFontanelle, "but—"

"But what?" asked Tanni.

"Madame must understand," said the little Hoka. "It is only that I am so French."

"*Monsieur l'Ambassadeur de la Terre Alexander Braithwaite Jones!*" said the commandant of the Legion formally.

Alex stepped forward with equal stiffness. The commandant adjusted his épaulettes, stood on tiptoe, and pinned the red rosette on the man's chest.

"*Mon brave!*" said the commandant.

He kissed Alex on both cheeks.

Humans and Hokas present were treated to the sight of the Cultural Development Plenipotentiary, representative and official arm of the United Commonwealths, which is the mightiest state within an Interbeing League of a hundred thousand suns, blushing like a schoolboy.

Interlude VI

**Plenipotentiary of the
Interbeing League
Planet Toka**

HEADQUARTERS OFFICE   CITY OF MIXUMAXU

9/9/86

Mr. Hardman Terwilliger
2011 Maori Towers
League City, N.Z., Sol III

Dear Hardman,

This is a somewhat hasty note, but you'll soon see the reasons for that. Briefly, I'm shipping out for Earth in a few weeks, and the preparations are keeping me busier than a one-armed octopus.

The fact is, I've changed my mind about resigning my position here. Exposure to your man Brassard, while generally instructive, has convinced me that possibly the Hokas would be better off under my wing than someone else's.

Also, those doubts I've expressed to you are being resolved. Thinking over all my years here, I see them as basically a sturdy, brave, independent little folk; their protean imaginativeness merely plays like a brilliant flickering light over a fundamental solid strength.

"Cultural imperialism" or not, I don't think the Service program—in my hands, anyhow—can hurt them. At worst, it will only involve them in a certain amount of waste motion. Their very adaptability is a protection against losing their racial heritage. It is, also, the special talent by which they may one day succeed us as the political leaders of the galaxy. Don't laugh at the thought! Feel free to shudder, but don't laugh.

What also bothered me was the feeling that I was accomplishing nothing. I didn't want to be a party to the Hokas remaining in Class D for the standard minimum fifty years. They have met every other requirement for upgrading—at least to Class C. It's quite possible that I may see them attain full status in my own lifetime, which would make all my troubles worthwhile.

Accordingly, I used the threat of resigning, even after I'd changed my mind, as a club on Parr. So he's waived the fifty-year rule, and I'm taking a Hoka delegation to Earth to apply for advancement.

We have a Galactic Series Baseball game coming

up shortly, but after that I'll be on my way. And when you meet my Hokas again, I'm sure you'll be amazed at how civilized they've become. I do think I've pounded some sanity into them—even if it has been my own sanity, pulled up by the roots!

Must close now. Be seeing you. Our love to Dory.

Best,
Alex

Joy in Mudville

"Pla-a-a-ay *ball*!"

The long cry echoed through the park as Alexander Jones, plenipotentiary of the Interbeing League to the planet Toka, came through the bleacher entrance. Out on the field the pitcher wound up in a furry whirl of arms and legs and let go. Somehow the batter managed to shift his toothpick, grip the bat, and make ready while the ball was streaking at him. There was a clean crisp *smack* and the ball disappeared. The batter selected a fresh toothpick, stuck it in his mouth, jammed his hands in his pockets, and started a leisurely stroll around the diamond.

Alexander Jones was not watching this. He had heard the crack of the bat and seen the ball vanish; but following that there had been only a vague impression of something that roared by him and smashed into the bench above in a shower of splinters. As a former Interstellar Survey man, Alex was *ex officio* a reservist in the Solar Guard, and the promptness and decisiveness with which he hit the dirt now would have brought tears of fond pride to the eyes of his superior officers had they been there to see it.

However, they were not, and after holding his position for several seconds, Alex lifted a cautious head. Nobody else was up to bat; it looked safe to rise. He dusted himself off while glancing over the field.

It was spotted with small round forms, tubby, golden-furred, ursine-faced, the Hoka natives of the planet Toka. They were all in uniform, the outfit of long red underwear, shortsleeved shirts, loose abbreviated, trousers, and peaked caps which had been traditional for baseball since it was invented back on Earth. Even if most of the races throughout the known Galaxy which now played the game were not even remotely human, they all wore some variation of the costume. Alexander Jones often wondered if his kind might not, in the long run, go down in history less as the originators of space travel and the present leaders of the Interbeing League than as the creators of baseball.

Mighty Casey, the planet's star batter, had completed his home run—or home saunter—and returned to the benches. Lefty was warming up before he tried himself against The Babe. Professor, the intellectual outfielder, was at his post, keeping one eye on the diamond while the other studied a biography of the legendary George Herman Ruth. Beyond the bleachers, the high tile roofs of Mixumaxu lifted into a sunny sky. The Teddies were practicing, the day was warm, the lark on the wing, the snail on the thorn.

Putzy, the manager of the team, trotted worriedly

up to Alex. He had been called something like Wishtu before the craze reached his planet; but the Hokas, perhaps the most adaptable race in the universe, the most enthusiastic innovators, had taken over names, language—everything!—from their human idols. Though of course they tended to be too literal-minded . . .

"Ya all right?" he demanded. He had carefully cultivated hoarseness into his squeaky voice. "Ya didn't get a concussion or nuttin'?"

"I don't think so, " answered Alex a little shakily. "What happened?"

"Ah, it wuz just mighty Casey," said Putzy. "We allus try a new pitcher out on him. Shows him he's gotta woik when he's up wit' duh Teddies."

"Er—yes," said Alex, mapping his brow. "He isn't going to hit any more this way, is he?"

"He knocks dat kind every time," said Putzy with pardonable smugness.

"Every time?" retorted Alex maliciously. "Did you ever hear the original poem of 'Casey At the Bat'?"

Putzy leaped forward, clapped a furry hand to Alex's mouth, and warned in a shaking whisper: "Don't never say dat! Geez, boss, ya don't know what duh sound of dat pome does to Casey. He ain't never got over dat day in Mudville!"

Alex winced. He might have known it. The Hoka mind was about as *sui generis as* a mind can get: quick, intelligent, eager, but so imaginative that it could hardly distinguish between fact and fiction and rarely bothered. Remembering other facets of Hoka-assimilated Earth culture—the Wild West, the Space Patrol, Sherlock Holmes, the Spanish Main, *la Légion Étrangère*—Alex might have known that the one who had adopted the role of mighty Casey would get so hypnotized by it as to start believing the ballad had happened to him personally.

"Never mind," he said. "I came over to get you. The Sarennians just arrived at the spaceport and their manager's due at my office in half an hour. I want you there to meet him."

"Okay," said Putzy, sticking an enormous cigar into his mouth. Alex shuddered as he lit up; tobacco grown on Toka gets strong enough to walk. They strolled out together, the pudgy little Hoka barely reaching the waist of the lean young human. Alex's runabout was waiting; it swung them above the walled city toward the flashy new skyscraper of the League Mission.

Seen from above, the town was a curious blend of the ancient and the ultramodern. As a technologically backward race, the Hokas were supposed to be introduced gradually to Galactic civilization; until they had developed so far, they were to be gently guarded from harming themselves or being harmed by any of the more advanced peoples. Alex, as League plenipotentiary, had the job of guide and guardian. It paid well and was quite a distinction; but he sometimes wondered if it wasn't making him old before his time. If the Hokas were just a little less individualistic and unpredictable—

The runabout set itself down on a landing flange of the skyscraper and Alex led the way inside. Ella, his native secretary, nodded at him from an electrowriter. There was a cigaret in her lipsticked mouth, but the effect of her tight blouse was somewhat spoiled for him by the fact that Hokas have twice the lactational equipment of humans. She was competent, but her last job had been with Mixumaxu's leading Private Eye.

Entering the inner office with Putzy, Alex flopped into a chair and put his feet on the desk. "Sit down," he invited. "Now look, before the Sarennian manager comes, I wart to have a serious talk with you. It's about financing the team."

"We're doing okay," said Putzy, chewing on his cigar.

"Yes," said Alex grimly. "I know all about that. Your arrangement with these self-appointed outlaws in the so-called Sherwood Forest."

"It's fair enough," said Putzy. "Dey all get free passes."

"Nevertheless," said Alex after gulping for air, "things have got to be put on a more regular basis. Earth Headquarters likes the idea of you . . . people playing ball, it's a good way to get you accustomed to meeting other races, but *I'm* responsible for your accounts. Now I have a plan which is a little irregular, but I do have discretionary powers." He reached for some papers. "As you know, there are valuable uranium deposits on this planet which are being held in trust for your people; they're being robotmined, and the proceeds have been going into the general planetary development fund. But there are enough other sources of income for that, so I've decided to divert the uranium mines to the Teddies' use. That will give you an income out of which to pay for necessities." He paused an I and frowned. "—and that does *not* include toothpicks for Casey!"

"But he's gotta have toot'picks!" cried the manage, shocked. "How kin he waggle a toot'pick wit'out—"

"He can buy his own," said Alex sternly. "Salaries are paid to the team, you know. The same goes for that bookworm outfielder of yours, Professor—let him pay for his own books if he must read while he plays."

"Okay, okay. But we gotta have a likker fund. Duh boys gotta have deir snort."

Alex gave in on that. The fieriness of the Hoka distillation and the capacity of its creators were a Galactic legend. "All right. Sign here, Putzy. Under the law, native property has to be in native hands, so this gives you title to those mines, with the right to receive income from them and dispose of it as you see fit. Sometime next week I'll show you how to keep books."

The manager scrawled his name as Ella stuck her head in the door. She never would use the office annunciator. "A monster to see you, chief," she said in a loud whisper.

"Ask him to wait a minute, will you?" said Alex. He turned to Putzy. "Now look, please be as polite as you can when the Sarennian comes in. I don't want any trouble."

"What's duh lowdown on dem, anyway?" inquired Putzy. "All I know is we play 'em here next mont' for duh Sector pennant."

"They—well, I don't know." Alex coughed. "Just between us, I don't like them much. It isn't their appearance, of course; I've been friends with weirder beings than they are. It's something in their culture, something ruthless. . . . They're highly civilized, full members of the League and so on, but it's all that the rest of the planets can do to restrain their expansionism. By hook or by crook, they want to take over the leadership." He brightened. "Oh, well, we're only going to play ball with them."

"*Only?*" cried Putzy, aghast. "What's so only about it? Man, dis is for duh Sector pennant. Dis ain't no bush-league braggle. Dis is a crooshul serious!"

Alex shrugged. "All right, so it is." But he could

sympathize with his charges. The Hokas had come far and fast in a mere ten years. It would mean a lot to them to win Sector championship.

The Galactic Series necessarily operated under some rather special rules. In a civilization embracing thousands of stars and still expanding, one year just wasn't enough to settle a tournament. The Series had been going on for more than two centuries now. On the planets local teams contended in the sub-series for regional championships; regions fought it out for continental victories, and continents settled the planetary supremacy. Then there were whole systems, and series between systems, all going on simultaneously. . . . Alex's brain reeled at the thought.

Extrapolating present expansion of the League frontiers, sociologists estimated that the play-off for the Galactic Pennant would occur in about 500 years. It looked very much as if the Toka Teddies might be in the running then. In one short decade, their energy and enthusiasm had made them ready to play Sarenn for the Sector pennant. The sector embraced a good thousand stars, but Toka had by-passed most of these by defeating previously established multistellar champions.

"If we lose," said Putzy gloomily, "back to duh bush leagues for anudder ten-twen'y years, and mebbe well never get a chanst at duh big game." He cheered up. "Ah, who's worrying? Casey ain't been struck out yet, and Lefty got a coive pitch dat's outta dis univoise."

Alex pressed a button and spoke into the annunciator. "Send the gentlebeing in, Ella." He rose politely; after all, Ush Karuza, manager of the Sarenn Snakes, was a sort of ambassador.

The monster squished in. He stood well over two meters high, on long, clawed legs; half a dozen ropy tentacles ending in strong boneless fingers circled his darkly gleaming body under the ridged, blubbery-faced head. Bulging eyes regarded Alex with a cold, speculative stare, but he bowed courteously enough. "Your sservant, ssir," he murmured in tolerably good English.

"Welcome . . . ah . . . Mr. Karuza," said Alex. "May I introduce Putzy Ballswatter, the manager of the Teddies? Won't you sit down?"

Putzy rose and the two beings nodded distantly at each other. Ush Karuza sniffed and unfolded a trapeze-like arrangement he was carrying. When he had draped himself over this, he lay waiting.

"Well," said Alex, swinging into the little speech he had prepared, "I'm sure you two will get along famously—"

Putzy, who had been staring at Ush Karuza, muttered something to himself.

"Did you say something, Putzy? " asked Alex.

"Nuts!" said Putzy.

"Hiss!" hissed the Sarennian.

"Well, as I was saying," continued Alex hurriedly, "you'll get along famously as you ready yourselves for the big contest—"

Putzy seemed on the verge of speaking again.

"—in your *separate* training camps," went on Alex loudly, "at *good* distances from each other—" Under the rules, a team playing off its own world had to have a month's training on the other planet to accustom itself to the new conditions. There was also a handicapping system so complicated that no human brain could master it.

Alex knew what the trouble was this time. It was

something he had kept carefully to himself since first learning that the Teddies were to play the Snakes. The fact was that the Sarennians bore a slight but unfortunate resemblance to the Slissii, the reptile race which had been the Hokas' chief rival for control of Toka from time immemorial till men arrived to help out; and the fur on the little manager's neck had risen visibly at the mere sight of his opposite number.

What was worse, Ush Karuza seemed to be experiencing a like reaction toward Putzy. Even as Alex watched, the tentacled monster produced a small bottle which he opened and wafted gently before his nose like a disdainful dandy of the Louis Quinze period on Earth. For a second, Alex merely blinked, and then a whiff from the bottle reached his own nostrils. He gagged.

Putzy's sensitive nose was wrinkling too. Ush Karuza came as close to smirking as a being with fangs in its mouth could.

"Ah . . . merely a little butyl mercaptan, ssirss," he hissed. "Our atmosphere containss a ssimilar compound. It iss nessessary to our metabolissm. Quite harmless, to man and Hoka."

"Um . . . ugh . . . ah?" said Alex brightly. Out of the corner of his eye he saw Putzy grind out his dead cigar in the ashtray and dig another one twice the size out of his baggy uniform shirt. He fired it up. Butyl mercaptan sallied forth to meet and mingle with blue noisome clouds of smoke.

"Ah sssso!" mumbled Karuza furiously and began to waft his bottle more energetically.

Puff! Puff! Puff! went Putzy.

"Gentlebeings, gentlebeings, please!" wheezed Alex, taking the heavy paperweight away from the Hoka.

Venomously hissing, Ush Karuza was uncorking a second bottle while Putzy crammed more cigars into his mouth.

Things were off to a fine start.

Alexander Jones came staggering home to his official residence that night in a mood to be comforted by his beautiful blonde wife, Tanni. But the house was empty, she having taken the children for a few days to the Hoka Bermuda for its annual sack by pirates (a notable social event on Toka), and dinner was served by the Admirable Crichton with his usual nerve-wracking ostentation. It was only afterward, sitting alone in the study with a Scotch and soda, that Alex's ganglia stopped vibrating.

The study was a comfortable book-lined room with a cheerful fire, and when he had slipped into a dressing gown and placed himself before the desk, Alex realized that privacy was just what he needed. He pressed the door-lock button, opened a secret drawer, and got out a sheaf of papers.

Let not the finger of scorn be pointed at Alexander Jones. The most amiable, conscientious, thoroughly normal young men still have their hidden vices; perhaps these outlets are what keep them on their orbits, and surely Alex had more troubles than most who shoulder the Earthman's burden. What the universe needs is more candor, more tolerance and understanding of human weakness. The truth is that Alexander Jones was a poet.

Like most great creative artists, he was frustrated by the paradoxes of public taste. As a Solar Guardsman, he had achieved immortality by his poetic gifts. It was he who had originated the limerick about the spaceman and girl in free fall, as well as the

Ballad of the Transparent Spacesuits, and these shall live forever. Yet they were merely the sparks of his careless youth and he now winced to recall them. His spirit was with the Avantist Revival; his idols had never been known outside of a select clique: Rimbaud, Baudelaire, cummings, Eliot, Cogswell. From time to time the interstellar mails carried manuscripts signed J. Alexander to the offices of *microcosm: the minuscule magazine*. So far, they had also carried the manuscripts back. But a shoulderer of the Earthman's burden is not easily discouraged.

Alex took a long drink, placed stylus to paper, and began writing:

> *the circumambient snake surrounds the pal-*
> *pitating tarry fever-dream of uncertain dis-*
> *tortions and Siva screams and mutters*
> *unheard vacillations: now? then?*
> *Perhaps later, it is hot today.—*

The visio set interrupted him with a buzz. He swore and pressed the *Accept* button. The features of a rather woozy-looking Hoka appeared on the screen.

"Hi-yah, bosh," said the apparition.

"Putzy!" cried Alex. "You're drunk!"

"I am not," Putzy replied indignantly, momentarily reeling out of screen range, "Shober as a judge," he said, reappearing. "Coupla liters ish all I had. Wouldn't make a pup drunk. It's dis yer stuff Ush Karuza smokes when he's shelebratin'. Dese Sarennians don' drink. Dey just smokes uh stuff. Makes me kinda light-headed—smellin' it—" Putzy went over backwards.

Climbing back into view, he said with heavy gravity: "I called y'up t' tell ya shumfin. You said be nice to Karuza, di'n'ya?"

"Yes?" said Alex, a dreadful premonition seizing him.

"Thash what I thought ya said. Well, listen. Like yuh said, we wen' out for li'l drink. Had li'l talk, like yuh said we should. We got t' talkin' shop, shee, an' I tol' him 'bout dose uranium mine rights. Right away he wan'ed ta bet me some salt mines on Sarenn against 'em. So I did."

"You did?" yelped Alex.

"Sure I did. Signed duh papers an' all. Di'n' ya say be nice to him? But listen—" Putzy beckoned mysteriously and Alex leaned forward, shaking. Putzy went on in a whisper. "Here's duh t'ing. Not on'y has I made him happy, but we got us some salt mines."

"How come?" moaned Alex.

"Because!" said Putzy strongly, driving his point home with a stubby finger jabbed into the screen before him. "Because he don' know it yet, but duh Teddies is gonna win."

"Is that so?" barked Alex.

"Sure, ah' yuh know why?"

Alex shook his head numbly. "No, why?"

"Because," said Putzy triumphantly, "duh Snakes is gonna lose."

He beamed. "Jush t'ought ya'd like to know, bosh. So long."

"Hey!" screamed Alex. "Come back here!"

He was too late. The screen was blank.

"Oh, *no!*" he gasped. "Not this!"

For a wild instant, his only thought was of *quotation at the waterfront*. It had been shaping up so nicely!

Wouldn't he ever get a chance to write something really significant?

Then he settled back to realities and wished he hadn't.

Tottering to his office the next morning after a sleepless night, he took an athetrine tablet and called the Mission library to send up Volume GAK-GAR of *Basic Interstellar Law*. When he received it, he turned to the section on gambling between beings from different planets. He had to find out if the bet Putzy had made with Karuza could be legally collected or not. The legislation in question turned out to be full of such witty statements as, "The above shall apply to all cases covered by Smith vs. Xptui except in such cases as are covered by Sections XCI through CXXIII inclusive"—each of these with its own quota of exceptions and references. After two hours, he was still no closer to an answer.

He sighed, sent Ella out for more coffee, and was just settling down to a fresh assault on the problem when there was a sort of swirl in the air before him and a semi-humanoid specimen with an enormous bald head topping a spindly little body materialized in his visitors' chair.

"Greetings, youth!" boomed the newcomer. "My visualization of the cosmic all implies that you are surprised. Do not be so. Be a advised that I am Nicor of Rishana, who is to umpire the forthcoming contest between Toka and Sarenn."

Alex recovered from his astonishment. The Rishanans, the most intellectual race in the known Galaxy, were almost legends. They could be lured from their home only by a problem impossible for lesser races to solve. Such was any game governed by the 27 huge volumes of the Interstellar Baseball Association rules; as a result, Rishanans invariably officiated in the Series as umpires.

Otherwise they ignored the rest of the Galaxy and were ignored by it. Undoubtedly they had a lot on the ball—for instance, whatever tiny machine or inborn psionic ability permitted them to project themselves through space at will; but since nobody really misses the brains he doesn't have, the rest of the League had never fallen prey to any sort of inferiority complex. Indeed, most beings felt rather sorry for the poor dwarfs. Since the Rishanans felt rather sorry for the poor morons, everybody was happy.

Inspiration came to Alex. "May I ask you a question, sir?" he begged.

"Of course you may ask a question," snapped Nicor. "Any ego may ask a question. What you really wish to know is whether I will answer the question." He paused and looked uncertain. "Or have you already asked me the question? Time is a variable, you know."

"No, I didn't know," said Alex politely.

"Yes, indeed," thundered the voice of that incredible ancient being. "As determined by Sonrak's hypothesis. But come, come, youth—the question."

"Oh, er, yes." Alex pointed to the law book. "I'm having a little trouble with a small point here. Just a—heh! heh!—a theoretical question, you know, sir. If a Hoka bet a Sarennian some Tokan land, and lost, could the—er—say the Sarennian collect?"

"Certainly," snapped Nicor. "That is, he would collect by respective substitute."

"I beg your pardon?"

"You need not apologize for inferior mentality. In

effect, the Hokas, being wards of the League, would be protected; but as plenipotentiary and responsible individual, you would have to pay the winner an equivalent amount."

"What?" cried Alex as the assessed valuation of the uranium mines—a fourteen-digit figure—reeled before him.

He heard the explanation through a blur. The extreme libertarians who had drawn up the League Constitution had protected ordinary citizens right and left but deliberately placed high officials on a limb. In this case, a judgment in equity would send him to the Sarennian salt mines for—oh, in view of the new longevity techniques, about fifty years, turning his wages over to Ush Karuza. The working conditions were not too bad unless one happened to have a distaste for the odor of the mercaptans.

"Well, well, enough of this pleasant but unprofitable chit-chat, youth," finished Nicor. "Let us be off to the ball game."

"What game?" asked Alex weakly. "The pennant game isn't for another month."

"Tut-tut," improved Nicor. "Don't interrupt. I am, of course, both forgiving and gracious. Perhaps you think an intellectual like myself has no sense of humor. So many beings fall into the misapprehension. Certainly I have a sense of humor. Of course it is more subtle than yours; and naturally I am not amused by the crude horseplay of lesser intelligences. In fact," went on Nicor, his brow darkening, "that is the main trouble with beings of small development. They do not take the cosmic all seriously enough. No dignity, youth, no dignity."

"But wait a minute—" broke in Alex.

"Don't interrupt! As an intelligence of the quaternary class, you cannot possibly make an interruption of sufficient importance to interfere with a statement emanating from an intelligence of my class. As I was saying . . . Dignity. Dignity! That is what is so painfully lacking in the younger races." A thundercloud gathered on his face. "When I think of the presumption of those few rash individuals who have dared to question my—MY!— decisions upon the baseball field—But I am sure your charges will be guilty of no such indiscretion."

Alex rocked in his chair. If there was any sport the Hokas loved with a pure and undying love, it was umpire-baiting.

"As for your quaint belief that this is not the day of the game," continued Nicor, "I could hardly expect you to know. You irresponsible children never know. When I was your age, I used to have to get up every morning and figure time as a variable to fourteen decimal places before I could start my day's calculations. We didn't have Sonraks in those days to help us. The trouble with you present youths is that you have it too easy. Surely you do not think I would put myself in the ridiculous position of having to realign myself for thirty days in the future? Naturally, I devoted only one point eight percent of my reasoning power to this business of establishing my spatio-temporal coordinates, but it is inconceivable that I should fail. No, no, rest assured that this is the day of the game."

Alex pointed a mute finger at the chronopiece on the wall. Nicor whirled and stared at it.

"What?" he roared with a volume that shook the office. "Am I to be given the lie by a mechanical? Am I to be outfaced by a planet? Am I to be maladjusted by a cosmic integral of the square root of minus one over log log tangent X, theta R squared over N dx from zero to infinity? Blast Sonrak! Damn the mis-placed decimal point! Time is not a variable!"

And with an explosion that rocked the room, he vanished.

Now, it seemed, everything depended on the Teddies winning the game. Alex visited the Hoka ball park and tried to make Putzy institute more rigorous training. The Hokan idea of practice was to let Casey swat a few wild ones while the basemen and fielders sat down, puffing cigars, tilting jugs to their lips, and chatting lightly of this and that. To Alex's protests that the Snakes were bound to get some hits when they came up to bat, Putzy retorted that Lefty would fan them or, failing that, fielders with the speed of the Professor would easily tag them out. Alex gave up.

He made an excuse to drop in on the Sarennian training camp. The visitors were good, no denying that: their main advantage was their terrific tentacle spread, handy for nabbing flying balls; and when the pitcher was winding up, you couldn't see what kind of pitch was coming among all those arms, or even what arm it was coming from. But they lacked the Hoka swiftness and hitting power. Alex—who had spent long hours under a hypnoteacher cramming himself with baseball lore—decided that one set of advantages just about offset the other, so that there would be no handicapping.

Ush Karuza looked positively gloating under his superficial good manners, and Alex began to get suspicious. Considering the ambitions of Sarenn, there was probably more at stake than the pennant and a bet. Returning to his office, the man consulted the Service roster and found that a Sarennian was now at the top of the list of those waiting for ambassadorial vacancies and, if Toka's plenipotentiary were removed, would probably get the job. Sarenn being fairly close to the Tokan sun while Earth was far away, it wouldn't take long for the new chief to gain complete control of the planet for his people without attracting too much attention at Headquarters.

And a plenipotentiary sent to the salt mines would naturally not retain his position.

Alex looked hollowly into space. He didn't even have Tanni to comfort him; she had messaged an intention to stay on a while in Bermuda and he agreed, not wishing to torment her with worry which might turn out to be needless. His carefully guided planet was headed for tyrannous foreign rule; he was headed for the same; *microcosm* had just returned *Greeks En Brochette.* . . .

There is an old saying that, "The optimist declares this is the best of all possible worlds; the pessimist is afraid he's right." Alex agreed.

The big day dawned bright and clear and hot. Since early morning, a colorful throng of Hokas had been flocking into the ball park. They had come not only from Mixumaxu and its neighboring city-states, but reflected the varied impact of human culture on their entire planet. A booted and spurred cowboy sat next to a top-hatted Victorian gentleman; a knight in armor clanked past a tubby Space Patrolman; a sashed character with a skull and crossbones on his cocked hat grumbled saltily, "Scupper my mizzenmast!" as he tripped on his cutlass. One part of the stands was reserved for

Sarennian spectators, a silent and impassive mass of tentacles.

As Alex walked across the field to his official seat in the Hoka dugout, he scowled. The substitutes were all present and accounted for, but where was the regular team?

"Hot dogs, pop cawn, soda pop!" bawled a vendor in the stands above. "Getcha pop here, folks. Can't kill duh umpire wit'out a pop bottle!"

Alex's worried eyes traveled across the dusty ground to the center of the infield. Nicor of Rishana was already there, leaning on the bookcase containing the 27 volumes of rules. There was a grim look on his face which might have been caused by thoughts of Sonrak, and a slightly withdrawn expression in his eyes as he mentally scanned the field from all necessary points of view. This psionic ability had enabled the number of umpires to be reduced to one, even as the easy exhaustion of some races had forced changes in the rules governing substitutions.

"Where's our team?" muttered Alex. "They're late already."

The buzz from the bleachers became a chant. "We want the Teddies. We want the Teddies. We want the Teddies."

Then there was it ragged cheer as the famous nine came into sight—not from the locker room, but from the main gate. Even at that distance, Alex saw how they staggered. Leading the way Ush Karuza, looking smug and supporting Putzy, who was singing something about somebody called Adeline. Alex broke into a cold sweat.

Putzy lurched up to him while the rest of the team was calling cheery greetings to their friends in the

stands and forcing autographed balls on them.
"Hi-ya," burbled the Hoka manager, collapsing into
Alex's arms. "I gotta tell ya shumfin. We got dese
Sarennians all wrong. Good ol' Ush, he's all right.
Ya know what he done? He took us all out dis mornin'
an' stood us to duh bigges' dinner in town. All duh
steak an' French fries we could eat. Whoops!" He
lost his grip and sat down suddenly. "T'ink I'll take
li'l nap." His beady eyes closed.

Alex glared at the Snake manager. "Is this your idea
of fair play?" he asked. "Drugging our team. Umpire!"

Nicor flickered in mid-air and appeared beside
them. "What is it, youth?"

"This—" Alex pointed shakily at Ush Karuza. "This
gentlebeing took our men out and drugged them with
that stuff he smokes."

"My dear ssir! " protested the monster. "It iss merely
a mild sstimulant that we Ssarennianss ssmoke for
pleasure. I am not accountable if it affectss our little
friendss."

Alex opened his mouth indignantly. "Down, youth!"
snapped Nicor. "There is nothing in the rules covering
pre-game festivities." He returned to midfield.

Another Sarennian pushed forward a great wheeled
tank. "Ice cream," announced Ush Karuza grandly.
"Help yoursselfss, my friendss!" As the Hokas threw
themselves on it with besotted cries of glee, lie pulled
a book out of his pouch and gave it to the Professor.
"And for you," he added, "a brand-new biography
of Tyruss Cobb, sspecially prepared by the Ssarennian
Sstate Department."

"Oh, boy!" The small, bespectacled Hoka sat down
and began reading it at once. Ush Karuza oozed off
with every appearance of satisfaction. Alex buried
his face in his hands.

Nicor of Rishana spoke into his wrist microphone, and his voice boomed over the park: "Come, youths! My visualization demands that you now play ball!"

The spectators cheered. The band, somewhat confused, broke into *Auld Lang Syne*. The Toka Teddies wobbled out onto the field. Putzy sat up and muttered something about not feeling so good.

The Snakes, as visitors, were first up to bat. Their star hitter, Shimpur Sumis, wrapped his tentacles around his club and waved it gleefully. Lefty, the Teddy pitcher, found his way to the mound and began turning around to get his position. He kept on turning.

"Play ball, youth!" thundered the umpire. Shimpur Sumis yawned.

It seemed to infuriate Lefty. He sent his ball spinning in faster than Alex could follow. Either because he wasn't quite himself, or because he hadn't allowed for the greater reach of Sarennian tentacles, Shimpur Sumis connected with a solid hit. The ball smacked into left field. The monster dropped his bat and galumphed toward first base.

"Grab it, Professor!" screamed Alex.

The intellectual outfielder was too immersed in his new book to notice. The ball shot past him. His fans howled, "Wake up, ya bum! Grab dat ball!"

Shimpur Sumis rounded second.

A Hoka near Alex, clad in doublet and hose and feathered cap, leaped up, fitted an arrow to his longbow, and let fly. The Professor yelled as it pinked him, glared around, saw the ball, and loped after it. By a miracle, he got it back to the catcher just as Sumis went by third. The Sarennian retreated, grinning smugly.

The next one stepped up to bat. Lefty sent a whizzer past him. The ball smacked into the catcher's mitt.

"Ball one!" cried Nicor.

"Whaddaya mean, ball one?" squeaked Lefty, spinning around in a rage. "Dat wuz a strike if I ever seen one."

"A strike," said Nicor, glowering, "must pass between waist and shoulders."

"Yeah, but he ain't got any waist *or* any shoulders," protested Lefty.

"Hmmm, yes, so I see." Nicor pulled one of the fat volumes out of the bookcase beside him and consulted it. Then he took forth a transit and sighted on the batter. The crowd rumbled impatiently.

"The equivalent median line," said Nicor at last, "yields the incontrovertible result that the missile so injudiciously aimed was, indeed, ball one."

Alex shuddered. Putzy turned green under his fur.

The next ball met a hard-swinging bat. Again it zoomed by the immersed Professor. Again the archer fired. This time the Professor was ready. He plucked the arrow out of the air as it neared him and continued reading. Both Sarennians loped home. Their rooters set up a football-style cheer:

Hiss, hiss, hiss!
Who iss better than thiss?
Squirmy worm, destiny's germ
TEAM!!!

The next Sarennian went out on a pop fly just behind third. The one after that made it to first. But Lefty, even when pitching on hope and instinct, was not a hurler to be despised. The fifth Sarennian up to bat barely got a piece of the ball and both he and the Snake on base were put out in a wobbly double play.

The Teddies came to bat. They were uniformly ineffective with the single exception of mighty Casey, who, as Putzy was too sick to tell him not to, tried to fulfill a longstanding ambition to lay down a bunt, but only succeeded in bunting the ball over the left field fence. Score one run for the Teddies.

The next four innings were a rout. The regular Teddy team got even sicker and had to be taken out, and against the substitutes, the Sarennians made blissful scores. At the end of the first half of the fifth inning, the board read seven to one in favor of the Snakes.

By the second half of the fifth, the original team members were weak but recovered, and ready to take the field again with blood in their eyes, Casey was first up, and with a valiant return to his usual nonchalance, he put his hands in his pockets and sauntered toward the plate, a toothpick in his mouth and scorn in his eye. He whipped into his batting stance just as the Sarennian pitcher let go. There was a blur, a crack, and he was strolling off along the baseline, nodding graciously to his fans.

But for him it had been a poor and a weak hit. The Sarennian left fielder reached forth an interminable tentacle and nabbed it as it came smoking along the ground. He whirled and shot it back toward first base. Casey saw it coming. and broke into a panting run. He thundered into first together with the ball.

"Out!" said Nicor, appearing at the bag.

"Out???" screamed Casey, skidding to a stop and coming back. "I wuz in dere ahead o' duh ball wit' enough time fer a nap."

"I say *out*," ruled Nicor. "Do not dispute with a superbrain—Time! Don't mention that word *time* to me!"

"Why, ya blind, bloody, concrete-skulled superbrain!"

Pop bottles began to fly from the stands, bursting to fragments in the air as the small robot-controlled anti-aircraft guns mounted on the right field fence went into action. Nicor ignored the bombardment and settled the discussion by flickering back into position behind the pitcher's mound.

The game continued. The Teddies were still a little weak and uncertain. The Hoka following Casey was caught out at shortstop and the next Hoka sent a high fly into right field where it was easily taken for the putout.

The Snakes came up to bat in the first half of the sixth inning. Lefty, turned white-hot with determination, retired the opposing side without gain by three straight strikeouts. The Hokas took over at the plate and the first six men up scored two men and loaded the bases. The score stood at seven to three with Casey yet to bat, and the Snakes called time out.

"What is the occasion, youth?" demanded Nicor of Ush Karuza.

The Sarennian smirked. "I find I musst invoke one of the handicapping ruless, ssir," he answered. "Article XLIII, Ssection 3, Paragraph 22-b. In effect, it iss that a certain gass iss necessary to our player'ss metabolissm. It being a mercaptan, completely non-toxic in small dosess ass you know, we may ssimply releasse it without sslowing the game down by wearing masskss and handicapping the Hokass."

"There are psychosomatic effects," objected Nicor. "I refer to the nauseous stench involved."

"I do not believe the ruless ssay anything about such side issuess, answered Karuza smugly.

Nicor went back to the books. At last he nodded.

"I fear you are right," he added sadly. "But in the name of sportsmanship—"

Ush Karuza turned purple with rage and swelled up alarmingly. "Ssssir! How dare you!" he hissed. "Article CCXXXII. Amendment Number 546, paragraph 3-a, explissitly sstatess that Ssarennianss are incapable of the conssept of Ssportssmanship and sspessifically exemptss them from observing it."

"Oh." Nicor looked crestfallen. He checked. "True," he said bitterly.

Alex felt ill already. This looked like the end.

A great generator was wheeled into an upwind position on the field. It began to fume. Alex caught a whiff and felt his stomach rise in revolt. There could only be a few parts per million in the air, but it was enough!

"Oof!" groaned Putzy beside him. "Lemme outta here."

"You stay," said Alex desperately, grabbing him. "Play up, play up, and play the game!"

Nicor turned a delicate green. "My visualization of the cosmic all suggests I am going to be sick," he muttered.

Putzy opened a box of cigars and passed them around to his team. "Dis may help ya fer a little while," he said. "Now get in dere and fight!" Tears rose in his eyes. "Me aged grandmudder is sitting at home, boys, old and sick, laying dere amongst her roses and lavender waiting for yuh to bring home duh pennant. It'll kill duh sweet old lady if ya lose—"

"Ah, shaddap!" said his grandmother, leaning out of her place in the stands beside him and stuffing her knitting in his mouth.

Alex fumed away on his own cigaret, trying to drown

the smell that curled around him. There must be *some* way to escape those salt mines!

With the mercaptan turning his stomach upside down on top of the effects of the drug, Casey still batted in the man on third on a sacrifice fly. The Hoka following him struck out. Retired, the Teddies lurched out onto the field and took another pasting. The score climbed against them—six Sarenn runs in the seventh, seven in the eighth, with the brief one-two-three interlude of the Teddies at bat hardly noticeable in the Snakes' slugging festival. When the Hokas came up again in the top of the eighth, they were trailing twenty to four.

Alex chewed his fingernails. There *must* be an answer to this! There must be some counter irritant, something which would get the Hoka back to the careless energy and childlike enthusiasm which served them so well . . . Counter-agents! The idea flared in his head.

He snatched at the water boy's arm. "Bring us something to drink!" he commanded. The little ursinoid sped away, to return with a slopping bucket which Alex knew very well did not contain water.

"Time out!" he yelled. "The Hokas request time out."

"What for, youth?" asked Nicor faintly.

"They need alcohol to protect themselves against the effects of the Sarennian gas. It's okay by the rule books, I'm sure."

Nicor brightened a little. "It does protect?" he inquired. "Then, youth, you may bring me some too."

Ush Karuza jittered about in a rage while the Teddies gathered weakly around the bucket and dipped their noses into it. Even by Hoka standards, they got it down fast. Nicor scowled at his complimentary beaker, sipped, winced and gasped. "*This* is necessary to them?" he cried. "I have seen halogen breathers, I have seen energy eaters, I have seen drinkers of molten lead, but here is the race that shall rule the sevagram!"

Casey lifted his dripping black snout. "Urp, he said. "Gotta toot'pick?"

"Play ball!" hollered Ush Karuza wrathfully.

The Babe waved casually at Putzy. "We'll get 'em," he said confidently, and connected with the first pitch for a clean single to left. The Professor came up with his book in one hand, stuck it under his arm just long enough to belt one out of the park, and walked home with his nose back in his book.

"Geez!" he muttered reverently. "Dat Cobb could sure play *ball*!"

Lefty stepped up to bat with an evil gleam in his eye. The Sarennian star pitcher launched a ferocious fast ball across the middle. Lefty let it go by. "Ooooof!" said the catcher.

"Strike one," said Nicor.

Time out to replace one catcher.

There was no second strike. Lefty bounced the next pitch off the right field wall for a stand-up triple.

Casey sneered and sauntered out to the plate. Grabbing the end of the Sarennian catcher's fourth tentacle, he began picking his teeth with it.

"Halt! Stop! Foul!" shrieked Karuza. "He *bit* my player!"

Some of Alex's hard-won baseball knowledge came to his aid. "Article XLI, Section 5, Paragraph 17-a: 'Players may take such nourishment as is required during the game,' " he flung back.

"But not off *my* players!" wailed Karuza.

Nicor weaved over to his books and consulted them. "I am afraid I can find nothing forbidding cannibalism," he announced. "It must never have occurred to the commission. Tsk, tsk."

The pitcher let fly. Casey set his bat end-on on the plate and jumped up to balance on to of it. "Strike one!" called Nicor.

"Nope," said Casey owlishly. "Yuh mean ball one, ump. Duh ball went under m'waist. Under m'feet, in fack!"

"So it did," agreed Nicor imperturbably "Ball one!"

"The ruless—" sputtered Ush Karuza.

"Nothing in the rules against balancing on top of a bat, youth." Nicor scratched his bulging head. "I do believe the commission will have to call a special meeting after this game."

The Sarennian pitcher wound up again. As the ball zoomed toward him, Casey swung the mightiest swing in Toka's history. The Snakes' second baseman saw the ball screaming at him and dropped to the ground in terror. A bolder monster in the outfield raised his glove and caught it. Or perhaps one should say it caught him—he was lifted off the ground described a beautiful arc, and landed three meters away. The ball went merrily on to cave in a section of the fence beyond.

Casey, who had been spinning on one heel unable to stop, came to a halt and staggered around the bases. He had plenty of time, because the Sarennians had to dig the ball out from between two planks.

Time out while the Snakes replaced one unconscious outfielder and one second baseman with a bad case of the shakes.

The rest of the Hokas followed the example of their star players and sailed twice completely through their lineup before being retired with a score of 19 to the Snakes' 20 at the end of the eighth. The crowd, including Alex, was going wild.

Shimpur Sumis came up to bat with a haughty look suggesting that he alone could settle the matter. Lefty, who was higher than a kite, threw him a ball so fast that it exploded on being struck. Nicor consulted his library for the rule on exploding balls, found none, and called it a strike . . . though he admitted that his visualization was not very complete today. Sumis' abused tentacles could not handle the bat well enough to keep him from being struck out.

Ush Karuza snarled and went over to the mercaptan generator and opened the valves wide. A thick, nearly visible stream of vapor rolled across the field to envelop the Hoka pitcher.

Lefty was too drunk to care. He sent off his famous curve. Then he gaped at it. So did the Snake batter. So did Alex. No—the ball couldn't possibly be where it was!

It landed in the catcher's mitt. "Strike one!" announced Nicor.

The next pitch was even more unbelievable than the last. It defied all known natural law and went in a sine curve. "Strike two!"

The batter flailed wildly the third time. Alex distinctly saw the club go through the ball, but nothing happened.

"Strike three!" said Nicor. "Youth, you are now external to the n-dimensional sociological hypersphere!"

"Huh?" asked Putzy.

"He means, 'You're out,' " translated Alex happily.

"Foul!" bawled Ush Karuza. "They're using black magic."

"There is nothing in the rules against magic," said Nicor.

"I just t'row a damn good coive, dat's all," said Lefty belligerently.

The next Sarennian fared no better. By that time Alex had figured out the situation. "The thick stream of mercaptan vapor has a refractive index appreciably different from air," he told Putzy. "No wonder it produces optical illusions. Hoist by their own petard!"

Putzy seemed dubious. "If dat least means what I t'ink it means," he said, "you shouldn't oughtta say it in front of me grandmudder."

The Teddies came to take their turn at bat. It was the last half of the ninth inning. The score stood at 19-20 with the Teddies trailing. The batting order at that moment stood: first The Babe, then the Professor, then Lefty, and then Casey. The Sarennians looked grim, but the Hokas in the stands, who had resorted to their potent pocket flasks while the team was getting their liquor from the water boy, were wildly jubilant. As The Babe picked up his bat and strode to the plate they began a cheer which finally died away to an awful silence as the whole crowd held its breath.

The Sarennian pitcher was clearly determined to let no hits be gotten off him. He wound up and let fly.

From the stands rose a mighty groan of horror, interspersed with shrill hoots of glee from the Sarennian section. For the stream of mercaptan vapor was still flowing past the pitcher *and all three balls wove a daisy chain past the plate!*

"Strike three!" cried Nicor. "Out!"

Sadly, The Babe came back. The stands were in an uproar. It looked as if open battle might break out between the Hoka and Sarennian fans. Alex cringed on his bench.

The Professor went up to the plate. The ball looped crazily by him. "Strike one!"

A long moan of agony went up from the Hokas.

"Strike two!"

The Professor braced himself. There was a wild, almost berserk gleam in his spectacles. The Sarennian pitcher writhed and twirled his tentacles with contemptuous confidence. The ball shot forward.

The Professor threw himself and his bat to meet it.

There was a tiny *tick*. The ball popped out of the vapor fog and trickled along the ground toward third base There were only a few seconds of time before it was caught, but that was all the Professor's famous legs needed. There was a whiz, a blur, an explosion of dust, and the Hoka was safe at first.

The tying run was on, and there were two outs left to bring it home.

Lefty took his time selecting his bat. He swung it heavily a few times to test the balance and then slowly stalked up to the plate. The pitcher wound up. He threw. The stands groaned.

"*Strike one!*" thundered Nicor in a voice of doom.

The Sarennian catcher strolled out to return the ball to the pitcher. They conferred for a few seconds.

With the batter back in position, the pitcher wound up again. The ball snapped out of his mass of tentacles, flickered, and appeared in the catcher's mitt.

"Strike two!"

"Casey," said Putzy in a shaking tone, "get ready, boy."

Alex turned to look at the Teddies' mainstay. To his surprise, the little batter seemed cool and calm. "Relax, Putzy," Casey said. "It's in duh bag. All I gotta do is knock us bot' home."

"But dose pitches!" said Putzy.

"Lissen!" said Casey with some heat. "Lissen, ya

don't t'ink I ever bodders to watch d' pitcher, do yuh? All I pays attention to is duh ball from duh time it gets to about two meters away from me. And duh ball gotta be straight den, or duh ump calls it a foul. Dey can't fool me none."

Slowly, hope began to dawn on Putzy's furry face. He was even smiling as Nicor called "Strike three!" and Lefty returned glumly from the plate.

Casey got to his feet and began his customary nonchalant stroll toward the batter's box. At first the crowd merely gaped at him in astonishment; but then, drawing courage from his apparent confidence, they raised a swelling cheer that rocked the stands. He doffed his cap and kissed his hand to the fans, waved, rubbed his hands in the dirt and took up his stance. Alex saw, through a vision blurred by tenseness, that the Sarennian pitcher was already losing heart at sight of this overweening opponent.

"Time out!" screamed Ush Karuza.

For a moment the park was held in agonized silence. Then a mounting growl like that of a Boomeringian sea-bear disturbed at its meal commenced and grew.

"For what reason, youth?" asked Nicor.

"Article XXXVI, Ssection 8, Paragraph 19-k," said Ush Karuza defiantly. "Any manager may encourage hiss team by verbal meanss."

Nicor checked. "Correct," he said. "You may proceed."

There was a scurry from the Sarennian dugout and a public address system was wheeled onto the field and its microphone set up before a small tape player. As the stands waited silently to see what this new move might portend, Ush Karuza switched it on. There was a hissing noise as the machine warmed up.

At the plate, Casey smiled indulgently.

And then the hissing stopped and a voice boomed over the park. It was not a Sarennian voice, but human; and the first words it uttered wiped the smile from Casey's lips and fell on the field like the hand of doom. For the voice was reciting, and the first words were:

> *It looked extremely rocky*
> *for the Mudville nine that day:*
> *The score stood two to four*
> *with but one inning left to play.*
> *So when Cooney died at second . . .*

"Oh, no!" wailed Putzy. "It's *it!*"

"What's it?" choked Alex.

"Dat pome—'*Casey At duh Bat*'—oooh, lookit poor Casey now—" The manager pointed a trembling finger at the Teddies' last hope, who was shaking with unbearable sobs as he stood at the plate.

"I protest!" screamed Alex, leaping from the bench and running wildly out to where Nicor stood.

"You have no right to protest," snapped the umpire, "You are merely a spectator."

"Den I pertest!" roared Putzy, skidding to a halt beside Alex. "Turn dat t'ing off!"

At the plate, Casey was melting down in his own tears as the tape swung into the fifth stanza.

> *Then from the gladdened*
> *multitude went up a joyous yell.*
> *It rumbled in the mountaintops,*
> *it rattled in the dell,*
> *It struck upon the hillside*
> *and rebounded on the flat.*

> *For Casey, mighty Casey,*
> *was advancing to the bat*

Casey was flat on the ground now, making feeble pawing motions as if he would dig his grave where he lay, crawl in, and die.

"Your protest is out of order," said Nicor.

Ush Karuza oozed oily sympathy. "I am afraid your batter iss not feeling well," he muttered.

> *. . . And when the writhing pitcher*
> *ground his ball into his hip,*
> *Defiance gleamed in Casey's eye,*
> *a sneer curled Casey's lip. . . .*

Abandoning the umpire, Putzy ran to his collapsed star and tried to lift him from the ground. "Fer cripessake, Casey," he pleaded. "Stan' up. Just get us one little hit. Dat's all I ask."

"I can't," choked Casey. "Muh heart ain't in it no more. Dey trusted me in Mudville and I let 'em down."

The stillness over the park was broken only by his sobs and the inexorable recorded voice.

> *. . . Close by the sturdy batsman,*
> *the ball unheeded sped.*
> *"That ain't my style," said Casey.*
> *'Strike one!" the umpire said. . . .*

Like a drowning man, Alex saw his whole life parade by him: Tanni, the children, Earth, Toka. It was not what he wanted. He wanted some way out of this inferno.

No other batter had a chance; the Teddies were

too demoralized. But what to do, what to do? Surely he, Alexander Jones, had some means of helping, some talent—He gnawed trembling fingers as the poem tolled its way to its dreadful conclusion.

> . . . *And now the air is shattered*
> *with the force of Casey's blow!*

Damn all poets!

> *Oh, somewhere in this favored land*
> *the sun is shining bright,*
> *The band is playing somewhere*
> *and somewhere hearts are light,*
> *And somewhere men are laughing,*
> *and somewhere children shout,*
> *But there is no joy in Mudville—*

Poetry!

—MIGHTY CASEY HAS STRUCK OUT!

"Yipe!" said Alex.

There was one other outstanding ability which Ensign Alexander Jones had shown in the Guard besides hitting the dirt. And that was that when the occasion arose, he was very quick off the mark when there was something to be run to, or from. Therefore, just as some weeks earlier the promptitude with which he nosedived would have pleased his superiors, so now they would have joyed to see the speed with which he covered the distance between the umpire's post and the public address system. Even the Professor would have been pushed to match his velocity; and the way he stiff-armed the lone

Sarennian guarding the recorder was a privilege to observe.

He snatched up the microphone and panted into it. "Go on, boss!" yelled Putzy, unsure what his adored plenipotentiary intended but ready to back him up.

"Pant, pant, pant," boomed Alex over the field.

Ush Karuza ran to stop him. "Hold, youth!" ordered Nicor. "He has a right to use the machine."

"Pant, pant," panted Alex, and began to improvise:

> *"But hold (pant), what strikes the umpire,*
> *what causes him to glare*
> *With fiery (pant, pant) look and awful eye*
> *upon the pitcher there?*
> *And Casey takes the catcher by the collar*
> *with his hand,*
> *He hales him to the (pant) umpire*
> *and together there they stand."*

Beside the plate, the Hoka Casey lifted his head in wonder, and wiping the tears from his eyes, stared openmouthed at Alex.

The human had had his dark suspicions the way Lefty was struck out last time. No chance to prove that, but he could weave it into his revenge.

> *'I bid you look,' cried Casey, 'I bid you*
> *search him well.*
> *For such as these our fine fair game*
> *they soon would sound its knell—!' "*

Alex hesitated, looking a trifle confused. "Dat's my plenipotentiary who said dat!" cried Putzy's grandmother; and thus heartened, he proceeded.

> *"The umpire checks them over*
> *and the villains' faces fall*
> *When out from each one's pocket he pulls*
> *forth A HIDDEN BALL!*
> *" 'Oh, shame!' cries out the Mudville crowd.*
> *The echoes answer, 'Shame!'*
> *'That such a dirty low-down trick should*
> *blight our Casey's name.*
> *The pitcher only faked his throw,*
> *the catcher faked his catch.*
> *The cowards knew that such as they*
> *were never Casey's match.' "*

"You untentacled mammal!" raged Ush Karuza. "You sslimeless, conformation of bone flesh!"

Alex had long ago discovered that mankind rarely reacts to insults couched in nonhuman terms. It did not offend him at all to be told that he was slimeless.

The Teddies' Casey was sitting up by the plate now and beaming. Alex took a deep breath and went on:

> *" 'Now take your places once again.*
> *Once more!' the umpire cried.*
> *'And your next pitches will be fair*
> *or else I have your hide.*
> *Now take your places once again,*
> *to places one and all!'*
> *And as soon as they were ready,*
> *the umpire cried, 'Play ball!' "*

The Hoka Casey was up on his feet and clutching his bat. His eyes were riveted on Alex. And as the

last two stanzas came out his little form hunched and
twisted through the motions Alex described.

> "And now the pitcher takes his stance,
>   his face is black and grim
> And he starts his furious windup
>   with a fearful verve and vim.
> And now he rocks back on his heel;
>   and now he lets it fly.
> The ball comes sizzling forward
>   watched by Casey's steely eye.
>
> "For Casey does not tremble,
>   mighty Casey does not balk,
> Though it's clear the ball is high and wide,
>   and they aim to make him walk.
> He steps forward in the batter's box,
>   his bat's a lambent flame.
> Crack! Smash! The ball flies o'er the fence—
>   AND CASEY WINS THE GAME!"

The stands were going crazy. Hokas of all shapes,
sizes, and descriptions came pouring down from their
seats to mob and congratulate—

—Casey, of course.

Who else was responsible for the Mudville win?

To Hokan taste, it was almost an anticlimax after
the glorious victory of the fictional Casey when the
factual one playfully tapped a home run over the left
field fence and won the Sector pennant.

In spite of custom, Alexander Jones did not preside
over the wild festivities that night. He felt he deserved
a quiet evening at home, alone with a tall drink and
quotation at the waterfront.

Tanni would be coming back soon, and much as

he longed to see her, he knew she would give him
no chance to produce something really significant—
some poem reflecting the realities of Life.

SAREN	2	1	1	1	2	0	6	7	0	20
TOKA	1	0	0	0	0	3	0	15	2	21

Undiplomatic Immunity

I was born with a dull, sickening thud. Had I but known what an aching void yawned before me, I would never have started down that lonely road.

"Well—er—" said Alexander Jones, putting down the sheet of paper. "It's . . . um . . . interesting. But don't you think some of the phrases are a little, hm, hackneyed?"

"Of course," said the Hoka with the tweed coat and calabash pipe. He leaned back in his chair and cocked his feet up on the electrowriter: a meter or so tall, round-bellied, golden-furred, ursinoid, an outsize teddy bear with stubby hands and eager button eyes. His name was W. Shakespeare Marlowe. "Don't you see, it is precisely by the use of the hackneyed phrase, the integral unit of language itself, that I create the Myth."

Alex, who was a tall and lanky young human, sighed. That was what came of letting a Hoka read 20th-century criticism. "But why did you stop there?" he asked.

"I have to leave something to the reader's imagination," pointed out the writer. "That's the quintessence of art. Think how dull and prosaic it would have been if I had gone on to describe the rest of my life."

"Oh," said Alex weakly. "I see."

"Those are the same views intrinsic to my essay, *The Novel As An Art Form.* I have it here—" W. Shakespeare Marlowe produced another sheet from his pocket. "Observe, it says: *'The Novel As An Art Form,* by W. Shakespeare Marlowe. Paragraph. The novel *is* an art form. Period. The end.' Succinct, isn't it?"

"Very," said Alex.

"I knew you'd understand. I call it the new look in writing. Actually, it has its roots in Hemingway. But I refined it to its present form. You see, the trouble with writers has always been that they wrote too much. It cut down their production."

"Cut it down?" asked Alex uncertainly.

"Of course. Look at Twain, Dickens, Melville—a mere few dozen books. Whereas I often write a dozen novels in one day."

"Oh, no!" groaned Alex.

"Quite," said the Hoka, sticking his hands in his pockets and puffing complacently on his pipe.

They were alone in the outer office of the Tokan delegation's suite. A broad window revealed the spectacular towers of League City, spearing into the serene late-afternoon sky of New Zealand, Earth. A webwork of elevated mobilroads knitted the pinnacles together, from the soaring bulk of this official hostel to the immense hall where the Council of the Interbeing League met.

From the adjoining room came subdued squeaks

of excitement. Alex wondered what the other Hokas were up to. So far he had kept them out of trouble, but . . .

W. Shakespeare Marlowe, his secretary, was a very mild case, having merely gone overboard for authorship. But the energy, enthusiasm, and literal-mindedness of Alex's charges could lead to their playing any role that struck their fancy with an almost hypnotized solemnity. It was fortunate that the Tokan business stood high on the agenda of the present Council session: the less time on Earth they had, the less chance for some disastrous escapade.

Alex glanced at the wall chrono. He was supposed to meet informally with Commissioner Parr in a few minutes, and had already dressed for the occasion in suitably dignified crimson tunic and green slacks. "We'd better be going, Marlowe," he said. The little Hoka stumped happily out with him.

Two slideways and a dropshaft brought them to a tasteful suite in which cocktails and canapés were laid out. Adalbert Parr, the Chief Cultural Commissioner, received them: a big, portly man with a florid face and wavy gray hair. He bowed stiffly, shook hands, and widened his eyes as Marlowe whipped out a pad and took notes. Then, with regulation heartiness, he waved at the others present.

"We were only to get acquainted, Plenipotentiary Jones," he said. "May I present the chief delegates from three planets in your sector? His Excellency, Representative His Highness Prince Idebar of Worben."

The Worbenites were from a fairly terrestroid planet, a highly civilized race, and Prince Idebar was known as one of the shrewdest diplomats in the Galaxy. He was tall, with sleek black hair, his face aged but still keen and aquiline, his carriage erect; indeed, to be completely human-looking he would only have had to trim his ears and remove his horns and spiked tail. The females of his species were less manlike. "Delighted, sir," he murmured.

"No more than I, sir," replied Alex with equal urbanity.

They bowed. Alex jumped back as the horns swept by his nose.

"Ahem!" said Parr. "May I present His Excellency, Tantho the Hairy, leader of the delegation from Porkelans."

This being was two meters high, barrelshaped, with enormous four-fingered hands at the end of short, muscular arms. He wore only a pocketed belt, but long blue fur covered his body. Two small eyes peered out of a face mostly hair, with just a suggestion of snout. "Most pleased," he rumbled in the official English of the League.

"Her Excellency, Miss Zuleika MacTavish of Bagdadburgh," intoned Parr.

As Her Excellency came into view around the bulk of Tantho, Alex had a sense of being hit with a perfumed blackjack. The Scottish-Arabic colony, founded by a rather puritanical group, had followed the usual law of reaction to interesting extremes. Zuleika MacTavish was tall and willowy, with flowing brown hair and great liquid eyes and a wide soft mouth and . . . well, the few wisps of colored translucency making up her native costume gave even an old married man like Alex a slight impulse to throw back his head and howl.

However, plenipotentiaries do not howl, or slaver, at beautiful representatives from neighboring planetary systems. Not if they want to stay on good terms with the Cultural Office of Earth Headquarters and—most particularly—their wives. So Alex goggled and sputtered in what he hoped was a suitably diplomatic manner, and scarcely noticed the dark, hawk-faced Colin MacHussein who was introduced as the delegate's special assistant.

"Please sit down, gentlebeings," said Parr. A servant offered a tray of drinks. Alex reached for an interesting-looking green one. Prince Idebar muttered an alarmed *"Garrasht!"* and caught his arm and warned:

"Excuse me, sir. That happens to be made from the jithna leaf of my planet. I believe it is chemically quite similar to poison ivy." Alex shuddered his thanks, and Idebar took the drink himself and sipped with practiced grace.

"Oh, His Highness has no reason to murder you," said Zuleika MacTavish acridly. She took a cigaret from her belt pouch and a long holder from her décolletage. Alex came out of a reverie in which he wished he could be—temporarily, of course—a cigaret holder, to hear Parr exclaim:

"Please! We save the, ah, disagreements for the agenda. This is merely a social gathering. My own concern is with Plenipotentiary Jones's planet, Toka, but I thought an exchange of views with his neighbors out in Sector Seven might be . . . enlightening. He is here to see about getting the autochthones upgraded."

Alex nodded. "The Hokas have met the requirements for Class C by establishing a planet-wide peace authority," he said—careful not to add a description of a meeting of teddy bears from nations modeled on the Wild West, Victorian England, the East Roman Empire, King Arthur's realm, and others. "Guiding them is, of course, my task, and I believe they are now ready for Class C." That was mostly a technicality, involving science scholarships for qualified natives, but an essential step on the path to full autonomy and membership in the Interbeing League.

The catch was, there were too many planets in process of becoming civilized, each a complicated special case. The League Council voted on their status, but in practice, of necessity, always followed the recommendation of the Commissioner. Which meant that Parr had to be convinced. Alex prayed that Worben, Porkelans, and Bagdadburgh had no objections to the upgrading. Quite apart from the Hokas themselves, it would mean a substantial raise in salary for him.

However, the little session was uneventful. The diplomats made polite noises and then returned happily to throwing courteous venom at each other. Alex got a distinct impression that there was trouble between Bagdadburgh on the one hand and Worben and Porkelans on the other. It was with some relief that he finally excused himself.

W. Shakespeare Marlowe followed him cheerily down the hall. "I can never thank you enough for bringing me along," he burbled. "I have notes for three new novels . . . sensational! The *haut monde*, wild, dissipated, the orgies as world-weary, cynical beings flog their jaded senses with ever new and more fantastic pleasures—"

"I thought they were rather dull," said Alex, with regret.

"It is the business of the artist to select and rearrange his material," said Marlowe firmly. "How else shall he portray the essence of Life?"

The main door to the Hoka suite opened before them and Alex trod in. He had left his delegates alone all day while he went through some necessary red tape, and had barely noticed that they sent out for some special items. Now, as he entered the living room, he stopped dead.

"Yipe!" he said.

Three Hokas sat around a table drinking tea. Two of them had adorned their rotund forms with archaic striped trousers and cutaway coats; top hats lay beside them. The third was completely muffled in a long black coat with its collar turned up, his beady eyes peering out from beneath a black slouch hat. They were being waited on by a fourth in chauffeur's uniform.

"What is this?" cried Alex. "Tharaxu—"

"The name," said one of the Hokas in cutaway, "is now Allenby. Foreign Office, don't y'know. Come join us in a spot of tea."

Alex's gaze roved wildly about the room. He saw numerous books from the hostel's extensive library. The authors were unfamiliar to him—Eric Ambler, E. Phillips Oppenheim, Sax Rohmer—they must be centuries old. The Hokas had apparently dialed for novels about the diplomatic service and—

He clenched his teeth and sat down. "I don't believe I've met the other gentlemen," he said in a hollow voice.

"Forgive me, old chap," said Allenby. "More tea, Bert."

The chauffeur poured.

"Who's Bert?" inquired Alex.

"Our chauffeur, of course," said Allenby. "Foreign Office has 'em, don't y'know." He bowed at the other cutaway. "Heinrichs."

"Heinrichs?"

"Code expert," said Allenby, gazing distantly at Heinrichs. "One of these efficient German types."

Heinrichs beamed. He had always been nearsighted and worn contact lenses; these he had now discarded for two monocles.

"Code?" choked Alex.

"Naturally," said Allenby. "My dear old chap (more tea, Bert. Thanks), surely you don't imagine we'd dare communicate with the home office except in code?"

"Oh," said Alex. Allenby sipped at his tea. Marlowe took notes. "And . . . er . . . this other gentleman?" said Alex when it became clear that the Hoka in the black hat was not going to be introduced.

Allenby looked around the room, leaned over the table, put a furry hand to his mouth, and whispered: "That's Z."

"Z?"

"Z," breathed Allenby. "You remember Z, of course. The chap who was so useful to us at the time of the Balkan crisis."

"Oh," said Alex.

He was too late. The Hokas were already off on their own path. He could only play along. "Well, gentlemen," he sighed, "you must not forget that this delegation has an important job to do—a very important job."

"Hear, hear," cheered Marlowe.

"The future of Toka depends on it," said Alex earnestly. "If we don't get upgraded this time, we can't apply again for twenty years."

"Roight!" said Bert.

"Bert!" said Allenby.

"Sorry, guv'nor," said Bert.

"We have to remember that we are on trial—"

"More tea, Bert," said Allenby.

"Yes, sir."

"On trial, I say. The future of Toka depends on our making a favorable impression. You must remember—"

"Knockout drops, Bert."

" 'Ere you are, sir."

Alex frowned, but was too busy explaining to inquire what was meant. "In most cases," he went on, "there is a delicate situation existing just under the surface of polite intercourse—"

"Let me give you a fresh cup of tea, old bean," said Allenby.

"Thanks," said Alex. "As I was saying, there are conflicts—" He took a swallow from his cup. "There can be situations that—"

The floor came up and hit him.

He struggled back to consciousness to find himself neatly laid out on a couch, and the suite empty. Two hours had passed; it was now 2030 o'clock. He felt like retreaded oatmeal.

After a while he managed to get to his feet, stagger to the bathroom, and gulp down an athetrine tablet. The pains vanished and his head cleared.

"Omigawd!" said Alex. "The Hokas!" He went out the door at full gallop.

Each floor of the hundred-story hostel—this was the 93d—had its own lounge. Alex burst into this room and found its comfortable chairs deserted, its robobar humming softly as it polished glasses . . . no sign of his charges. He was about to dash on, he knew not whither, when a glorious shape undulated through the rear entrance, paused, and sped forward. The soft eyes of Zuleika MacTavish fluttered incredible lashes at him and the soft hands with their luminous nail polish gripped his.

"Oh . . . Plenipotentiary Jones," she whispered "I was hoping I could find you alone."

"You were?" squeaked Alex.

"Please," she said. "I'm in desperate need of help."

Alex, who had been pawing at the floor in his eagerness to be off, began to paw a little more slowly. Not that the situation wasn't bad, with the Hokas on the loose; but after all, any gentleman who called himself a gentleman—

"Well, er, hruff!" he coughed. "If there's anything I can do—"

Zuleika leaned toward him, still several centimeters removed but slightly indenting his tunic. "It's not for myself, it's for Bagdadburgh," she pleaded. "There's so few of us, and those awful Worbenites and Porkelugians—" Suddenly her eyes were swimming with tears, and Alex put a fatherly arm around her.

"There, there," he began.

A shrill voice exploded behind him. "I say!"

Alex jerked free of the ambassadress and turned to confront the stem gaze of Allenby.

"Oh, er, good evening," he mumbled.

"Beg your pardon, old grapefruit," said the small Hoka frostily. "Your presence is required at the suite."

"Alex," breathed Zuleika, "I just have to talk with you."

"Yes, yes," said the man. "Later . . . to be sure, later—"

Zuleika gave him a thousand-watt smile through a mist of tears and walked slowly off. Alex stared after her, trying to recall the equations of simple harmonic motion. Allenby tugged at his sleeve. As they left, he found himself blushing, and the more angry he got on that account the more he blushed.

"Well, Allenby," he said gruffly.

"Well," repeated Allenby.

"Charming young lady," said Alex in a frantic tone.

"Yes. I rather imagine you feel like a father toward her."

"Why, of course. How did you know?"

"We," said the Hoka wisely, "know their methods."

"Methods?" asked Alex in bewilderment. "Whose methods?"

"You force me to be blunt, old parsnip," said Allenby. "The methods of beautiful spies. . . . Hist! Not another word till we're back. These walls have ears, don't y'know."

"Oh, no!" groaned Alex as he realized he had been cast in the role of Colonel Blimp.

"Play up, play up, and play the game!" said Allenby, patting him on the arm. "Stiff upper lip. Bite the bullet." With a courteous gesture, he produced a bullet from his cutaway and offered it.

"Play up yourself!" screamed Alex. "Now you listen to me—"

The slideway had borne them around a corner, and they saw Commissioner Parr's ponderous form on the opposite strip. He waved agitatedly at them and stepped onto the motionless central band. "Plenipotentiary Jones!" he barked. "What do you make of this?"

And he thrust under Alex's nose a large, ornate Oriental dagger.

"Found it stuck in my door," went on Parr. "Pinning down a note." He held out the message, and Alex read:
WHERE ARE THE SECRET PAPERS?

"Ulp," said Alex.

"Do you know whose idea of a joke this is?" rumbled Parr. He glared suspiciously at Allenby. "Have you seen this knife before?"

"I?" asked the Hoka. "Can't say I have, old cabbage." He helped himself to a pinch of snuff.

"Well . . . it's odd, to say the very least." Parr bowed stiffly, got back onto the westbound strip, and dwindled down the hall. Alex and Allenby continued east in a chilled silence.

The human found the suite in a state of hideous confusion. Its tables were heaped with paper of all sorts and varieties, and Heinrichs was busily examining these with a magnifying glass. Bert was making tea, Marlowe was writing, and Z sat muttering into his slouch hat.

"*Ach!*" said Heinrichs, looking up. "Vere vas der *hochwohlgeborene Bevollmächtigter* Jones?"

"With," said Allenby in tones of deepest deprecation, "*her.*"

"Her?"

"*Her,* herself!"

"Now cut it out!" roared Alex. "Now listen to me! I won't have this—I positively forbid—" Suddenly and belatedly he realized from the happy expressions on the furry faces that he was once more sliding into the character they had determined he should play.

As he stood sputtering, Marlowe looked up and said eagerly: "What do you think of this, Jones? I'm making a new translation of the *Iliad.*"

"You are?" asked Alex blankly.

"Yes, indeed," beamed Marlowe. "I have chosen to represent the timeless spirit of Homer by using the metrical form most characteristic of our age, a rapid, mellifluous—well, hear for yourself." He cleared his throat and read:

"*I sing of the wrath of Achilles,
which gave the Achaeans the willies.
Help me tell, O my muse,*

how Troy got the goose
and of quarrels which really were dillies."

Alex was saved from making noises like a critic by the buzzing of the visiphone. He pressed the button and Parr's thunderous face popped into the screen. "Plenipotentiary Jones!" he said. "Would you come down to my apartment right away, please?"

Alex nodded and clicked off, wondering what had happened now.

"Z," said Allenby, "attend the Chief."

"Und better you take mine Luger," said Heinrichs, withdrawing a young cannon from his top hat.

"No!" cried Alex. But as he sped out, Z followed relentlessly.

It occurred to the human as he went down the corridor that he could at least get an explanation of what had been going on. "Z," he said firmly, "I want an explanation of what has been going on. In the first place, what was the idea of giving me knockout drops?"

"Policy, sir," said Z.

"Policy?" Alex snapped his mouth shut. Oh, no, he thought, he wasn't going to get into one of those brain-tangling discussions this time. "What about that dagger and note?" he demanded.

"Sir?" asked Z cautiously.

"Do you know anything about that?"

"What can one say?"

Alex stared at him, but he volunteered nothing further. "Well," asked the man finally, "what *can* one say?"

"Exactly," said Z mournfully.

"Exactly *what*, for the love of Saturn?" snarled Alex.

"Exactly nothing."

Alex choked. "All right," he said. "Tell me one thing. Just one thing. What's this all about? What's supposed to be going on?"

"Ah," said Z darkly. "Who can tell?"

"Can't you?"

"Sir!" cried Z reproachfully, drawing himself up. "I'm in the secret service. I never tell."

Before Alex could think of a reply, they were at the Commissioner's suite. Grouped around a table were Parr, Prince Idebar of Worben, Tantho the Hairy of Porkelans, and Zuleika MacTavish of Bagdadburgh. An air of tension prevailed.

"Oh, good evening, Jones," said Parr distantly. "Ah . . . this is one of your delegation?"

"Um, yes," said Alex. "Commissioner, Your Excellencies, Mr. Z."

"How do you do, Mr. Zee?" said Parr.

"One has one's methods," said Z mysteriously.

Parr looked a bit startled, but turned to Alex. "I asked you here because your delegation and Their Excellencies all have accommodations on the 93d floor, and no one else. Possibly we can throw some light on a, ah, very delicate and unfortunate situation. It seems that Their Excellencies have had their suites broken into and stripped of papers."

"Aha!" said Z.

They all stared at the Hoka. "What?" asked Tantho.

"Just aha," said Z. He pulled an Oriental dagger from his sleeve and began idly to clean his fingernails with its tip. Parr's eyes narrowed, but before he could speak, Zuleika flared:

"Can't you see, these, these *gentlebeings* were out to find what they could in my quarters, and just pretended to have their own broken into as well?"

"Your young Excellency," crackled Prince Idebar,

"may I point out that a planet must resent slurs on its accredited representatives?"

"Please!" said Parr. "We only wish to get to the bottom of this. I suggest that the Interstellar Bureau of Investigation—"

"No!" snapped Tantho and Zuleika, while Idebar murmured: "I am afraid that that impossible."

"Ah—" began Z, but Alex hastily clapped a hand over his muzzle and babbled: "I'd better check my own place. I didn't notice any signs of burgling, but . . . I'll let you know—" With a sick grin, he hurried Z out.

"—and furthermore," stormed Alex when he was back in his suite, "breaking into the quarters of Council delegates is a territorial violation. I never saw anything like this! How did you—"

"Aow, naow," said Bert modestly.

"You, Bert?" whispered Alex.

"Of course, old onion," said Allenby proudly. "Bert is an ex-master criminal (now reformed, right, Bert?) and it was jolly old child's play for him, eh, what, what, what?"

"But those locks are finger-sensitive—pickproof!" said Alex.

"Simple, h'it were," said Bert. "H'I took me little h'ax—" He reached inside his uniform with a flourish and brought out an object like a giant jackknife with a hundred blades; from the body he snapped a small but wicked-looking axhead. "—then h'I took me little gouge"—he unfolded something like an icepick—"and me little jimmy, me little bryce and bit—"

Alex turned slightly green. "I see, I see," he groaned. "You needn't go into details."

"H'I picked those locks orl roight. H'I'd like ter see the lock h'I couldn't pick—"

"Bert!" reproved Allenby.

"Roight, guv'nor. Sorry, guv'nor." Bert lapsed into silence.

"—Anyway," said Alex after drawing a deep breath, "breaking into private offices and so forth . . . filling up our rooms with stuff like this—" He grabbed a handful of papers from under Heinrichs' magnifying glass. "What is this, anyhow? Here—

" *'Dear Miss MacTavish: This is to notify you that payment on your account for three black silk negligees, Size 12, and four pairs Upthrust brassieres, 107 cm. large, is now overdue—'* Hrump, we won't go into this. Hum." Alex cleared his throat and hastily shuffled the documents. "What's this, a private letter? Don't you know that one of the worst invasions of privacy is to read somebody's else's—um, I see the Worbenites have adopted English as their own international language— *'Dearest Iddykins—'* Good Lord, *Iddykins!* 'Dearest Iddykins, I had a dream last night and I dreamed you were speaking in the chamber of Earth but they had the ventilation turned up for the Chokgins representative. There you were, with nothing but your lightweight underwear on. For eighty years I've begged and prayed you to dress sensibly in your long woollies, you know you get the sniffles so easily, and I've tried to be a good wife to you but the moment you are out of my sight you cast caution to the winds—' "* Catching sight of the interested Hoka faces ringing him in, Alex broke off and cried wildly: "What do you want with this stuff?"

"Ve must decode," said Heinrichs.

"Ve must?" echoed Alex. "No . . . I mean—these aren't in code, dammit!"

"*Ja,* dey are."

"No, *no,* NO!"

"My dear old artichoke," said Allenby, "with all due respect, who is the code expert here, you or Heinrichs?"

"Heinrichs, of course!" roared Alex. "I mean—no, that's not what I mean. What I mean is— Now do don't get me off on *that!* The point is, this is a complete farce. There's nothing going on here"—the door chimed and Alex backed toward it, talking as he went—"that requires daggers in doors, burgling—come in—reading personal papers and so forth—come in, I said—and so on, and now that I have you here I'm going to show you that this business of intriguing is just something you've dreamed up—"

Becoming impatient, he opened the door manually. Leaning against the jamb, his face shaded by the tartan burnoose, was the silent and faintly sinister Colin MacHussein.

"Oh," said Alex. "What is it?"

To the Hokas' unbounded delight, MacHussein started to lean forward as if to whisper confidentially in his ear. The only problem was that he kept on leaning, further and further, until with a rush he ended face down on the carpet.

"MacHussein!" gasped Alex.

The Bagdadburgian did not reply. But for this seeming rudeness he had a good excuse. It consisted of a headgear the back of which was matted with blood.

Alex spun around and counted his Hokas. They were all present. He sat down and buried his face in his hands.

" 'Ere, sir," said Bert sympathetically. " 'Ave a nice 'ot cup of tea.

"Thank you," said Alex in a weak voice, accepting it. Then, cautiously: "No knockout drops, are there?"

"Aow, no, sir. Cream and sugar, two lumps."

"Thank you," repeated Alex and drank. "It's good."

"Thank you, sir. Bucks yer h'up h'in a tight spot, a bit of tea, don't it, sir?"

"Yes," said Alex. "Yes, indeed. When it's been a bad day ever since morning and when a man's been murd—" He leaped as if stung. "WHAT," he screamed, "AM I DOING SITTING HERE AND DRINKING TEA?"

"Thirsty, perhaps?" suggested Marlowe.

Alex slammed down the cup and saucer, shoving aside Z, who was about to search for secret papers. To the plenipotentiary's immense relief, the man was alive: it was the unpleasant but not grave effect of a powerful supersonic stun beam fired at short range.

"The body, of course, will have to be disposed of," said Z.

"No!" Alex began to function again. "Get out—all of you. Go get Parr, get a doctor, but for heaven's sake don't tell anyone what's happened. Get out!"

They got.

Left alone, Alex tried to remember his first-aid training. There wasn't much he could do except leave MacHussein undisturbed. The usual result of supersonic stunning was amnesia covering the past several hours. . . . He grew aware that this fumbling had gotten blood all over his tunic and slacks. Hastily he went to the bathroom, stripped off the clothes, washed his hands, and donned a robe. As he came out, the door chimed again. "Parr," he muttered, and aloud: "Come in."

Zuleika MacTavish sine-waved through, closing the door behind her. Deep, agitated breathing expanded her chest, which was not something Alex would have considered possible had he thought about it dispassionately. "Alex!" she said in a frantic whisper. "There's not a minute to lose. I have to talk to you!"

"Oh—" Alex jittered about. "Well, er, sit down, but—"

"This is no time to sit down." she followed him across the room, completely overlooking the corpse-like MacHussein. "This is the eleventh hour. Alex," she said, cornering him and seizing the lapel of his robe, "I know about you. I know your record. You have your heart in the right place."

"I do?" asked Alex feebly.

"Yes," said Zuleika. "Like me."

"Um . . . to be sure," mumbled Alex.

"You are the only man who can help me," cried Zuleika, throwing herself on his shoulder and bursting into tears.

"There, there," said Alex. He meant to pat her gently on the back, but somehow his hand slipped. "There, there, there." Getting no result from this, he disentangled himself, went to the brandy decanter, and poured out a stiff drink. She accepted it blindly and tossed it off at one gulp.

"It can't be that bad—" Alex was saying, when he was interrupted by a strangled, though ladylike, snort. Zuleika's finely molded face squeezed up, both hands flew to her throat, and she began to stagger around the room making ineffectual noises.

"What is it?" yelped Alex. Smitten with a horrible suspicion, he sniffed at the decanter. It was . . . yes, for his ambassadorial brandy the Hokas had substituted their native liquor, a 180-proof liquid dynamite which—"Omigawd! I'm sorry! Excuse me! 'Ere, 'ave a nice cup of 'ot—No, no, I mean, ice water—"

Zuleika downed it shakily, brushed aside his babbled apologies, and said with a new and fascinating huskiness in her voice: "No matter. Too much else to do. Prince Idebar and those awful Porkelugians—Goldfarb's Planet—you've got to help me! The whole future of Bagdadburgh depends on it!"

Alex found himself so busy unraveling her explanation that he forgot both MacHussein and the notoriously sudden wallop which Hoka brew delivers. Goldfarb's Planet was a terrestroid world out in Sector Seven; having no aborigines, it was open for colonization, but the award lay with the Council. Bagdadburgh, with a rapidly increasing population (if Zuleika was representative of its womenfolk, thought Alex, he could understand why they had a population problem), needed it badly, and would normally have been granted the title. Porkelans was also asking for it, but the reason was a mystery: their population was static. However, the Bagdadburgian intelligence service had discovered that Prince Idebar of Worben intended to support the Porkelugian claim—and his influence was so great that he was bound to get what he wanted unless he was blocked.

"But what's in it for Worben?" wondered Alex. "I know their present leaders belong to the Expansionist Party and they'd like more territory but they already have the legal limit of colonies."

"The Porkelugian government is corrupt," said Zuleika fiercely. "Tantho and his associates . . . bribed . . . betraying their own planet. Bribed by dirty Worbenite neodymium."

"Um . . . wait . . . you mean if Porkelans gets Goldfarb's Planet—"

"The Tantho gang would admit Worbenite settlers.

In a few years, there'd be so many settlers they could
vote for autonomy. But the Goldfarbian government
would be a Worbenite puppet. We know it, I tell you.
Tantho is selling out his planet for Worbenite
neodymium. Would I touch their tainted money? I
would not. You would not. But Tantho will. He does.
He touches their tainted money every day. I'll bet
he's sitting in his suite right now touching Worbenite
money."

"But how do you know all this?"

"We got spies," hissed Zuleika. "We found out . . .
Tantho an' Idebar got a written agreement about
it. Don't trust even each other . . . got a regular
contract . . . tainted money." She looked at him with
vague, though lovely, brown eyes. "You wouldn't
touch Worbenite money, would you?"

"N-no," said Alex. "I guess not. Not if it's tainted."

"Private contrac'. . . . would be proof we need to
bust rotten con—conshpi—plot. Bust it wide open.
Colin s'posed to steal contrac'. Special agent of ours.
Where's Colin?" Zuleika peered about in a charming
misty fashion. "Will you help me, Alesh?"

"I, well—"

"Oh, thank you, Alesh!" cried Zuleika, staggering
a trifle. "Tha's y'r name, isn' nit? Oh, Alesh, hol'onna
me, I feel a li'l dizzy—"

The door chimed.

"Hurray for Bagdadburgh!" whooped Zuleika.
"Bagdadburgh, my ain planet! Would I stop at
anything for Bagdadburgh?" she demanded of the
empty air. "No!" she answered with a ringing cry,
dramatically seizing the front of her wispy tunic
and ripping it across. Then she stumbled over
MacHussein, looked down, whitened, screamed, and
fell into Alex's arms.

The door opened and Commissioner Parr strode in with several Hokas. He stopped dead.

Alex stared at him, dumbfounded. He could see no reason why the Commissioner should look at him with loathing. Then, glancing at a full-length mirror across the room, he reeled. In its crystal depths he saw a man in a dressing gown clutching a hiccoughing girl with torn tunic while at his feet another man lay weltering in blood and behind him two tables groaned under stolen papers.

"Commissioner!" bawled Alex in tones of anguish. "You don't think—you can't believe—Commissioner!"

"Please, Mr. Jones," said Parr loftily, withdrawing. "Don't paw me."

Alex had been protesting his innocence for a couple of minutes now. The Commissioner did not appear to be convinced. He stood in the middle of the room and stared coldly at Alex while MacHussein lay on the floor and Zuleika lolled in a chair. Even the Hokas were silent.

"But it's not what it looks like!" gibbered Alex.

"Hiccup!" said Zuleika.

"*I* didn't stun this man!" cried Alex. "I sent for you myself—"

"And the representative?" asked Parr scornfully. "I imagine she, too, fell through the door in her present condition?"

"No! She just took a drink, that's all."

"Which you gave her."

"Well, yes, but—"

"Ha!"

"I gave her the wrong thing."

"Indeed you did."

"Whoops!" said Zuleika faintly. "Porkelans, Worben—

poke 'em inna nose. Throw'm to the bushcats."

"Now, Mr. Jones," said Parr, "you still have the status of your office and, therefore, diplomatic immunity. My hands are tied. But I shall, of course, make urgent recommendations to my superiors tomorrow to the effect that Toka badly needs a new plenipotentiary and, as the result of—to put it in as kindly a light as possible—your incompetence, the planet is not yet ready for advancement in grade."

If he had been perfectly fair, Alex might have agreed that Parr had a case. But it was his job, his reputation, and his Hokas that were at stake. He clutched at a straw. "You don't understand," he said. "I discovered there was an illegal conspiracy between the Worben and Porkelans delegates. Since the IBI can't act against diplomats, I had to use my own status to get the proof."

He flattered himself it was a good speech, but Parr gave him only the thinnest of smiles. "If such proof is forthcoming," said the Commissioner, "naturally I will reconsider. May I see it?"

"I—well—I haven't got all of it yet—"

"I thought not. It is my duty to inform Their Excellencies of the situation, and the aspersions you have cast on them must, of course, be taken into account in judging your case. Good evening, Mr. Jones." Parr bowed and went out.

Alex sat down and grabbed at the decanter. Before he could sort out his whirling thoughts, Marlowe trotted in with the hotel physician.

"Ah," said the doctor cheerily bending over MacHussein, "a stun beam. Tsk-tsk. But we're feeling much better now, aren't we?" Getting no response, he removed the burnoose and examined the injury.

Marlowe peered over his shoulder. "I am writing

a novel about the medical profession," he squeaked. "Heroic, unselfish—"

The doctor reached for his stethoscope. It wasn't there. Z was peering into it for secret papers. "Hey!" said the doctor. Marlowe took busy notes as man and Hoka wrestled for the instrument. Winning the fight, the doctor checked his patient and prepared an athetrine injection. "This'll bring him around," he explained. "He should be all right when he wakes up."

"Aha!" said Z. "When he starts his drugged babbling—"

"Aren't you going to operate?" asked Marlowe, handing the physician a scalpel from his bag.

"For God's sake, no!"

"Not even a little operation?"

"No, I said! Get out of my way!"

"You have the soul of an editor," said Marlowe. "Instead of a novel, I think I shall write an exposé."

Somehow the doctor got MacHussein injected, bandaged, and laid out on a couch. He departed muttering.

Alex had recovered his wits enough to give Zuleika a soberpill. They stared grimly at each other.

"Well," said Alex, "I just hope you were right about that contract, and that we can find it. Otherwise—"

The girl nodded. "No less than four of our best secret agents learned of its existence just before I left for Earth," she said. "It'll be here somewhere— the Embassy Building Offices aren't private enough, and naturally it must remain secret to all but a few."

"But why did you—Damn it," protested Alex, " this is serious and I have to think. Will you *please* get another tunic?"

Zuleika looked down and blushed. She was, of

course, wearing her Upthrust brassiere, 107 cm. large, but it was made of Sheerglo fabric, which happens to be perfectly transparent. Hastily she went to the closet and borrowed one of Alex's tunics. He was a reasonably athletic young man, but it was still a tight fit around the chest.

"Why did you drag me into this?" moaned Alex.

"I had to have someone," she pleaded. "You see, I was getting suspicious of Colin. He has been a secret agent of Bagdadburgh for years, but since we reached Earth I saw him too often talking with Idebar. I turned to you because you, well, you looked so strong and self-reliant and . . . oh, I'm *so* grateful to you—"

"Hrumf!" said Alex. "Never mind. Quite all right."

Zuleika swayed closer. "The whole future of my planet depends on finding that contract," she whispered. "I would do *anything* to get it—to get your help—"

"Now . . . now, wait . . . I've got a wife and . . . and children on Toka and—and—" Alex backed up. His collar felt tight. "Just take it easy."

"After that reception today, Colin disappeared," went on Zuleika. "I got desperate and came here. It was hard to believe anything wrong about him; he's worked with me for years, and always been such a perfect gentleman, though with his looks he could— Never mind." She sighed. "Of course, his being attacked like this proves I was mistaken." She laid her hands on Alex's shoulders and searched his eyes with her own. "But we still need your help."

"And I guess I need yours," agreed the man. "If we can find that contract, it'll clear us, but—"

"I'll be quite frank with you," said Zuleika. "We were going to burgle their apartments, but apparently your Hokas beat us to it, though how you knew even before I told you—" She regarded him worshipfully.

"Oh, well," said Alex with due modesty. "One has a knack—*Hey!*"

Zuleika jumped. This made her quiver. This in turn distracted Alex so much that he could not go on for a few seconds. Then he turned excitedly to the stolen papers. "But the contract must be *here!*" he shouted. "We're saved!"

"Whee!" said Bert, doing a swan dive into the nearest stack.

It took only a few minutes in spite of the Hokas' help. After that there were several more minutes of frantic re-searching. At the end, Hokas and humans regarded each other rather bleakly.

There was no contract. There was not even a protocol.

"I found a treaty on import quotas of rugglepthongs," said Allenby with an air of having done his best.

Colin MacHussein groaned and stirred. Zuleika went to the couch and sat down, laid his head on her breast and stroked his hair. "There, there," she crooned.

MacHussein blinked his eyes open. *"Garrasht!"* he mumbled. "What—oh—" He grew aware them. "What happened?"

"Does it hurt much?" asked Zuleika softly. "Here, lie back and rest."

"No, I'm all right," said MacHussein crisply. He sat up. "But everything else is wrong. You haven't found that contract, have you?"

"No," said Alex. "What happened to you?"

"I don't know." MacHussein frowned, concentrating. "My memory stops several hours ago. Amnesiac effect, you know. But where did all this litter come from?"

Alex explained. "Apparently the contract isn't in this hotel after all," he finished.

MacHussein shook his head. "It would have to be, for their purposes. Have to be available for reference. But they knew we'd lift it if we could, so they must simply have hidden it better than we realized."

Bert bristled. "They couldn't 'ide nothink from me!"

"Afraid they did. We'll just have to try once more." Alex opened the door and peered out, to meet the unmistakable chilled-steel gaze of an IBI man. Others patrolled the slideways as far as he could see.

"Er . . . we don I need protection," said Alex weakly.

"No, sir," said the IBI agent. "You don't."

Alex closed the door.

"Hist!" said Z, at the window.

"Hist yourself," said Alex bitterly. "We *can't* get to their rooms now."

"There are," said Z, "other methods."

"What other methods?"

"I cannot tell," said Z.

However, he could act, for he opened the window. Alex went over and looked out. A meter below was a flange, some 20 centimeters wide, running around the tower for the benefit of the window-cleaning machines. Beneath, except for other flanges, was a good 400 meters of sky terminating in some very hard-looking pavement.

"Ulp!" said Alex.

"*En avant*, old turnip," said Allenby with revolting cheerfulness. Carefully he donned his top hat, put a fresh carnation in his buttonhole, stuck a rolled umbrella under one arm, and vaulted out onto the ledge.

MacHussein swallowed. "I'd better stay and hold the fort," he offered.

"No—" Alex gave up. There was no escape for him, unless he wanted the Hokas to go off with no one to control them. But he took some satisfaction in pushing MacHussein to the window. "Miss MacTavish is the one to stay behind."

"Nonsense!" said Zuleika. "I told you I would do anything for my planet."

"Even on a window ledge?" asked Marlowe, interested.

"Even on a window ledge," she declared.

Alex got out into a fresh night wind that nipped his bare shanks but cooled his ears somewhat. Allenby was ahead of him; Bert, happily snapping and unsnapping tools from his instrument, came after; Zuleika, Z, MacHussein, and Marlowe followed.

Under better conditions Alex might have enjoyed the view. The great city sprawled for kilometers around, its arrogant pinnacles reaching for the stars, its roadways a faerie web of lights; far off, under a low moon, he could see the snowy heights of Mount Aorangi. But hugging a slick plastic wall with his heels sticking out over the edge of nothing—

"Naow 'ere, guv'nor," said Bert, "h'is the neatest bit of 'it h'all. See, h'I h'unfold this little drill, turn this little wheel, h'insert the nitro with this little 'ypodermic—clever, eh?" He nudged Alex knowingly in the ribs.

"Yipe!" said Alex.

There was a low wail behind him, Zuleika was shuffling along with her face to the wall. For her, though, this was not very practical.

"Turn me around, somebody!" she begged.

"Right-o," said Allenby gallantly. He reached past

Alex and Bert with his umbrella. "Hold on to the end of this and step off the ledge; I'll swing you over to me. We Hokas are quite strong."

Alex assured her of this, and she obeyed. Then she vanished as the handle and the ferrule parted company. "Oh, piffle," said Allenby in an annoyed tone. "I forgot this was also a sword cane. Sorry, old girl."

Just in time, Bert grabbed her hair. This overbalanced Bert, who snatched at Alex. Alex clutched after Allenby, who also toppled but managed to throw his umbrella up for Z. The secret agent got it and went over the brink, dragging MacHussein along. Marlowe got MacHussein by the left foot and hooked his free elbow under the windowsill so he could take notes. Not till he had finished this did he use the really astonishing Hoka strength to draw himself back through the window and then haul in the rest. The most irritating part of it all was that as he pulled in the living rope, he piped forth a deep-sea chanty.

"Not making much progress, are we?" asked Allenby with undiminished good humor. His eye fell on Heinrichs, seated with paper and pencil. "Stop that and come along with us!"

"But I iss decoding!" protested Heinrichs.

"You can decode as we go," said Allenby sternly. He wheeled about and went over the sill again. There was nothing to do but follow him.

This time the path was negotiated without incident. They rounded the corner of the building and saw ahead of them the windows of the Porkelugian and Worbenite suites. The former glowed with light; the latter, beyond them, were dark.

The windows were broad enough so that the whole party could stand looking in. The upper transoms were open, and words drifted out—conversation between Prince Idebar, Tantho the Hairy, and Commissioner Parr, who were sitting about with drinks and cigars.

"—most kind of you, sir, to warn us about those Hokas," said Tantho.

"Oh, just doing my duty," said Parr. "But I'm sorry I can't legally recover those papers for you until Jones has been fired."

"No matter," said Idebar, waving his tail airily. "I assure you we are not so foolish as to leave confidential documents where any unscrupulous hireling could find them. We have our methods."

This was too much for Z. He whipped out a dagger and tossed it expertly up, through the transom and across the room, to stick quivering in the wall before Tantho's sheepdog nose.

"What's that?" roared Parr, leaping to his feet.

Z pulled down his slouch hat and rubbed his hands. "We too have our methods," he said with a fiendish cackle.

It is disconcerting, to say the least, to be having a private chat on the 93d floor of an official building, and then suddenly to have daggers quivering in the wall and see five teddy bear noses flattened against your windowpane. When one nose is surmounted by a top hat, one by a black slouch, one by a chauffeur's cap, and one by two gleaming monocles, the effect is positively unnerving.

"What kind of place is this, anyway?" stormed Tantho with a not unjustifiable huffiness.

"Spies!" hissed Idebar, gliding forward.

"Spies yourself!" said Zuleika.

"Cut that out!" said Alex raggedly. "We've got to—"

Allenby was already scuttling down the flange to the Worbenite windows. The rest followed. Bert got to work cutting out the livingroom pane. Behind them, Parr looked out, bellowing like a wounded bull. "Thieves! Barbarians! You'll get psychorevision for this, Jones! You—"

"Not so fast, please," squeaked Marlowe, busily taking notes.

"He iss schpeaking in ein zimple double-transposition cipher," decided Heinrichs, looking over Marlowe's shoulder.

"—and naow me little saw," said Bert, "and me little roll of tape, and me little—"

The pane gave way with a crash, and the burglars scrambled through. There was only the vaguest possible illumination from outdoors, but as he fumbled for the switch Alex could see MacHussein's shadowy form atremble. "Sunspots, what a day!" stammered the Bagdadburgian. "I need a drink—" He groped over to a barely visible decanter and put it to his lips and shuddered with relief.

Alex turned on the lights as the outer door opened. An IBI man looked in. Z sent a dagger whisking past him. The IBI man withdrew and Alex scurried about locking all the doors.

Feet thundered in the corridor. "Open up!" bawled Tantho.

Alex groaned. "We've got to find that contract fast," he chattered, staring at the wild disorder left by the previous Hoka visit . . . or visitation. "They'll break in— and for all we know, it's in the Porkelugian suite—"

Allenby glared at an inoffensive chair, broke off its tail-rest, and ripped the cushion with his sword cane. "Not here," he announced.

"Of course it isn't," said Z. "Don't you know secret

documents are always left in plain sight?" His eyes glittered around. "Aha! I've found it!" He snatched a framed paper off the wall. Alex took it with shaking hands and read:

WHEREAS H. H. IDEBAR FANJ HURTHGL HAS SATISFACTORILY COMPLETED THE REQUIREMENTS FOR THE DEGREE OF MASTER OF ARTS IN THE FIELD OF GLOGSNORGLING, NOW THEREFORE BY AUTHORITY OF THE REGENTS . . .

"It vill haff to be decoded, of course," said Heinrichs.

The door glowed as someone turned a raybeam on it.

"Too late," said Alex dully.

The door fell, and Parr, Idebar, Tantho, and a dozen grim-faced IBI men rushed through. Alex stared down the muzzles of their Holmans and raised his hands.

"I've got you now, Jones!" raged Parr. "Diplomatic immunity or no, I'm going to have you locked away till—"

"We are not disposed to be malicious, Commissioner," said Idebar with his usual suavity. "Obviously Jones is a public menace, but we see no reason to press charges against the others."

"Aha!" said Z darkly.

"Guilty conscience, eh, what?" observed Allenby.

"To be sure," said Z. He tugged at Parr's sleeve. "Commissioner."

"What now?" demanded Parr, turning like a large elephant baited by a very small dog.

"Arrest that man," said Z, pointing to MacHussein.

"What for?" sputtered Parr.

"On suspicion."

"Suspicion of what? Who's suspicious of him?"

"I am," said Z with a sinister overtone.

"Now listen," screamed Parr, "that man was attacked himself—"

"Aha!" said Z. "That proves it."

"Proves what?"

"My suspicions."

"What suspicions?"

"None of your business," said Z, looking distrustfully at the Commissioner.

"My dear sir," broke in Idebar, "may I inquire what this is all about?"

Z turned to Allenby. "May he?"

"It should be referred to the home office," said Allenby. "But a field agent has to stick his neck out now and then, what? Damme, I *will* stick my neck out. He may."

"Go ahead, Your Excellency," bowed Z.

"I *was* going ahead," choked Idebar. "Mister . . . Mr. Jones, will you do something about these—these—"

"Allenby, what's the meaning of this?" gasped Alex.

The elegantly dressed Hoka extracted a handkerchief from his pocket and flicked invisible dust from his sleeve. "My dear old mangel-wurzel," he said, "must we do *all* the work? We have ransacked three suites, issued a mysterious warning, questioned eighteen members of the hostel staff, decoded thirty-four documents, and gathered everyone here for the dénouement. Having done this, we now sit back and wait for you to do what is yours to wit, reveal what is behind all this." He beamed, took a pinch of snuff, and added to MacHussein: "Sorry, old chap. You played the Great Game well."

The Bagdadburgian grinned and shrugged. "Let's get this over with, Commissioner," he suggested. "I could use some sleep."

Alex's brain leapfrogged. "Hey!" he cried.

"Arrest Jones," said Parr to the IBI agents. "I'll take the responsibility."

"Hold on there!" said Alex. He was still panting and shivering with the revelation that had burst on him. "Parr, I told you there was an illegal contract between Idebar and Tantho. That's the truth—and I now know where it is!"

"Oh, Alex," crooned Zuleika.

The man flung his arm dramatically out. The effect was somewhat spoiled by his knocking over a floor lamp, and in any event it is difficult to cut a heroic figure in a bathrobe, but he pointed at MacHussein and said with triumph: "You've got it!"

"You're raving!" said Idebar.

"Not very well trained in elocution, is he?" whispered Allenby to Marlowe.

"No," agreed the Hoka writer. "The proper phrase is, of course: 'You're mad, I tell you—mad, mad!' "

Alex backed away, speaking fast, as the IBI men closed in. "MacHussein isn't a human at all. He's a Worbenite. Do a little surgery on a Worbenite, he'll took just like an Arab. I can prove it. When he woke up, he used a Worbenite oath; I'd heard Idebar use it earlier. Well, anyone could do that, of course, but it's one point. Then Zulei—Her Excellency said he had been a perfect gentleman in all the years of working closely with her. And she was holding his head in a very uh, comfortable position—but he sat up immediately and said he felt fine. Does that sound like a *human* male? Finally, when we broke in here just now it was quite dark, but he went right to the decanter and drank from it. How could he know it was brandy and not the jithna drink which would poison a human? The answer is, he couldn't . . . and he didn't care, because he's immune!"

"I really feel sorry for anyone in your mental state, Jones," purred Idebar. "Why, MacHussein himself was stunned."

"Yes." Alex was backed into a corner now. He picked up the lamp and used it to fend off the IBI agents. "That was to divert Zuleika's growing suspicion from him and make us look bad to Parr. You must have been alarmed when your suite was raided, and been fairly sure the Hokas did it, so you wanted us under suspicion and therefore, you hoped, immobilized. Actually, MacHussein was planted on Bagdadburgh years ago, to work his way up and be in a position to thwart—Leggo there!" He wrested the lamp from an agent's hand and swatted him.

"I shall file an official protest against your unbridled language," said Tantho with dignity.

Bert took out his giant burglar tool, joggled Prince Idebar's elbow, and tried to interest the elder statesman in a lecture on lockpicking.

"You knew Zuleika's agents would be trying to get that document," went on Alex. "You knew they might find it in any hiding place or waylay anyone carrying it—except one person, their own trusted comrade, MacHussein! He's carrying it right now!"

The dark-faced man sneered and turned to go. "I won't bother answering that," he said. "Goodnight."

It was a mistake. Allenby made a beautiful flying tackle, shouting something about the playing fields of Eton. Bert picked him up by the ankles and shook him. And as he lay dazed, Z extracted the paper with a grand flourish and snapped it before Parr's eyes.

There was a long silence.

"Well?" said Parr when he had finished reading.

"Sleight-of-hand," blustered Tantho. "Planted on him."

Idebar nodded, elevating his brows. "There is also the matter of diplomatic immunity," he said in an ice-slick voice.

Parr reddened. "Yes," he said. "There is. I can't do anything to punish you—nobody can. But I can tell the Council what I saw. That will settle who gets Goldfarb's Planet." He bowed heavily at Alex. "My apologies, Plenipotentiary Jones. I shall file an account of this daring exploit in your already distinguished record and, of course, recommend Toka for upgrading. Good evening, gentlebeings."

He went out. His IBI troop followed. There was another silence, broken only by Alex's wheezing. This was choked off by a long and passionate kiss, after which it resumed somewhat more noisily.

Prince Idebar stalked up to him. "Congratulations," he said with a vitriolic note. "You have, ah—"

"—foiled me," suggested Marlowe.

"Thank you. You have foiled—"

"Perhaps 'checkmated'?"

"Checkmated me, then. Thank you!" gritted Prince Idebar.

"Quite all right," said Marlowe.

"Jones," said Idebar, "you have won. But I am not without influence, even now, and I shall certainly not let you continue your career unmolested."

Alex smiled sweetly. "I have diplomatic immunity," he said.

"If you think that will help—"

"I think it will . . . Iddykins."

The Worbenite started. "What?"

"Iddykins," said Alex. "There is the little matter of your winter underwear, Iddykins. Tell me, are you wearing it now? You have a very devoted wife, Iddykins, and I can think of several news services which would be happy to print a sample of her devotion . . . shall we say, a letter?"

"Um . . . yes." Idebar's aristocratic face purpled. "You do have the upper hand, it seems. Very well, sir." He stalked out, his tail lashing his ankles.

Tantho the Hairy started to follow. Alex grabbed his arm and pointed to the semiconscious MacHussein. "Better take him along," advised the human. "He's no more use to you, and might as well return to Worben. They can regenerate his normal appearance there."

Zuleika giggled. "I imagine," she said, "he'll be the first humanoid male in history who actually wanted to grow horns."

Alex blushed and led his Hokas out. Zuleika looked as if she might continue that line of thought, and he valued his own marriage.

FROM: Chief of Tokan Secret Service

TO: Operative X-7
        Room 13
        The Sign of the Cloak and Dagger
        Mixumaxu, U.X.

CODE: 24-J-298-q

1. Your secret report on the Interbeing League, as described to the Hoka delegation, is now in my hands.

2. Good work, X-7. Stand by for further orders.

3. Further orders: It is the opinion of this department that one of the delegates to the Council of the Interbeing League on Earth is none other than the interstellar criminal and arch spy-ring master known only as Y.

4. You know what to do.

                              (signed)
                              The Chief

DAVID WEBER

continued 🐾

EXPLORE OUR WEB SITE